Dracaena Marginata

Dracaena Marginata

To Dana with love ...

Donald Greco

(Uncle Don)

Donald Greco

Other novels in Donald Greco's Youngstown Quintet Series:

Abramo's Gift
Tommy the Quarterback

ISBN: 1497336511
ISBN 13: 9781497336513
Library of Congress Control Number: 2013915482
CreateSpace Independent Publishing Platform
North Charleston, South Carolina

To Joe, S.J., Casey, and Angie for inspiring this story

Part 1: Yesterday

RIGLEY AND I LOVED to build those fires as big as we could. Every night after school: hurry home, change, and run outside. Build a big fire. Sometimes we'd sit and watch it blaze; sometimes we'd roast old dried-out cattails from the summer and use them for gas guns. Sometimes we'd be hunters looking for squirrels and rats, or chickens that strayed out of the coops, and then we'd try to smoke them out like the Green Hornet did.

Mom used to give me lickings because she thought I was smoking all the time. But I never did too much; never could find cigarettes. Once in a while Rigley used to get some for us; he learned how to steal them, I guess.

In spring we'd go down by the creek and catch crabs and polliwogs. Crabs are funny. When you smash them, they're yellow inside, like mustard. I never did much like polliwogs. Rigley liked to keep them, though. He told me they'd be frogs someday, but I never believed him; they were too soft, and they always died. We never saw no frogs, either.

Sometimes, on the creek bank, if you cleared away the mud, you'd get nice clay. We made cups and ashtrays with it and put them in the sun to dry. We never used the cups, though; they got too sloppy when we put water in them.

We did lots of things in those days, and Rigley always did them better than me. One time a funny thing happened at Bev's house. He was bending over and I pushed him down. I never saw him get so mad. He screamed and cried, and started running after me, calling me a son of a bitch. I figured I was faster and could get away from him, but he kept still coming, really catching up. Man, I was scared. I fell down and started crawling; my leg really hurt, and I couldn't breathe. But there he was, and the only thing I could do was duck, so I covered my head with my hands and arms, and turned my back. It wouldn't hurt so much in the back. I thought he'd kill me, he was so big, but all he did was hit me once with his fist, not very hard either. Then he called me a goddamn son of a bitch and walked away.

I followed him back to Bev's house, but her mother chased us home because she said we were crazy and I was bad for hurting Rigley.

When we walked home, Rigley said, "Why'd you do that, Sandy?"

"I don't know," I said.

"Don't do it no more, huh? I never saw you push me, and that ain't fair."

Sometimes we'd build castles in my sandbox and make wars with my little army men. Rigley showed me how to wet the sand and make a ramp for my tanks to go into the castle. I always won the wars. Hell, they were my tanks and my sand.

One day he wanted to win, and I said no. He filled up one of my buckets with wet sand and started spinning it around faster and faster. Then he just let go, and the thing smashed into the ground and broke open. I cried and screamed, and my sister, Gini, came outside.

"What's wrong?" she said.

"Rigley broke my bucket!"

"You big dummy! Get out of here!" she said. She chased him with a broom and he ran like hell. She was more mad at me than him,

2

I think. "Can't you play with someone other than that crazy hillbilly?" she said.

There really wasn't anybody else. Rigley lived close, and he never played with anyone but me. Yeah, sometimes even I didn't like him. But mostly he was nice enough.

Gini said Rigley stunk. People were saying stuff like that all the time, like he needs a haircut, and how come I play with him. But I never smelled nothing, so it never bothered me.

When Bowen's store put out wood that their stoves and refrigerators came in, he and I would get it and make a hut. But it was always over behind Rigley's house, because his yard was messed up already, and I couldn't have huts in my yard. But then, in our club, he was always president and I was always vice president. Sometimes his cousin, Nathan, would come over to visit, and he and Rigley would check me off the list so I wasn't in the club anymore.. It seemed like every time someone new came around to play, Rigley would check me off the list.

Rigley taught me how to trade funny books, too. We used to have big stacks, and we'd trade all around. If you said, "First pick!" you'd get a chance to trade first. We traded with a little colored kid named Daniel every Saturday afternoon. Daniel was always quiet. He never even liked to come up on my porch. We'd always have to go down the steps and trade, so he could go away real fast when we were done.

One day Nathan was with us and Daniel came up with a lot of books. When he went away, Nathan asked me, "How come you trade with niggers? I bet those nigger funny books got germs all over them. You and Rigley are dumb asses."

We walked away from him. "I hate Nathan," Rigley said. "I wish he wasn't my cousin."

Nathan kept calling us names. He said Rigley was a big fat dummy and I was a greasy dago. I didn't know what that meant, but

I knew I wasn't supposed to like it. Then Nathan ran up to us and hit Rigley in the head with a funny book. Rigley was really mad and called him a goddamn son of a bitch.

"You guys are stupid," Nathan said. "Look. See this book? I stoled it from that nigger. And you trade with him all the time, Sandy. I bet he stoled hundreds of books from you."

I thought about that after I went home. Those niggers steal a lot. I bet Daniel made me like him just so he could catch me off guard and rob me.

The next time Daniel came up to trade, I counted all the books in my stack before I went down on the steps, and then I counted them again after we were done. They were all there, and I couldn't figure it out. Maybe he knew I was mad about something, 'cause I didn't talk to him very much. Maybe he just knew I was watching him, so he didn't steal any.

Anyway, the next time he came up to trade, I screwed him good. While we were talking, I mixed up some of our books, so we both had books in the same stack. "Hey, they're all mixed up, Daniel. You sure you have the right ones?" I counted them all and separated them into two stacks, his and mine. "Here, we're done with this part; let me put mine away."

I took that part of my stack up to the porch. I had one of his books in it. "You want to come up on the porch, Daniel?" I asked him. He said no, but that was my plan; I knew he wouldn't come up. He sure acted funny when he was up around our neighborhood.

So I went back down and we finished trading our other piles. He looked at me funny. I was smiling all the time, but didn't talk much. That big nigger. When he was done, he stacked the books, put them on his head, and walked away, just like he always did. I didn't say nothing, just watched him go.

Then all of a sudden he turned around, knelt down, and looked through all his books. Then he looked at me for a long time. I stared back, just grinning. He walked up to me and said, "I think I got a book missing."

"Maybe you left it home," I said.

"No, I had it in my stack." He looked at me kind of funny.

"How many books did you have?" I asked.

"I don't know," he said. "I didn't count 'em."

"Then how do you know you have one missing?" What a dumb ass.

"It seem like I 'member one." He kept looking at me, making me nervous. Then he looked up at the porch. "Let's go up there."

"No," I said, "it ain't there."

"Yeah, let's look anyhow."

"I said there ain't nothing up there."

He ran up to the porch. Before I got to him, he scattered my stack and found his book. I didn't say anything.

"You said you didn't have it."

"I made a mistake."

"You ain't supposed to steal. It say in the Bible never to steal."

"Steal? Are you kidding? I didn't steal anything."

"You stole my funny book."

"Steal, huh? What do niggers know about the Bible anyway? Go on. Get out of here."

"You were my friend and you stole a book. You think just Catholics go to church? Niggers go to church, too. Least we know it's wrong to steal."

Daniel never came back to trade anymore. At first I was glad; I didn't need his damn books. But later that summer, at Coolidge Field, I tried to talk to him. "Come on. Everything'll be up and up. No tricks. Come up Saturday."

"Okay. See you Saturday."

I waited all day Saturday, but he never came. The next time I saw him, he said his mother had him go to the store, so he couldn't come. He never came again, and I asked him lots of times, too.

What bothered me was that nigger thought he was better than me. Imagine. A stealing, fighting, switchblade-cutting nigger calling me a crook. And that damned Nathan. I was okay until he came along and made me just like him. Daniel wasn't my friend anymore 'cause I listened to that son of a bitch. Well, I wasn't making that mistake again.

One day the Bowen Furniture Company put out some things from their store. We used to take all that stuff they put out, before the trash men got it, especially the wooden crates.

"Look here, Rigley. Look at this funny plant."

"Oh, that's a cactus."

"No it ain't. Look, it's got palm leaves. Hey, maybe we can make our own palm, like for Palm Sunday, huh?"

"That old dumb plant ain't gonna grow. It's broke; look there." He held up the leaves and showed a crack. "That's gonna die."

"Well, I'm gonna see. Let's go ask Mr. Bowen about it." I walked around the building and Rigley followed me inside. Jake, the clean-up man, hollered at us.

"What're you kids doing in here?" He was always mad about something. He never liked anybody.

"Do you know what kind of plant this is, Jake?" I asked.

"Were you back by that dock? How many times I have to tell you kids to stay out of there? Next time I see you out there I'm gonna beat the shit out of you; then I'm gonna call the cops."

"Shut up, Jake," Rigley said. "We ain't scared of you."

"You get the hell out of here, you big dummy. You should be in a cage."

"I want to talk to Mr. Bowen," I said.

"I said get out of here!" Jake said, really nasty.

"Jake, you ain't nothing but a goddamn son of a bitch. Don't call me dummy," Rigley said.

Jake looked like he was going crazy. His face got red and his eyes looked all screwed up in his head. He started coming.

"Rigley," I shouted, "are you crazy?"

We ran toward the door with Jake right after us. All of a sudden there was Mr. Bowen standing in the doorway, a real big guy, and he wasn't very happy either. He looked down at us kind of mean.

"What's wrong, Jake?"

Jake answered. "Well, these damned kids, Mr. Bowen; they keep coming around taking things all the time."

Bowen looked at me. "What things, Sandy?"

"Nothing, Mr. Bowen, honest. Rigley, did we take anything?"

"No, sir. Jake just started chasin' us."

"What's that in your hand, then?"

"We got this out back; honest. Right, Rigley?"

"Yeah. Look, it's broke."

Bowen looked at Jake. "What happened to that, Jake? What was it doing outside?"

Jake didn't want to answer. "Well...uh...It was broke, Mr. Bowen."

"How, Jake?"

"Well, when we unloaded them I put 'em all on the ledge near the dock, and, well...I knocked one over."

"Those plants cost thirty dollars apiece, Jake. Did you tell Sam you broke it?" Jake didn't answer. "Did you, Jake?"

"No, sir."

Mr. Bowen just looked at him for a little bit. Then he said, "Get back to work."

Jake walked away real fast. I was glad he got in trouble. Mr. Bowen looked at us. "Sandy, you kids aren't supposed to play near that dock. You know that."

"We weren't playing, Mr. Bowen. We just came up for some wood and found this plant. You want it back, Mr. Bowen?"

"That plant's no good anymore, Sandy. Once it's broken, it won't grow again; it's too delicate."

"I can try to make it grow; it's not dead yet," I said.

"Well...if you want it, you can have it. Here, let me see...."

I brought it to him.

"Put some paper around here, then tape it. Maybe you can make it grow. Try, at least." He smiled. "I know you'll take better care of it than Jake did."

"What kind is it?" asked Rigley.

"It's a *Dracaena marginata*."

"How do you say that?" I asked. He said it again slow.

Rigley mumbled, "Drismus alata."

"Does your mother know you go by that dock, Rigley?" asked Mr. Bowen.

"No, sir."

"All right. Next time I see either of you near that dock, I'm coming down to talk to both your mothers; understand?"

"Yes, sir."

We left. Rigley carried the plant with us. Mr. Bowen knew we weren't going to stay away from that dock, not with all that nice wood back there.

Nathan came with us one day to build a hut down the creek. We took our palm tree with us; it was supposed to mean we were on an island where pirates lived. Nathan had a big strap that he wore, so he was the pirate and we were slaves. Rigley was his slave, and the two of them were going to make me a prisoner. I didn't like playing that way. Hell, I was better than Nathan. Why should I be his slave? Rigley didn't care. We began sword fighting and jumping off the little hills in the mill yard. We'd pretend the hills were pirate ships and try to knock each other off. But I never let Nathan knock me off a hill. I kept pushing him back each time he tried, and he was really mad. Then he started whipping me with that big belt. Once he hit me in the shoulder and I caught it. He pulled and so did I. When I let go he fell down.

"Go get him, Rigley!" he shouted. "Don't let him do that. Hear me, Rigley? You're a slave. Go get him, you dummy!"

"That ain't fair, Rigley," I shouted. "Two against one!"

"Go get him, Rigley. Get him, slave!"

Rigley picked up the belt and started swinging like crazy, but I was too fast for him. My sword was a little branch that I could block his swings with. The belt was big, and I had to jump around, on and off the hills like Captain Blood in the movies. I stumbled one time and hurt my knee like hell.

"Wait! Time out; I'm hurt." I wasn't kidding.

Nathan was still screaming, calling Rigley dummy and laughing. "Get him, Rigley," he kept screaming.

Rigley was standing over me listening; I thought he was giving me time out, but the crazy nut started swinging again, and he caught me right across the face. Boy, it really hurt. But once he did it, it was easier for him to swing again, and again. He stopped only when he saw me crying.

Nathan picked up the plant and held it way over his head like he was going to bash my brains in. I could hardly see him throw it, but it caught me in the shoulder and the thing bounced and rolled and fell apart.

"Look at the crybaby," Nathan said to Rigley. Rigley was laughing too.

I ran all the way home. Mom and Gini heard me running up the steps and stopped me at the door.

"Rigley hit me," I said. They could see the tears.

"Where did you get all those red marks all over you? My God, look at your face! Why did he hit you like that?" Mom said.

"Rigley and Nathan...they had a big strap." I was really crying then.

"Let's go," my mom said.

"No, Mom. I don't want to go up there. His father's crazy. He'll kill us if we make him mad!"

"Don't worry about it; she'll handle him," Gini said.

When we got there I was scared. Rigley had told me how crazy his dad was. His mother came to the door and then out on the porch.

"Look what that kid of yours did to Sandy," Mom shouted.

"My Rigley don't do things like that."

Gini turned to me. "Sandy? Did he? Tell her."

"Yeah, Mrs. Potter. He and Nathan were playing with me this afternoon."

Mr. Potter came out then, and I got really scared.

"Let's go, Mom," I said, "I don't want to talk to him."

Rigley's mom looked mean. "Damn right, you little liar! He'll fix your sissy ass for you."

"What's the matter?" said his father.

Mom was tough, too. "Potter, you see what Rigley did? Am I gonna have to come over here all summer because Rigley and that crazy cousin of his keep beating Sandy up?"

"Why don't you people get the hell off my porch? Bad enough I got Rigley, then I have a pissy little dago kid come around crying all the time."

"Listen to me, Potter. If you can't control that kid of yours so that he stops doing these crazy things to Sandy, I'm gonna call the Humane Society. Understand?"

He just looked nasty at Mom for a second. "You think it's easy, huh? Having a dumb kid like Rigley? Well, he ain't coming in your goddamn high-class dago yard no more. And you keep that little bastard of yours home, too," he said.

I thought Mom was going crazy. Gini held her arm. "Let's get out of here, Ma. No use talking to these hillbillies," she said.

That was it, man. I wasn't allowed to play with Rigley anymore. For a while I didn't go over his house and he didn't come over mine. I used to see him go back and forth to the store, but he'd look at me, then look away.

One night, I remember, I was going past his house when I heard a lot of noise. I went around to the side window by the driveway and I could see his father beating him something terrible. Rigley was crying and running around; sometimes he screamed. His old man was hitting him with his fists. Rigley fell down and his dad just kept hitting him. I watched for a minute; I never saw a lickin' like that.

I went home and felt bad. Rigley never did anything so bad to deserve that. His father was a son of a bitch; I hated him. He never said anything; just looked mean and drank his beer.

I looked at Mom and Grandma. They were different; Rigley's mom wasn't like them at all. I don't know. Maybe because they were poor, maybe that was why they always seemed mad, and never talked much, never laughed.

Grandma was falling asleep in the chair, her crochet needle dangling from the thread. Mom was folding clothes. Dad was smoking and reading the paper. He wouldn't hit me like Rigley's dad.

That night I dreamed of Rigley dying and I woke up crying. It was a real funny feeling. Poor Rigley.

—∞∞—

I got pretty lonely after a while. There weren't any other kids to play with around our street. One day he was coming back from the store carrying some milk under his arm; he always carried it like it was a loaf of bread. I called him to cross the street.

"My mom won't let me play with you no more…said you dagos are all stealers and killers, next thing worst to niggers."

"Aw, you don't believe that, do you? I heard the same stuff about hillbillies, and you ain't so bad."

"Who you been playing with?" he asked.

"Nobody. How 'bout you?"

"Nobody…Just Nathan when he comes over, but I don't like him, that son of a bitch."

"Where are you going now?" I asked.

"Taking this milk home. Then I ain't doing nothing."

"You want to go down the creek?"

"Yeah. How we gonna go?"

"Well…I'll see if I can go down myself. Then I'll meet you by the old blast furnace, okay? Only don't bring Nathan."

"Okay. I'll be down in a little bit," he said.

After that, we'd sneak around and give signals like the Lone Ranger and Tonto, instead of knocking or calling at the house. Tonto always made a sound like some kind of bird, then the Lone Ranger knew he was there.

Soon Rigley was coming around again. And I was going over his house. My mom saw us one day and didn't say nothing, so I guess it was okay. His mother saw us too, but she never remembered when she said something.

Then one day Rigley came over my house, and I went to the back door. He said, "Here," and handed me my old plant. "You can take care of it now. I think it'll be okay; I had to patch it up."

The stem was skinny and drying out and it was dying. "Where'd you get this?" I asked.

"You know that day I kept strappin' you? Well, I felt bad 'cause I did it; I like you more than Nathan. So I went down the creek and got the plant 'cause you liked it. I had a hard time keeping it alive."

"Thanks," I said. Imagine him going all the way down there, probably after his old man beat him up, even.

"How do you say that?" he said. "Slow."

"*Dracaena marginata.*"

"Dras...am...lata." He looked at me funny. "Say it again."

"I'll go slow, okay?"

"Yeah."

"Dra."   "Dra."

"See."   "See."

"Na."   "Na."

"Mar."   "Mar."

"Gin."   "Gin."

"Ata."   "Ata."

"Okay, put it all together," I said.

"Dra...sme...nis...a...tala."

"No! Just say the first part."

He couldn't say it all together. I kept saying it slow again and again, but he never got it right. Next day, the same thing. It took a long time before he got tired.

13

He kept asking me to say it slow. "Rigley, I ain't no teacher. I get tired saying that all the time. What do you want to know a big word like that for anyway? People think we're crazy."

"'Cause I like them Italian words. Ain't nobody in my family knows it—my sister, my ma, nobody. My pop heard me say it and he got mad. Said he didn't want me learning no dago words. Come on, say it again."

We were sitting on my porch one day and Rigley told me his sister taught him a new game called jacks. He had a little ball and a bunch of little things that looked like Hitler crosses. He took a long time to tell me the rules; he forgot things all the time. When we started playing, I was pretty good. I could get almost all the jacks when I tried. Rigley wasn't good as me, but he liked the game. It helped us pass the time when we didn't have nothing to do.

One day it was raining and we were playing jacks on my front porch. Beverly, the girl next door, saw us. "What are you playing? Jacks?"

"Yeah. So what?"

"So that's a girl's game, you big queers."

"Shut up, Bev," I said. "How do you know it's a girl's game?"

"I know 'cause I have jacks myself. My sister and I play it all the time. Wait and see, you big sissies; I'll go get 'em right now." She ran inside.

"Rigley, don't you lie to me. Is this a girl's game?"

"Well…I saw my sister play it."

"Yeah, but she's just like a boy; she plays anything."

"I don't know. What are you asking me for?"

"'Cause you're the one who showed me this dumb game first of all."

"Well, you said you liked it."

"Yeah, but then I didn't know it was a sissy game. Damn you, Rigley!"

Beverly brought the jacks outside. "Here," she said. "Now do you believe me, you queers?"

"You're a dumb ass, Beverly," said Rigley.

It stopped raining. Bev and her sister were playing down by the driveway near the street. Just then a car was coming and when it got near them, the driver blew his horn real loud and it scared hell out of Bev. She was kinda stooped down and when the horn blew, she fell backward and got her panties all dirty. I was glad; Rigley and I laughed our heads off. Bev was really screaming, not because she fell down, but because we saw her and started laughing.

My grandmother came out. "What has happened?" she asked in Italian. She always talked to me in Italian.

"Nothing. She got scared by a horn and fell down."

Bev was still crying when her mother came outside. "What happened?" she asked. "Stop that screaming!"

"They pushed me down," she said, pointing to us. I almost went crazy.

"Why that dirty little liar. We didn't do that!" I said to her mom.

"Yes they did, Mommy. They pushed me down and I almost got hit. And then they ran away." She started to cry again.

"Mrs. Morelli, Sandy should be ashamed of himself," said Bev's mother. "Those guys are too rough. I wish you'd keep them away from my girls."

"How many times I have to tell you? Leave them girls alone. Did you go there?" Grandma said.

"But we didn't do it, Grandma!" I said. I was really mad at Bev. "She's a dirty liar, Gram, a rotten, no good—"

She hit me before I finished. My grandma had a way of hitting that almost knocked my head off. And I never saw it coming, either. She'd hit up on the sides of my face or the back of the head. Bev loved it, too. Rigley ran for home.

When we got back in the house, I said, "Grandma, why'd you hit me? You know she was lying."

"I know," she said softly as she sat down.

"You know?"

"Yes."

"But how come you hit me, then?"

"I don't like the way you talk. If they're animals, do you have to be one, too? And talk like *bestie*? Like some of those American kids talk? Answer me!"

"No, Grandma."

It was no use. She was always right, even if I didn't do anything bad; if she hit me, I was being a *cafone* or a *bestia*.

There was a guy who used to come every day to the beer garden up the corner from our house. He would stay for hours and get real drunk every time he came. And he used to drive a big old open-back truck and park it in front of our house.

I never liked that truck, 'cause it looked like it would fall apart. And it really messed things up. We could never play catch all summer, because every afternoon that truck was in front of our house. And the driver always had stuff in the back that other people would throw away. Junk. He was the guy they called the "junk man."

And he usually had people in the truck. One was a dirty, skinny guy who always wore a ratty old hat shaped like the new one my grandpa used to wear when he got dressed up. This guy was short and old and used to cuss at us if we came near the truck.

But there was another guy in the truck, too. He was a kid a little older than me—maybe the same age as Rigley. I hated those guys. The old one was nasty, just like the driver who owned the truck, and he looked like he was gonna die any minute. The kid was ugly and smelled bad. They both had dirty clothes and faces. And they would sit in the truck for hours every day, even when it was real hot, just waiting for that fat-ass driver to come out of the beer garden.

Then one day Rigley told me that the old guy died. I think he was right, 'cause I never saw the guy anymore. But the truck still kept coming all summer long; only this time the ugly kid would wait in the truck all alone, never talking to anyone, hour after hour.

One day it started to rain real hard and all the stuff in the truck got wet. When the father came out to the truck, he started yelling at the kid and slapping him around 'cause he didn't cover up the junk with a tarp that was in the back of the truck. He called the kid all kinds of names, and the kid answered him back and talked funny, like he was speaking another language, though I could understand some English words once in a while. His father made him help with the tarp and kept yelling at the kid until they got all the junk covered and then drove away.

The next day it started to rain again, and the kid got out of the truck and tried to put the tarp over the junk in the back all by himself. That was my chance. I came down off our porch and went up to the truck. He was still in back trying to spread out the tarp. I just stood there watching him.

When he was finally done, he jumped down from the truck and seemed surprised when he saw me. Man, he was smelly. His face was funny, too. It was the first time I was ever up that close to him, and his face looked crooked, like his jaws were lopsided. And one eye was bigger than the other one.

"What's your name, kid?" I said, nasty-like.

He answered me but I didn't know what he said. He just didn't talk good. Then he started to walk past me to get back in the truck. But I grabbed him and spun him around so he could look at me. He was taller than me, but he didn't seem strong. He felt like a girl, and he looked afraid. "Why do you always park here in front of my house?" I said. "So Rigley and me can't play catch?"

He didn't say anything; he just put his head down and hunched his shoulders and shook his head. Man, he was really dumb, and I was gonna bust him one in the face.

"Sandy, what are you doing?" It was my grandmother. She always spoke to me in Italian, because she couldn't say hardly any English words. "Sandy?"

"I don't like this kid, Grandma," I said in Italian. I looked back at the kid but I stood in front of him so he couldn't get into the truck. "He's dirty and he smells and he's ugly," I said, again in Italian.

"Don't touch him," she said.

"But—"

"I said don't touch him. He doesn't have a mother."

"What?" I didn't know what she meant. How could someone not have a mother?

"His mother is dead. Let him go, Sandy. Do not ever hurt him."

I looked back at the kid. Wow. He didn't have a mother. No wonder he looked so ratty.

"Come here, Sandy. Let him go," Grandma said. I stepped away and let him pass. He just looked at me and then got back into the truck.

I went up the steps to our porch. Grandma was waiting for me, and when I came near her she hugged me. "That was good," she said. "You never should hurt those poor creatures who have no one to love them."

That night I dreamed that my mom died. I woke up crying and thought about that kid in the truck. The next week, Grandma gave me two big slices of hot bread with butter and jelly to take to him. I didn't understand what he said, but it was some kind of thanks, I knew.

I never bothered him again, but whenever I saw him I always remembered my dream about my mother dying. The next summer the truck didn't come around anymore. Rigley told me that the dirty kid's father got drunk one time and was killed in a car wreck. We never knew what happened to the kid.

That summer was over fast. When we went back to school I didn't see Rigley much, because he went to Monroe and I went to St. Rocco's. After school we'd play together if it wasn't real cold and didn't get dark too early. Saturdays we'd play down by the creek; it was cold and frozen. The fish and animals were gone.

Those days my grandmother would feel sorry for Rigley. She was always worried because he never had a big coat on in the cold. He used to wear a long-sleeved shirt and two old sweaters. His shoes were always wet; he wore the cheap ones that used to look falling apart almost as soon as he put them on. He never caught cold, though.

Grandma would make soup and call us in. She always made sure Rigley got a lot. Sometimes, when she made bread, she'd give him a nice warm slice with butter and jelly. Rigley liked that stuff, and he sure liked my grandmother. But he was afraid of her because she yelled at me a lot and slapped me when I was bad.

Christmas was the funny time, though. When my cousins would come over and we'd be waiting for dinner and playing with our toys, I could see Rigley in his backyard all alone, sometimes walking, sometimes running, talking to himself, and hunching his shoulders up like he always did, like he was always cold, though every time my grandmother asked him he always said no.

Anyway, I'd look at him and then go back to playing. Later, I'd think about him again. He always had those same two sweaters on, the gray and the brown one, and a scarf around his neck. Christmas was just another day to him. I wondered if he ever believed in Santa Claus when he was little. I guess he didn't; Santa never came for him.

It's worse, I guess, when everyone watches you be lonely. It even seemed worse for me when Rigley played outside alone. Me, I was ashamed to get nice stuff, because Rigley always had the same old beat-up things. He'd look at mine and never say anything. His were good enough, he'd say.

Going to different schools changes people. It seemed sometimes like I didn't know Rigley during the school year. Then in the summer he and I would be good friends again, and it was fun.

I tried to teach him baseball because I was pretty good at it in school. But Rigley struck out every time I pitched to him. Sometimes we'd go down by the creek to Coolidge Field and watch Skinny Tom and his gang play the niggers. It always ended up in a fight.

They'd let me play sometimes when they needed another man, but no one would ever choose Rigley, so he'd just watch. Skinny Tom didn't like him. Sometimes as soon as he'd see him, he'd say, "Get out of here, Gorilla."

"I ain't leaving," Rigley would say. "This ain't your field, you son of a bitch."

I think Skinny Tom was a little scared of Rigley, 'cause he was six five and only thirteen years old. But he never bothered us; he just said something nasty to us whenever he could.

The niggers were better than his team; they could run faster and make more hits. Tom's team could hit the ball farther, but they couldn't score the runs. It was funny. Rigley used to cheer for the niggers. He went to school with them, and they all liked him.

One night about eight o'clock, we were walking our bikes back from Coolidge. Walking slow, talking to the niggers. I liked this one kid named Herbert, and I used to joke with him a lot. Rigley was behind me talking to someone else.

When I heard his bike fall, I didn't think anything of it. Then some of the kids started laughing. I turned and saw Rigley down on all fours, his head on the ground. I thought they were just messing around. But when I called Rigley, he didn't answer me.

I went over to him, "Come on, man; get up."

He kept staring at the ground. "I'm all dizzy," he said.

"Get up. Maybe you won't be dizzy with your head up." I helped him. He held on to my shoulder. "Can you walk?" I said.

"Yeah, I'm okay."

We walked a few steps that way; then he fell down again. That time I was a little scared.

"Rigley, are you sick? What's the matter?"

He looked real crazy. His eyes were half closed. He grabbed my hand and fell again. Then he used me to get up, and I helped him stand there for a few minutes.

"What'd you do? Faint?"

"No…Maybe I'm hungry, that's all…I'll be okay…just a little dizzy."

"Let's go to my house. My grandmother can feed you."

"No, I said."

"Are you hungry?"

"No."

When we got home, I asked him again if he wanted something to eat. He didn't want anything. "You eat something at home, okay?"

"Yeah."

"See you tomorrow, man," I said.

"Yeah."

Part II: The Secret

I WAS GETTING BIG, too. Not nearly as big as Rigley, but still, I was catching up to my dad. And I could go more places as I got older, like downtown to see a show. Rigley and I used to like to go to the Strand because it was cheap and they showed four cowboy movies on Sunday afternoon. My mother didn't like it because dirty kids and niggers used to go there. But I liked it. After the show, we used to go to Isaly's to have ice cream and talk to some kids from Thornhill High School.

One day we went down to a different theater, the Warner. Everybody was going to the show; it was *The Three Musketeers*, and had lots of sword fighting in it. One kid from Thornhill was waiting in line; he was the dirtiest guy I ever saw. He used to brag about how far he could spit. He was the hocker champion of Thornhill, and Rigley hated him.

"Get out of here, Marvin; you stink and you got germs," he said.

"Shut up, you damn hillbilly. Look who's talking, you special-class bastard."

Marvin tried to push him off balance. He knew Rigley never liked to fight. He always let people push him around until he got really mad; then you had to look out. But Marvin couldn't do much because

Rigley was so big and he was so small. So he spit on him. "Dumb special-class bastard!"

Rigley went crazy. He started chasing Marvin up the lobby. At the Warner the balcony stairs were always roped off, but they ran past the usher and right up the stairs.

"Rigley!" I screamed. "No, Rigley!"

He just kept on running after Marvin.

"You dumb ass, you're gonna get us in trouble," I said. I ran past the usher too.

The usher was calling somebody named Frank. He said we were sneaking upstairs. A policeman came running up the lobby, and two ushers ran up the other stairs and grabbed Rigley and Marvin. The cop caught me. When they brought Rigley and Marvin down, the cop yelled at us about being criminals, and what kind of boys were we, our parents should be ashamed.

"Now get out of here and don't come back," he said.

"We paid our money, you son of a bitch," Rigley said to the cop.

"Do you want to go to jail, kid?" he said.

Marvin was gone already. One of the ushers was a kid that Rigley knew at school, and Rigley started on him. "You slick-haired son of a bitch, you think you're a big shot at school with all them girlfriends? Don't you push me no more."

The kid just smiled, looking nasty; but the cop was getting mad as hell. "I'm telling you for the last time…"

"You tell Slick to come outside and I'll beat his ass," Rigley yelled at the cop.

I was moving Rigley out of the lobby when the cop started toward us.

"Let's go, Rigley. Jesus Christ!" I kept pulling on him till we got outside. He came to his senses then. "Come on," I said, "he's coming after us."

We ran about two blocks. Boy, was I mad at Rigley. "What the hell's wrong with you, man? Here we are—no money, no show, and you almost get us in jail. What'd you have to say that stuff to that cop for?"

"I'm sorry, Sandy, I just hate Marvin and that slick-haired kid. They always bother me at school all the time. I just got mad at everybody, I guess."

"You should be sorry. Now what am I gonna tell my mom? That I got thrown out of the Warner? You dumb ass! Now I have to piss around for a couple hours so I can tell her I saw a show when I get home."

"I'm real sorry, Sandy. I didn't mean to cause you any trouble."

"Aw, shut up!" I said as I kept walking. He was behind me.

"Don't be mad. I won't do it no more."

"Hell, you do it all the time. Every time I go someplace with you, you make somebody mad or scare them or something. You're really crazy, you know that? Just leave me alone; you make me sick."

I spent all that afternoon window shopping. He followed me all the time, only one or two store windows behind me. Sometimes he'd peep at me, like I didn't know he was there, just like a baby. I wondered if Marvin was right. Rigley was pretty dumb about some things; maybe he was in special class.

I turned around and surprised him. He was right behind me. "Rigley," I said, "are you in a special class?"

"No, I ain't in no special class."

"You sure?"

"Yeah, I'm sure. I should know."

"Then why did Marvin say that? You are in one, aren't you?"

"No. I told you before: I ain't in no special class! It's just for dumb kids and I ain't in it. Now quit asking me, you hear? Quit asking me. I ain't no dummy."

I knew all of a sudden that he really was in special class. It all seemed to fit now; he was smart and yet he was dumb. Sometimes he knew about things, how animals lived, how to inhale when you smoke, how to play dice under the bridge. He even understood the niggers when they talked. But he was never smart in school, and sometimes he acted like a baby. Still, he already did so many kind of things I never did, or never was allowed to do.

"Rigley, you know they could give us the electric chair for sneaking into a show?"

"Oh, they can't do that. You're lying." I was lying. "Can they do that, Sandy? Can they really do that? It don't seem right. Hey, let's get the hell out of here."

I didn't say anything; I just watched him while he was talking. Maybe he believed me; he seemed to think it back and forth.

"Let's go, Sandy. I don't want to stay in town anymore."

"Rigley, say *Dracaena marginata*." We still played the game after all those years.

"Drasmn..."

"*Dracaena marginata*," I said.

"Dran...a...mod..."

He couldn't say it. I felt funny on the way home. It was as if I had to learn about Rigley all over again. He wasn't like me at all.

I asked other kids about special class at Thornhill High School. One kid told me they didn't do anything. The teacher used to drink coffee and read the paper in the cafeteria a lot. The kids just fooled around and got into trouble.

Rigley told me once that some people take longer to learn things than others. But I don't know; sometimes they never learn anything...like Rigley with *Dracaena*. He said that mechanics never have to read, they just have to know how to fix cars and use wrenches and things. What a terrible thing to think about: my best friend, and I didn't even think he'd be a mechanic. Sometimes I thought he was too dumb to get any kind of job. But how could I tell him that? I had to act the same and think different, like I had a strange kind of secret. He even told me he wanted to be a fighter pilot if he got drafted. Oh, man!

—⊶⊷—

When I was fourteen years old, just out of ninth grade, I started caddying out the Meander Valley Country Club. New caddies always had a tough time; you really had to stay away from the big guys. I knew most of them; they were a goddamn scurvy bunch of bums from the North Side.

One kid was really bad; he was noisy and mean, always pushing guys and twisting their arms. Carlo, one of the guys I was with, said, "He's such a prick. How can somebody like that have a nice little brother? Did you know Jimmy Ryan's his brother?"

"No," I said, "I didn't know that. Does Jimmy come out here much?"

"Yeah, he comes, but he had to get new glasses again."

"No kidding? You suppose he's going blind?"

"I don't know, man. They're so thick now, he looks like a bug."

"Wonder why he's not out today?" I said.

"Hey, Sandy," said Carlo, "don't look at him now, but Harry's been staring at you. He has a hard-on for all new caddies."

Sure enough, he started after me. "Hey, you dago. Who the fuck let you in here?"

"Look, Harry. I never did anything to you. I don't want no trouble, okay?" I talked real quiet.

"I'm saying you're a dago wop pig bastard. How's that?"

"Aw, fuck you. Just leave me alone, huh?"

27

"Leave you alone? I'm gonna beat your greasy ass for you."

He hit me in the shoulder and it hurt like hell. He was a real nut and I didn't want to fight him. Son of a bitch loved to fight, especially someone younger than he was.

I pushed him in the chest all of a sudden and he fell backward. He didn't expect to fall and everybody laughed. Man, he screamed at me. "I'm gonna kill you now, fucker!"

I was running by that time. I never thought he was nutty enough to try to kill me; maybe he was. He was fast. He caught me as I ran down the far end of the caddy yard near the big trash drums. All the kids came running down and circled around us. They loved a good fight.

Harry hit me right in the jaw. It was the hardest punch I ever got in my life. I didn't even know who I was for a few seconds. I grabbed hold of him. He tried to get away, but I held on. My head was buried in his stomach and he was trying to box me around. Man, I was getting killed, but not as much as I expected. I realized I was stronger than he was, but he was a better boxer, light and fast, and tall.

"Let go, you queer. Goddamned chicken!"

We scuffled around the yard, but I never let go. Harry was beating my goddamn head in, but as least I had all my teeth. He tried to push me down on the ground so he'd have a better chance to make me let go. But I didn't let go, and he was getting madder every minute.

He tried to go behind me and I just brought my arm up over my head to protect myself before he hit me again. But what I did was flip him over and make him fall backward. He fell hard on his back. He tried to get up, but took a little more time than before, and I grabbed ahold of him again.

Anyway, we were rassling and I ended up with him on his hands and knees and me standing over him. I jumped right on him with all my might. He tried to force me up, but I hit the bastard a couple good blows right in the back. I hurt him that time. He got up real

28

slow, holding his back and groaning. But the bastard still came at me, only slower this time. He was getting weaker. I caught one arm and started swinging him around. He hit those cans like a steam engine, man. One was half empty and it fell backward. He went right with it down the bank and into the slimy green shit growing in the river. It couldn't have happened better: both Harry and the barrel going down the steep hill, tumbling like a goddamn avalanche.

The whole caddy yard loved it; everybody thought I was something special to take on that bastard. I played like I wasn't scared a bit. Hell, after getting my brains beat out, I deserved to be a hero.

Caddying that summer was nice. I became a regular out there and got out most of the time. The money wasn't much, but I made enough for some school clothes, and I didn't have to ask Mom for money to go the show.

But the summer was over fast, and it was time for school again. I was a sophomore at St. Alphonsus Liguori High School.

Autumn was a good time for me; it meant football and cool weather. School was tough, though. In grade school we had a small class, and everybody knew each other. But in high school each class was huge, and all of a sudden people didn't know me. Some of my old friends didn't hang around anymore. Everybody had new friends.

Mine were nice. Not so great at sports, or so smart, or so good looking, but they were the kind it was nice to be around.

Burton was my best friend. I met him when we tried out for football. Neither one of us knew how to play in a game with rules and penalties and things. We just knew how to stay in bounds, play fair, and try not to hurt someone on purpose. Well, we went out for the team and saw how much we had to know...and didn't get much of a chance to learn. Burt said that some kids trying out had been playing grade school football for five years. Everybody was supposed to know so much, and we didn't know anything.

Burt was an end. He was big and strong, but not too fast. I was a guard, and not too fast. Anyway, we made traveling squad for a few games. At least we could call ourselves football players.

One coach was a real bastard who hated us for some reason. At practice he hollered at us more than anyone else. We called him Hoppin' John. That was his first name. Every time we were playing in a game and someone would mess up a play, old John would hop and stomp all over the field. When the kid that made the mistake came off the field, John would put on a show for all the fans, bitching and stomping all around the kid.

Most people I knew thought he was an ass. Burt said he came from a big Catholic family in town—his brother was a priest—and John had a hard-on for everybody because he was always too skinny to play ball himself.

He had his favorites, though. He'd ride them home every night after practice. Burton and I used to go home that way, too. They always passed right by.

One night it was hot as hell and I was dead tired from running signal practice, so I asked him for a lift. He said, "Yeah, all right," and looked real disgusted. Burt and I sat in the back seat with some of the other guys. He never said a word to us all the way home. So I said piss on him; I wouldn't ask him again if I was fucking dying.

It was funny how I seemed so good to the kids around my house. I was the only one who went to Catholic school, and out for football. All of a sudden they seemed smaller to me. I'd go down the field and be a big shot, kicking, passing, beating the hell out of the ball.

There was a kid named Will who used to come down to Coolidge with some of the other guys from his neighborhood. They had their own team and they played dirty as hell. Sometimes, if you were on the bottom of a pile, they tried to scratch your face or kick you in the balls. There was one kid especially who used to piss me off. He was a halfback and he liked to run the ball, but every other play he'd put on a big act, like he was hurt.

"What's wrong now?" I'd ask.

"Oh, my leg, my leg!"

His buddy Will would always come over to him and help him up and talk to him, and he'd walk around to get the soreness out and jump up and down and run in place like he was one of the Cleveland Browns. It got to be a real joke; all the other guys would spend half their time waiting for him to recover.

"Who the hell do you think you are, Will, a doctor?" I said.

"Shut up, Sandy. He's really hurt this time."

"Aw, hurt my ass! That bastard's always hurt."

"If your guys wouldn't play so dirty, he'd be okay."

"Why don't you screw, Will? You know he's faking and so do I. How come you're so worried about that fairy? Look at Sam or Herman, how come they ain't all injured after every goddamn fucking play? Because they know you ain't gonna come around feeling sorry for them, that's why."

"Okay, Star, you think you're such a big deal when you come down here, kicking and passing. So how come you ain't first string, huh? You ain't nothing but a second-string lineman who hangs around retarded kids."

"Shut your goddamn mouth, Will! He's not retarded. And if you say any more I'll beat your ass, you and that fucking fairy. You ever try to cheat him at cards, Will? If he's so dumb, how come he can clean you all the time?"

"I ain't gonna show you how to pick your friends, Star. If you like dumb kids, that's your business."

Later that month we were playing a game on the flats of the old mill yard. I was doing a good job of mowing them down. I wasn't really a runner; I was slow and couldn't shift, but I could run through them. Will and his team were always after me; they tried to hurt me no matter who got the ball.

Will thought he was a great lover, always combing his hair; that's why I liked to beat his ass. He wanted to get me real bad, too, but it always took two of them to get me down, and they couldn't understand it.

As it got late, some of the kids had to go home because it was dark, so we played rough and tumble under one of the old street lights. I stayed because I liked doing what I was doing, running the ball. For a lineman it was fun.

Pretty soon it was me against Will's team, and he loved it. A few times someone pulled my hair or punched me in the face or balls when I was down. I was getting mad, because in rough and tumble it was supposed to be every man for himself. Will started calling me a baby.

Rigley was there watching me, but he never wanted to play. "Come on, man, they're beating my ass and I need help," I said.

"I ain't coming."

"Get in here, Rigley! You want to see me get stomped by all these queer bastards?"

"Just 'cause Will's a son of a bitch, that don't mean I should play ball," he said.

"Rigley, I need your help. I'd do it for you, wouldn't I?" I was talking real soft because I didn't want them to hear me.

"Yeah, I guess so."

"Okay. You help me when they all gang up on me. Get some of those guys off my back; they been piling on all night."

We played again. Each time I got the ball, the same thing happened; Rigley wasn't helping.

"Rigley, that little son of a bitch is scratching me when I'm down. Get him, will you?"

"Yeah."

Next time around, the same thing happened; the little kid they called Mule kept tripping Rigley and then piling on me.

"Rigley, kick that little bastard out of the way!"

"I can't get him, Sandy. I keep falling down. Damn ground is slippery."

They were hurting me and they knew it. Will loved seeing me fight the whole gang. I didn't know what to do. I was madder than hell because I could take any two of them and beat their ass. And Mule wouldn't dare try that scratching bullshit unless they had me way outnumbered.

I got nasty. They were trying to hurt me so I tried to hurt them back. I caught one of them in the stomach with my knee. But they got worse. When I was down, someone got me in the mouth and cracked my lip and it started bleeding like hell. Man, it hurt. My lip began to swell up and I was spitting all that goddamn blood out of my mouth. I was tired, too, man; Will's boys had wiped me out.

I looked over at Rigley and he was playing some kind of dumb game with Mule, laughing and pushing. He didn't even care how I was hurt, and that made me mad.

"You stupid, retarded son of a bitch!" I screamed at him.

He just looked at me really sad. Then all he did was walk away. The other guys laughed like hell. They not only beat me but they heard me call Rigley the same thing everybody else did. I called to him, but he didn't answer. He just waved his hand behind him like to say, The hell with you; you ain't no different than anybody else. You ain't no special friend.

"Rigley! I'm sorry, Rigley."

Everything was all quiet in the mill yard except for my voice. I looked back at Will and all the guys there. They were just watching and grinning. I fell into their trap, man, and they turned me against my own man. I just walked away.

I followed him home but he never even turned around. I was sorry then. Our secret was out. All those years I knew that he was different. Then when he heard me say it, I guess he finally knew it, too.

No one was home but Gini. She came downstairs and saw me sitting in the hall. I tried to look like nothing was wrong, but she knew I had been crying.

She came and sat on the stool and talked very soft. "What's wrong?"

"Nothing."

"Come on..." she said, putting her hand on my shoulder.

"I called Rigley a name," I said, not looking at her.

"What name?"

"I said he was retarded."

"Oh, Sandy," she said, kind of disgusted, "why'd you say that?"

"You know that kid Will from Curtis Street?"

"Yes."

"Well, we played rough and tumble tonight and it was me against his whole gang. Rigley saw me getting killed and never helped. He was just standing around, giggling and falling down while I got this fat lip here. Well, I got mad. And he really looked...retarded."

"So you called him that," she said. She sounded ashamed of me.

"Yeah, but I didn't mean it. Christ, I didn't mean it!"

"He really is, you know. Do you really think he's just like everybody else? Like you?"

It seemed strange to hear someone close to me say what I never even wanted to say to myself all those years. Everybody saw it in him all along, yet between us it was a secret.

I didn't answer. She sat beside me for a while and we didn't talk. Then she said, "Want some ice cream?"

Later, Rigley and I got over what I said. It seemed silly sometimes, like I made a big thing out of nothing. I don't think we ever mentioned it again.

<hr>

Burton and I had a lot of fun at school. I was in love with a varsity cheerleader, but she never even looked at me. She went with Jim McGinnis, president of the junior class, co-captain of the football team, too.

One time in the hall she asked me where the coaches' locker room was. I was trying to be cool, man. Inside I was screaming, "Say something, bastard! Come on; come on," but nothing cool came out. Maybe it was better that way. I just said, "Down the end of that hall," and shut up. At least I didn't make an ass of myself.

Funny the way things are. McGinnis could make tackles all day long, but when I tried to do it, I looked like a dummy. Speed, man. Being strong don't mean anything without speed. And worst of all, McGinnis was a nice guy; I couldn't even hate him for it.

One time she touched me. Man, I wanted that hand on my body forever. All she wanted was for me to pass a note to Jim for her in study hall. I told Burt she had the hots for me, and we both laughed. She never even saw us when we walked by her.

"Maybe his big cock is what she's after," Burt said.

"No, man. She's too clean; she probably never thinks about that kind of stuff. What a match: the kid with the whitest teeth going with the girl with the smoothest ass. And us two fuckers…all we do is end up chasing lowdown slutty broads."

"Bullshit, man, she wants to get laid just like everybody else. I can tell; she's doing it already."

I used to clown around a lot in some classes. She would laugh like all the other kids, but would never talk. I wondered what it would be like to take her to a dance in a nice car with a tuxedo on. Hell, it was a dream.

The year passed fast after football season and Christmas. Burt lived too far from me so I usually just saw him on weekends. I had some time on my hands at night so I spent it with Rigley. He'd come with me and we'd hang around down the Isaly store on Sloan Street; it had the best ice cream in town. Spring came soon. Then school was out.

I was fifteen and couldn't get a working permit, so I went back to Meander Valley to caddy. I grew a lot over sophomore year and felt like I could carry five bags instead of one. It was too bad I couldn't get a real job.

Ladies' day was usually bad. All those rich broads trying to be golfers. Some were nice, but some were like old Mrs. Burch, a real pain in the ass.

"Caddy, hold my cap," she would say in her bitchy, rich-lady voice. "Caddy, hold my jacket." She tipped lousy and bitched all around the course. And you did see the course, almost every goddamn square inch of it, especially the woods.

One day I caddied for her while she was playing a match. She sliced a ball into the woods on number fifteen just like that was where she was aiming, and I lost the goddamn thing. She kept me combing through those woods for twenty minutes. Man, my shoes were soaked, I was being chewed by bugs, and the bitch had the balls to call me stupid because I couldn't find a ball she hit fifty yards into a swamp.

I was so pissed at her that for the first time in my life I was going to steal a ball from her bag. Everybody else did it all the time. It was a real joke; you told your mom and dad or anybody else who'd ask that you found it in the woods. Yeah, nice shining balls without one smudge on them, all laying out in the woods like mushrooms waiting to be picked.

But her balls were the cheapest ones made, not even worth stealing. I was looking for Titleists or Spalding Dots, something you could sell easy, but she had nothing but shit in her bag.

She reported me to Rinky, the caddy master, because I lost her ball in the woods. He called me in to the pro shop after we were done.

"Look, man," I said, "you know what a hacker she is. She hit a ball straight into the swamp on fifteen and then got pissed because I couldn't find it."

"I'm not worried about the lost ball," he said. "But she said you were surly."

"What's that mean?"

"Acting pissed off all the time."

"Pissed off? I'm in the woods a half hour with the swamp rats sniffing at my cock looking for a cheap goddamn J.C. Higgins marshmallow ball. Wouldn't you be pissed? You ever see a son of a bitch find a ball hit fifty yards into that swamp?"

"You know these broads, Sandy; you have to kiss their ass."

"Well, fuck her. The world's going to hell and all that bitch is worried about is a tea-and-cookies golf match with a woman old enough to be in a rest home. Kiss ass? I don't say a word; I caddy good; I take all their shit. What more do they want?"

"That mouth of yours is gonna get you in trouble out here, kid. What do you come out here for if you feel like that?"

"Come on, Rinky. You know the only difference between them and us is money. And I ain't kissing nobody's ass for two and a quarter."

He shook his head. "You dagos fuck up everything you get into. Get the hell out of here." He smiled a little, so I knew Mrs. Burch didn't do me much damage; it was too early in the summer.

I didn't see Harry Ryan that second year. He never did bother me at all after our fight. Someone said he got a part-time job at the A&P.

More and more young guys were caddying. There were a lot from the North Side, Hubbard, and Liberty Township. We called them all farmers, and I guess some of them were.

The bastards used to be out there at seven in the morning. The fog wasn't even off the lake yet. Then we had to start going out early, too, if we wanted to get a loop.

I told Rigley to come out, too.

"No. I won't get out if I go."

"Sure you will. I know the caddy master. Come on. You could come out with me."

His mother was listening but I didn't know it. "Sandy," she said, "how much money you make out there?"

"Two and a quarter for eighteen holes. Then you get a quarter tip or a half dollar."

"In one day?"

"Yep."

"Rigley," she said, "you go out there and make some money."

"No, Ma, I don't want to go."

"You get out there tomorrow. I'm tired of you lying around the house. Don't be so goddamn lazy all the time!"

"Aw, Ma."

"Aw, nothing. Just go, that's all."

The next morning I went to get Rigley early. He didn't want to go still, but I dragged him. We hitchhiked and got a ride all the way. We were there about seven thirty.

The caddy yard was quiet and misty. The river was still and you couldn't even see the number eighteen green. It was chilly; the huge trees over the caddy yard made it all shady and cold. Some farmers were there already, but not many East Siders. We tried to play Ping-Pong, but Rigley wasn't very good; he just couldn't hit the ball back to me. So we started playing like babies; I'd hit the ball so it would bounce real high over the net and Rigley could hit it back. We did that a while and we started warming up. It wasn't much fun for me, but Rigley liked it a lot. We played till some East Side guys came in and started teasing me, then I quit.

A kid named Duke started on Rigley. Duke was small and fast and could box and dodge like a pro. Rigley seemed like an elephant next to him. Duke drove him nuts. Rigley tried to kick him, swing at him, spit at him, chase him, but nothing worked. It was funny as hell. They put on a show for the whole caddy yard. We laughed for an hour, till Duke got tired.

"Okay, you big fucker; I'm done," he said.

"Why'd you do those things to me, Duke?" Rigley said.

"Because you're a big, dumb son of a bitch, and bad enough we got farmers out here, now we got you fucking retards."

That made me mad. "Duke, you shut your goddamn mouth. You had your fun; now you had to spoil it."

Rigley just turned away and went to sit down at the far end of the caddy yard. Duke was still grinning; he got a few laughs with his "retard" remark. The more I looked at him, the more I wanted to strangle him. I started after the bastard and he stopped smiling then. I chased him but couldn't catch him.

"Duke, you mangy little prick, you're going in that fucking lake if you ever even look at Rigley again. Here me, Duke? You better get your fucking loops in the afternoon from now on."

Duke stayed away from me; he knew I'd get over being pissed in a while. He wouldn't call anyone a retard anymore either, though.

I went over to Rigley. "You okay?" I asked quietly.

"Yeah, I'm okay," he said.

"Don't worry about him, man. He's nothing but a pig."

"He won't leave me alone," Rigley said. "Nobody leaves me alone, Sandy."

We sat there for a long time. Burt came in the caddy yard about nine. I was surprised; he never came out very much. He waved at me to come over, but I shook my head. He saw Rigley and knew something was up.

About eleven o'clock, the members started to arrive, and Rinky started passing out loops. It didn't matter so much when you came, though if he didn't see you early enough, you were screwed. He decided if you got out and when you got out. Assholes got out in the late afternoon when it was real hot and all the hackers were playing.

Rinky had a bunch of cards in his hand. Everybody got quiet when he came into the yard. He nodded toward me; I got a loop.

"Rigley," I said, "I'll talk to him; maybe you'll get out with me."

Rinky handed me the card. "It's a good loop, kid. This guy tips a dollar."

"Who's in that foursome, Rinky?" I asked.

"Dr. Wilson, his guest, Tom Hines, and W.W. Carlson."

"How about putting Rigley out with me, Rinky? I can coach him along as we go."

"No," he said. "Maybe later."

"Rinky, it's his first time; maybe I can—"

"Does he know how to caddy or doesn't he?"

"Sure. I taught him, but—"

"But what? If he can't caddy, then he shouldn't be out here. If he can, he can wait till later. He's big enough, maybe he can double later this afternoon."

"This afternoon? Rinky, he was here at seven! Give him Dr. Wilson; he's a hacker and that big bag would kill almost anybody else."

"Morelli, do you want this loop or not?"

"But, Christ—"

"Do you want it or not?"

"Yeah," I said, disgusted, "I'll take it."

I went back to Rigley. "Look, I got a loop. I asked him about you, but he said later you'd probably get out. Okay?"

"Okay. Will you wait for me?" he said.

"No. I'm not sure when we'll tee off. Maybe I'll have to go out again. Anyway, we'd get all screwed up. I'll just see you at home."

"Okay."

It was a hot day. We were done with the front nine by one thirty—not a bad time. There was a refreshment stand between the number ten tee and the first tee. There were tables under the trees, and even a colored guy in a white coat serving drinks. What a life those people had. As we'd come down number nine, we could see the clubhouse sitting up on a hill. Right at the top there was a patio with round tables under big umbrellas. The pool was off to the side of that. The broads used to get suntans all along the side of the pool.

Hines was a good golfer, and most of the good ones tipped good. He was easy to caddy for, too. No chicken shit stuff, no "Hold my cigarette, caddy," or "Shag this ball, caddy." And, best of all, I stayed out of the woods. I never had to worry about losing a ball. (The ball fairy used to take them in the woods, we'd say. In their places, she'd leave a pile of dogshit.)

Anyway, coming down nine, we could see Hines's daughter and wife get out of the pool and stand on the hillside waving to him. What beautiful pieces of ass they were! They called to him after he putted out and he jogged up the hill to have a drink under an umbrella.

A lot of the members had younger wives. Even some of the rattiest, ugliest old members. They probably ditched their old ones after they made it big and grabbed some fine young ass. Anyway, at the pool they all seemed beautiful to me. I was just horny, I guess.

Dr. Wilson told all four caddies to order drinks at the refreshment stand. The spook in the white coat was nasty.

The others ordered orange drink. Me, like a dumb ass, I ordered chocolate milk and gave him a chance to fuck over a caddy.

"Sam," I said, "this milk is sour."

"Drink it, kid. Or get fucked."

"Sam!" I was mad, but trying to whisper. "You gave me this on purpose."

"Shut up, you little bastard!" He kept looking around like he was afraid someone would hear him.

"Sam, why do you always try to screw me? Quit fucking around; I'm thirsty."

"You piss me off, white boy. You always looking sour."

"If you caddied for some of the assholes I did, you'd be sour, too. Gimmie my milk."

"Hush up, boy, your man's coming."

"Sam, you prick, you give me that milk or I'll fill your gas tank up with so much sand, you'll think you were a fucking sheik!"

Sam was sweating then. Hines was talking to Wilson right near us.

"Come on, Sam," I whispered.

Sam said, "Fuck," under his breath and gave me some milk.

"See, Sam," I said, "I'm not always pissed; I smile sometimes." I made a big smile and showed my teeth, then gulped down my milk. Then we headed out on ten.

We got back about four o'clock. I was tired and it was hot as hell. I knew Rinky wouldn't let me go home. Shit! I wasn't like those other greedy bastards; I didn't ever want to be a rich caddy.

Rinky was waiting for me when I carried Hines's clubs into the pro shop. "You're going back out with Mr. and Mrs. Eliot Carson," he said.

"Who the hell are they?"

"Guests."

"Look, I'm tired, Rinky. How about if you give that loop to somebody else?"

"There's nobody here. I'm sending out all caddies who got out this morning, and you're one."

Well, I took the loop and caddied. It was hot as hell and they were hackers. And they went eighteen damn holes. Whenever two couples played it was a bitch. The foursomes were slow and they'd bullshit all around the course. It drives you crazy.

The one nice thing about caddying late is that around seven thirty everything is still and quiet; even the creek barely moves. And in late afternoon some tall birds come down to the lake and walk through the water. Some guys called them storks, but they weren't. They were pretty anyway.

Even with hackers, it was nice caddying, knowing you wouldn't be back out again, and that you made five bucks for that day.

Eliot Carson and his wife were friendly. She was beautiful, and they both called me "Sandy" instead of "caddy." It turned out to be a pretty nice day, and coming across number eighteen I was feeling good. The next day I'd be off; the course was closed on Mondays.

As I carried their bags down to the pro shop, the whole place was quiet. Ralph, the shop boy, was there. "Quiet as hell, Ralph," I said.

"Yeah...nice." He never used to talk much. It's funny about guys like that; sometimes he'd walk by as though he didn't know you; then sometimes, like then, he'd talk.

"That guest tip okay, Sandy?"

"Yeah, seventy-five cents. They were real decent, you know, Ralph? Hackers, but nice people. Didn't bitch; didn't give the caddies a hard time; just out there having some fun."

"Not all these people are bastards," he said as he shined their clubs.

"Yeah, once in a while you meet someone who doesn't think his money makes him better than you...Anybody else out yet?"

"Yeah, Big Sam, O'Brien, and some farmers; Booty and Jack should be about on fifteen. I saw another foursome coming down eleven about an hour ago."

"Hell, they'll be out on the turn hitching soon. I'd better get my ass out of here or I'll never get a ride."

"Yeah, see you."

I was thirsty and didn't want any pop, so I headed down the ramp toward the water pump. As I turned off the ramp, I could see the whole caddy yard—and Jesus Christ, there was Rigley! "What the hell are you doing here, Rigley?"

"Waiting for you."

"Waiting for me?"

"He told me to wait."

"Who did?"

"That guy with the blue hat."

"What'd he say?"

"He said that I'd get out later. Only when more kids came, they got out first."

"Did you say anything to him?"

"Yeah, I asked him if I was going out. He said I was new and probably no good."

"Fuck! Are you sure it was the guy in the blue hat? The oily bastard with the white shoes?"

"Yeah, that's him."

I was really pissed. "Come on, I'm gonna talk to Ralph." He was sweeping out the pro shop.

"Hey, Ralph, how come Rigley's still here in the yard?"

He didn't say anything; just kept on sweeping.

"Ralph, goddammit, what the fuck's he doing here?"

Ralph looked at Rigley, then at me. He acted like he really didn't want to answer. All he said was, "You know."

"No, I don't know. I don't know why Rinky didn't either put him out or send him home."

"Pete told him to keep him around in case they ran out of caddies, but to put everyone else out first."

"All the fucking farmers out first? Pete should stick to fucking members' wives and leave the caddies alone. What'd Rinky say?"

"He didn't say shit. Neither did I."

"Ralph, that was a lousy thing to do: keep him around the yard all fucking day."

"Hey, man, I don't know this kid." He nodded at Rigley. "All I know is that Pete's a prick, and he can fire me any time he wants to. And he can make it shitty for Rinky around here, too. Besides, you ought to cool it; the Old Man thinks you're a pretty good caddy. He's gonna take you out a few more times, and if you keep it up, you'll be his special."

"Ralph, at least the bastards can be decent. He came out here with me at seven thirty this morning, and hasn't eaten anything all fucking day."

"Look, Pete and you don't have no bitch, right? Stay clear of him and you'll be getting the best loops out here. The Old Man still plays four days a week."

"Man, Ralph, every time I see Pete in that blue hat and fag shoes, I want to bust him one."

"You're a hothead, Sandy. If you keep your mouth shut, you'll save everybody a lot of trouble. What the hell, maybe he'll get out next time. Lot of people don't get out the first day."

"Sure. And they go home at two o'clock, too. Well, you tell Rinky that's what he's gonna do from now on. If Pete don't have no caddies for his broads, then fuck him."

"Who are you, his manager?"

"Hey, man, you're not the one who sat out there in the yard all goddamn day. All you do is sweep this fucking shop and shine clubs. Well, you tell Rinky next time he wants somebody to caddy double for a late afternoon match, he can get a farmer. I ain't doing him favors anymore."

O'Brien and Big Sam and some other guys got in soon after I got through bitching at Ralph. They came down to the turn pissed because there was a whole gang of hitchhikers there, and it'd be hard to get a ride that late. When it was late, the members didn't leave so often, so no one stopped down at the turn to pick us up.

Sam and O'Brien thought they'd have a better chance out on the street, so they started walking down the long, winding drive. Rigley and I started down about a half hour later. When we got out on the road, O'Brien was waving at us to stay away. I gave him the finger and started thumbing. Man, those cars were passing us like we were hairy apes in jock straps. They blew right past Sam and O'Brien, too. We were there almost another half hour when they finally came up to us.

"Hey, Sandy, can we talk to you? Private?"

I looked at Rigley for a second; he didn't say anything, so I walked over to them. Sam spoke first. "Look, man, I know that big guy's your friend, but he's scaring the fucking cars away."

"Aw, horseshit, Sam. You come all the way back here just to hand me that?"

"I tell you he's too damned big. Ain't nobody gonna stop for someone who looks that old. And then if they don't pick you up, they won't pick us up."

"Hey, man, I don't want to hear this shit. That poor bastard has been out here since seven this morning, and fucking Pete wouldn't let Rinky put him out."

"Look, Sandy, I know you got first ride and everything, but we're never gonna get home, none of us," said O'Brien.

"Sandy," Sam said; they were talking low, trying not to make Rigley hear what they were saying. "How about if we hitch first and you guys go down the road? Then if we get a ride, we'll tell him you're one of us…if he asks."

I thought for a minute. They were trying to be decent; usually we'd end up beating each other's brains out. "Okay, we'll switch places. But if your driver asks, don't forget to tell him we're caddies."

They looked at each other as though they couldn't believe I agreed without a fight. "Okay," they said, and walked right past Rigley without a word…right to our spot.

"We goin' down the road?" Rigley said.

"Yeah, I owe them a favor so they asked me. We'll get a ride; don't worry. They said they'd tell the guy that picks them up that we're caddies, too."

"Shit! They ain't gonna help us. I know that O'Brien kid from school, and he don't give a shit about nobody. What the hell we doin' this for?"

"Shut up, will you? We'll get a ride."

Like hell we got a ride. It was getting dark. Sam and O'Brien got a ride right away; and when they rode by, they looked straight ahead. After a while we started walking down the road, and made it almost halfway home. Finally, one of the guys who worked with my father picked us up.

―――― ∞∞ ――――

Burt and I played baseball the next day. We saw two niggers on the same team fight and almost kill each other. One was called Willie, a real nice, big guy. He was first base on their team. Sonny was short-stop. We were killing them, nine to three, and Sonny kept calling Willie a fat pig and a motherfucker.

One time Willie missed a throw from Sonny to first; Sonny threw it low, and Willie lost it; it rolled into the high grass that grew around the creek alongside the field. Man, Sonny called him a fucking black nigger. Willie told him to shut up, and Sonny threw a glove right in his face. It must have hurt because Willie's nose started bleeding. He grabbed Sonny, picked him up, and threw him.

Sonny was tall and skinny, and thought he was another Sugar Ray Robinson. He started dancing around, but Willie grabbed the fucker and beat his ass again. Crazy Sonny started jabbing and dancing again, and Willie caught him again.

Finally, when Willie started walking away, Sonny grabbed a bat and hit him right across the back, just missing his head. Then the crazy prick was going to hit him again while he was down. Burt got to him first and gave him a low shot to the stomach that folded him in two.

"What the fuck's the matter with you, you skinny asshole?" he said as Sonny was rolling around on the ground. The other niggers started to bitch at Sonny then, too. Funny, while they were fighting, no one tried to stop it. I wondered if they would have let Sonny bash Willie's brains out. They're weird, man. They fight like animals, dirty as hell.

I went over to Willie to see if he was okay. He was all stooped over, his hands on his knees.

"I'm okay, man." He seemed surprised that I gave a damn. He just kept moving his shoulder around. It must have hurt like hell.

"Maybe your mother can have your doctor look at it," I said.

Willie looked at me funny. One of the niggers laughed out loud. "Yeah, Willie Boy, have your mama to take you to the doctor. Hey, Willie, go see that doctor man."

They all laughed like hell. Even Willie. I didn't think it was so goddamn funny; his shoulder might have been broke.

I went back to Burt, who was standing over Sonny. "Sonny," I said, "you could have killed him."

"Fuck him! Fuck that fat nigger!" he screamed.

Burt kicked him right in the ass. "A fair fight ain't enough, huh, asshole? You need a bat, too?"

"Aw, he's nothing but a little bitching pussy," I said. "All the time: Willie can't catch; the pitcher can't throw; the fucking fielders can't catch. Everybody stinks but this loudmouthed little prick. Hear me, Sonny. Next time you want to act like a pussy, you play somewhere else. And if you ever hit anybody with a bat again, Burt's going to cut your balls off with his switchblade. Show him, Burt."

Burt flashed the pearl-handled blade and flipped it out. "Get going, fucker," he said. "You're lucky we didn't let Willie stomp your brains out."

Sonny was all dirty from rolling around on the ground. He got up slow, and walked away without saying a word.

"Crazy fucker," Burt said, shaking his head. "He was really going to kill Willie."

"Yeah, and Willie's a nice guy. Too bad. All the niggers you ever hear about are pricks like Sonny. The good ones like Willie never say much."

"Yeah, Sonny ain't worth a shit."

"You know, Burt, I told Willie he ought to see a doctor and everybody laughed. You think he's ever been to a doctor?"

"No, man. They ain't got money for doctors like we do. You see those shacks they live in? Poor bastards probably never ate three meals a day in their life."

Next day, Burt and I went fishing at Council Park. It was fun doing things with him. Too bad he didn't live closer; it was just too damn hard to see him.

Rigley bothered me sometimes. He'd go places with me too, but anymore it wasn't the same. His mother was a pain in the ass, always bitching at him, wanting him to cut the grass or do some other shit he couldn't do. Every time I went over his house, it was the same story.

Sundays were really bad. It seemed like I spent half of every Sunday afternoon pissing around, trying to get Rigley to go to the show. One time he had to wait till his dad left so we could sneak down. Another time he had to mow the grass first, then if he did a good job, his mother might give him money for the show. But most of the time nothing happened, so I started going myself. I didn't need any of that bullshit every Sunday.

I hardly ever saw a cowboy show then, but I didn't care. I saw beautiful girls, and detective stories, and horse stories. They were a lot better than that same old crap down the Strand. Whenever I did go down there with Rigley, the film would break a few times and everybody would scream and throw stuff and stamp their feet. It seemed dirtier down there, too.

After a while I never asked Rigley anymore. As I got older, I started going out with Burt. I'd meet him downtown since he took a different bus.

I decided that Rigley had the fucking meanest, stingiest, rottenest parents in the whole world. His old man was the worst one. I'll bet that son of a bitch never did anything nice in his life. I never saw him smile, even at Rigley's mother. He was always looking mean, like some lousy, mangy old stray dog. You never knew what he was thinking whenever he looked at you. Sometimes he looked like he'd just as soon kill you. Other times he just had that dumb, pissed-off look, like a dog.

Anyway, Burt and I went fishing. It used to be an old swimming pool, the one the niggers had to swim in. Someone had knocked out two walls, so the water ran through and out of it. There were bluegills in there.

It sure was big. Years before, it was the only one in the park. Then when they built the new pool, the whites let the niggers swim in the old one. Then the niggers even gave it up. It was still nice if they'd have taken care of it. I don't know…Maybe I'd be pissed too if someone told me I couldn't swim in the new pool and had to stay in the old one with no bath house or anything. Especially if the whites were all like Rigley's father. Shit, he was even worse than most niggers.

We didn't get any bites so we started hill climbing like we used to do when we were younger. Some of that shale rock was a bitch to climb. Water used to drain out through some of it. It just trickled down and made the clay get slippery. It was fun as long as you didn't slip, and slide all the way down like Burt did, and have sharp rocks almost cut your balls off.

We played some shuffleboard, too. Then we stopped at the Royal Oaks, a nice little bar up by the park. Kids were allowed in the back room to eat; and they served great hot dogs. No one ever had any booze back there, just a pop drink called a pink lady. I think it was part orange and cherry. Anyway, we were gone all day. I told Mom I wouldn't be home so I'd eat at the Oaks. Mom took most of the money I made off my loops and saved it for me, but I always had enough left for the Royal Oaks.

Council Park was a long way from my house. Burt and I rode our bikes home together for a while, but then he had to turn off at East Broadway Avenue. I had about two miles to go alone. We had a good time, and I was tired and dirty. The sun was going down, and I was riding real slow, taking my time. I knew some of the people on Sloan Street, so I stopped to talk to them as I went along.

When I finally came to our street, I could see Rigley walking up Sloan.

"Hi," I said. "Where you been?"

"I ain't going out that golf course no more. Fuck it."

"What d'you mean? Were you out there today?"

"Yeah, and I ain't going no more."

"What the hell are you doing here so late?"

"That guy Pete told me to wait 'cause maybe some ladies would come out."

"Aw, shit! Ladies never come out that late."

"Yeah. I started home, and he came after me."

"You mean he chased you down at the turn?"

"Yeah. I didn't know his car. I thought it was a member stopping, but it was him, and he was mad. Said I was the only caddy there, and I had to go back."

"That fucking son of a bitch!" I said. "Who the hell told you to go out there alone anyway? Why didn't you ask me? There ain't never any loops on Tuesday."

"My old lady was bitching at me to go out. Besides, Pete said I'd get out more if I showed him how much I wanted to caddy."

"Why the fuck did you listen to Pete anyway? Rinky's the caddy master; Pete's just a goddamn assistant pro who gives lessons to rich broads."

"He said there was some ladies coming out at four o'clock, but they never came," Rigley said.

"Rigley, listen: You come with me tomorrow and I'll talk to Rinky again, okay?"

"You sure I'll get out, Sandy? My mom's pissed at me 'cause I ain't making no money. She don't think I ever go out there; she says I just go playing around down the creek."

"You be ready in the morning about seven, and we'll head out there. Tell your mother to pack a lunch, okay?"

"Yeah."

I couldn't believe that fucking Pete. What a prick to make him come out and stay all day on a Tuesday. He probably had a late golf date with a broad and it fell through. Rigley's so goddamn dumb!

Later that night I couldn't fall asleep. The moon was real bright and I could see it through the window near my bed. It was hot and sticky and quiet, except for the car doors slamming up at the beer garden. Everyone in the house was asleep.

I started thinking about Rigley. He sure got screwed those two days. Why in hell did the Lord ever make a poor bastard like that? What was going to happen to him?

Nobody let him alone. Me, I never bothered anybody. If a guy wanted to wear his fly open, that was his business. Why in the hell didn't everybody act the same way? What did they know about Rigley anyway? All they could say was that he looked funny, but hell, lots of people look funny.

Outside, the moon was smaller, but still bright. Once in a while I'd hear a cat, or a chicken clucking back at John's. The cars up the street seemed to be getting noisier.

I heard guys tell me I shouldn't mess around with Rigley at all. It wasn't cool, they said; he dragged me down, and I looked sort of weird, like he was my pet or something. Hell, I didn't want to be weird. But he was my friend, and I just couldn't leave him alone; people would eat him up. Then I'd be a real ball-less son of a bitch. But cool. Fuck it.

That morning we were out the course at seven thirty again. It was chilly as we sat on the benches. It was a mixed day, men and women coming out. I was hoping for a man; women never tipped as much, and it took sometimes six hours to play eighteen holes. They just drove you nuts more than men.

No one was playing cards in the yard; it was just too cold. Funny how the yard was always cooler; the huge trees all around kept all the sun out. It was always dusty and dark.

O'Brien and Sam came in. They looked sleepy and mean. I don't know how they ever understood each other; they almost never talked. They just sat around looking pissed and trying to be cool. Pauly and Jack came in, Jimmy Ryan, farmers. The whole place was filling up; it was going to be a big day.

Rinky came out of the locker room. The room was in the basement of the clubhouse and you had to come up some stairs to get to ground level. There was a long blacktop about thirty feet wide going all along the side of the clubhouse to the pro shop, which was a smaller building farther down the hill. In the morning, when caddies came in, they came along the walk between the clubhouse and the pro shop. Everything was blacktop except the caddy yard.

We all played a game, though I wasn't sure who knew it. We all acted like it didn't mean nothing to get a loop. We'd look around, or talk to each other like Rinky wasn't even there. Rinky knew the game, too, and he didn't mind playing it.

I saw Rigley looking right at him, hoping Rinky'd give him a card. Rinky always carried a handful of score cards with the names of members who were playing that day. If he gave you a card, that was your man. You went to the shop to pick up his bag from Ralph, then you went up the blacktop to wait. There were long benches all along the edge of the blacktop, from the locker room stairs almost down to the pro shop. On a busy day the benches would be lined with caddies and bags, sometimes almost fifty guys.

The members didn't like to golf too early on weekdays. Shit, they didn't have to. There wasn't any ball rack down at the tee where you had to sit around and wait till your ball came up to tee off. There was a schedule, and everyone went off on time. It wasn't like the city courses, where you had to fight your way on to the tee, and then for eighteen holes worry about some asshole driving a ball into the back of your head. No, man. There weren't thousands of people trying to golf out Meander Valley. There everybody was a big shot; everybody was polite.

"Rigley," I whispered, "don't look at him."

"Why?"

"Cause you look like a farmer, that's why."

"What if I don't get out again? Maybe he won't see me."

"I'll make him see you. Just wait a minute."

Rinky never really walked into the yard. He always came to the edge of the blacktop and stopped. Like I said, everybody pretended, but everyone knew he might be looking at them.

I never knew what the hell he was thinking. I never could figure out how he decided to give out the loops. There were always his
favorites; they got the best ones. But most of the time good caddies
got good loops. The bad caddies and the new ones, and the ones he
didn't like, got bad loops. Some days, when he felt shitty, he'd juggle
things around and fuck everything up. Good caddies got bad loops;
bad caddies and farmers, everything good.

Sometimes when he got cards early, he'd come down into the
yard, look around, wait for everything to get quiet, then walk away.
That used to piss everybody off. He started to do that this time. Then
he motioned to a couple of farmers. They came up, got the cards, and
went for the bags. Rinky walked away.

"Who'd they get, Sandy?" Pauly said.

"I don't know. It's probably Fox and Allen; they got here early."

"Looks like a big day, huh?"

"Yeah. There'll be better loops than Fox and Allen out. Rinky's
just trying to fuck everybody around again. He looked pissed about
something."

"He's always pissed anymore. Pete must be giving him a hard time."

"Yeah. The Old Man makes Pete handle a lot more members now."

"How can they stand that oily fucker?" Pauly said.

"Maybe they can't. Maybe they're giving him a hard time, and
he's laying it back on Rinky."

"Yeah. Rinky never used to be like that."

"Yeah, shit. And I have to talk to him."

"'Bout what?"

I nodded to Rigley. Pauly looked at him. "Think he'll get out?"

Rigley was over watching a washer-pitching game. "I don't know.
Rinky's pretty straight; maybe he'll listen to me this time."

"I heard about what Pete did to this kid." He nodded toward
Rigley. "It's a wonder he comes back."

"His old lady bitches about money all the time. She'll probably take every dime he makes."

"What are you busting your ass for him for?" Paul said. "You shouldn't keep getting them all pissed at you."

I didn't feel like going into all that with Pauly. "See you, Paul," I said. "I have to see Rinky."

"Sure, man." He was just glad he wasn't me, because he sure as hell wouldn't be trying to lay any shit on Rinky.

I caught up to him halfway up the walk. "Hey, Rinky, can I talk to you?"

"What do you want now, Sandy? I heard about all that shit you were laying on Ralph."

"All I want is for you to put that big kid out."

"Instead of you?" He was grinning a little nasty.

"No, not instead of me. With me."

"The Old Man told me he wants you today, Sandy; I sure as hell can't put him out with that foursome."

"I'll take care of him, Rinky, honest."

"Now look, I'm tired of saying it: he can't go out with you. Not one of the guys in that foursome wants to put up with a new caddy. And you know how the Old Man is when he's giving lessons to a member; one slip and your ass has had it."

"Okay, okay. But put him out with Paul or Jimmy Ryan, okay?"

"No," he said as he started walking away.

"Man, are you going to put him out, or are you going to pull the same shit you did the other day?"

"You know why I did that. There just wasn't anyone he could go out with."

"Why didn't you send him home then, Rinky?"

"Look, kid, I'm getting tired of all this. Now did he come out here to caddy or not?"

"Put him out and I'll never bother you again," I said.

"If he goes out, I don't get any more shit out of you, right?"

"That's it. But you gotta put him out a few times."

"Does he know anything? Really?"

"Yeah. He'd be good out there if you didn't give him a prick."

He smiled. "Okay, he's going out. And the first time he walks through a sand trap, I'm going to throw him the fuck out of here, understand?"

"You're a hell of a man, Rinky," I said. He walked away. Fucking Irishman.

I told Rigley he'd get out, and he was really glad. So we went down to pitch pennies and he was my pick-up man. He was good, too. A few times, when it was close, he had the pennies picked up before anyone could measure who was tightest to the wall. Everybody was pissed.

Finally Rinky came down and motioned to me. "You're gonna get out soon," I told Rigley. "Just wait a while and don't get into any trouble. And if you're not out by two o'clock, go home. Understand?"

"Why can't I wait for you?"

"Because I won't be back till two, that's why. Then maybe I'll have to go back out again. Besides, Rinky said you'd get out, so don't worry." He nodded. "Hey," I said.

"What?"

"You go home otherwise, okay?"

"Yeah."

"Okay. I'll see you tonight maybe. Then you can tell me all about your loop."

I picked up the Old Man's bag at the shop. Alban Christie, what a man. He still had some wooden-shaft clubs in his bag. It looked like a hacker's set, but boy could he golf. He never wasted time with practice swings and bullshit like that. All he did was walk up and hit the ball. And I don't think he ever hit a crooked one in his life.

I waited by the locker stairs for almost an hour. Some other caddies came up. There were all good ones in our foursome. One kid, named Simon, he was from the North Side, a nice, quiet kid; then Dominic Frazzini, who was a real clown; Pauly; and me. It would be fun going out.

The Old Man was the easiest guy in the world to caddy for. On the green you gave him his putter and driver and then went halfway up the next hole and waited under a tree until they teed off. And then he hit his drive straight down a pipeline to the middle of the fairway. He couldn't drive as far as some of the younger members, but he still hit the two-fifty-mark easily. I could have caddied fifty-four holes with no sweat.

The ladies were coming out, too. I could see them on the veranda drinking and smoking. Some were on the putting green. It was a good day; nice breeze. I'd get home early.

But for some reason, Dr. Birmingham in our foursome didn't show up. Our time came and went and still we were waiting down on the tee. It was beautiful down there. The tee had better grass than most greens on other courses. There were huge oak trees that shaded the whole tee. Number one sloped down away from the tee, and number eighteen ran into the back of it. There were park benches and tables all around the refreshment stand.

Everyone was joking and taking it easy. The Old Man and R.E. Watkins seemed to enjoy waiting for Birmingham; they were getting semismashed. It was going to be a lazy eighteen holes.

Samuel W. Bheemer was the other guy in our foursome. What a wild ass. He had an ulcer, so he never drank anything but milk, but he was always playing tricks on the Old Man and Watkins. All the caddies liked him because he used to tip big, but everybody in that foursome did, and he used to talk out loud about the asshole members that belonged to the club. Almost always the caddies agreed with him. It was as though he was a caddy himself; he knew the stingy ones, the biggest hackers, biggest pricks, biggest drunks, and biggest whores among the members' wives. And he said it, man; he said it right out, and didn't give a shit. Maybe because he owned a big machine shop, I don't know. All I know is, I wouldn't give a shit either if I had his money.

The Old Man called me. "Sandy, lad."

"Yes, sir, Mr. Christie." I could see him slowing down already.

"Go back up to the locker to see if Birmingham is here. Tell Pete if he's not here, we're going to tee off. Birmy can join us out on the course when he gets in. Give my bag to one of the other caddies till you get back."

"Yes, sir." I went back to the locker, knocked, and one of the butlers came to the door.

"Joe," I said, "is Pete here?"

"He's in the office; go on back," he said, pointing down the hall behind him.

A locker room with a rug, how about that? Pete was sitting in the office going over the match-play sheet for Saturday.

"Pete, the Old Man wants to know if Dr. Birmingham's here."

"Didn't they tee off yet? What the hell are they waiting for?"

"Birmingham, I told you."

He gave me a funny look. Some of those fuckers can tell when you don't like them. I don't think he liked me either, but neither of us said much. Maybe he heard about what I said to Ralph.

"I'll call upstairs," he said. He pressed a button on his phone and asked the clerk at the main desk if Birmingham was in. No he wasn't.

"The Old Man told me to tell you that they're going to tee off. Birmingham can join them out on the course."

"Okay. I'll tell him. Now get back down to the tee."

I just turned and walked out. Son of a bitch loved to give orders. I wonder what he thought I was going to do, go up on the veranda and have a drink? What an asshole!

As I came up the stairs from the clubhouse, Jimmy Ryan came running over to me. "Hey, Sandy, you hear about the trouble in the yard yet?"

"What trouble?"

"Rinky and Ralph had to keep that big guy of yours from killing Basil, Joe Romeo, and Duke."

"Fuck! What happened?"

"You know what pricks Basil and Duke are? Well, they talked your guy into a card game. Romeo just got here and he was looking for easy money, too. Well, they sat down to play, and in two hands cleaned him out. Sucker lost seventy-five cents. See, they made a deal: Basil and Duke take one hand, Romeo take the other one. No shit, the games didn't last three minutes! Before you know it, the big fucker was cleaned and Duke and Romeo just got up and walked away."

"Where was all the trouble?"

"Well, the big guy sat on the bench for a few minutes; I was watching the whole thing. All of a sudden he gets up and walks over to Duke and Romeo and says, 'You cheated; give me my money back.' Well, you know how Romeo talks like a hard man all the time? So he says, 'Man, you shouldn't play poker if you don't want to lose. Poker's a man's game.' The big guy—what's his name?"

"Rigley."

"Yeah, Rigley. Rigley asks him again, and Romeo says, 'Get fucked, zombie,' just like that—'zombie.' Duke started laughing that dumb ass laugh of his, and Romeo just turned his back on him. Well, the big fucker grabs Duke by one hand and swings him around and around like a goddamn doll, then lets him go, sliding down the hill.

You know all those stones down by the water pump? Well, Duke ate some of those stones and got the rest up his ass, man. You should have seen him: all bruised and cut up; it was beautiful. Then Rigley turned to old cool Romeo. Romeo didn't expect him to come after him, but he sure did. He grabbed him by the neck and the belt, and guess what? Wham! Down the hill with him, too.

"Basil, that little fucker, was like a little monkey, yipping and squealing. When he knew he was next, the bastard threw his money at Rigley and ran like hell around the other side of the lake."

"Did Rigley get his money from Duke and Romeo?" I asked.

"Yeah, he picked up Basil's money, every damn penny of it. When he turned to go after Duke and Romeo, the fuckers saw another ass-whipping coming, so they put some money down on the step and ran like hell into the shop.

"Man, Rinky was pissed. When those two bastards went into the shop, he came out storming. 'What the hell's going on here? What'd you do, kid?' he asked Rigley. Rigley said they cheated him. I told him, too. Me and a couple of farmers saw Basil, Duke, and Romeo screw him.

"He looked at Rigley for a minute and didn't say anything. We didn't know what he was gonna do. Then he pulled a card and gave Rigley a loop, just like that. I couldn't believe it; I thought he was gonna throw him out. Then he told Duke and Basil and Romeo that if he ever caught them easing a guy again, he'd send them home for good."

"Thanks for sticking up for Rigley, Jimmy," I said. "That fucking Romeo deserved that for a long time. It's just funny that Rigley ended up doing it."

"Well, I was glad those fuckers got caught by someone big enough. Romeo's been skinning farmers for years. You should have seen his face. Man, he was scared! He thought he was gonna die."

Jimmy went down for me to see if our foursome teed off already. I went down into the caddy yard to see Rigley. "How you doing, man?" I asked.

"I'm okay," he said. "Sandy?"

"What?"

"I got into trouble."

"What'd you do?"

"I played cards, and some guys took all my money. I thought it would be fun, but it was all gone so fast. I got pissed off then, 'cause I think they cheated. You know that little mean kid that was bothering me before?"

"Did you get a loop?"

"Ain't you mad?"

"No. Just don't play any goddamn cards anymore, okay?"

"No, I won't. Yeah, I got a loop, Sandy. Ralph told me to wait a while, 'cause he ain't coming out till later."

"Let me see the card," I said. Christ, he had M.B. Stratten. Rinky sure didn't give him a big break.

"Rigley, you listen to me now. This guy is a prick; he bitches like mad at all the caddies, so be careful. He slices balls a lot, so you have to watch on number seven and number fifteen, okay?"

"Yeah."

"Will you remember all that stuff I told you?"

"Yeah, I will."

"Remember to count every stroke, and rake the trap after he's done. Don't forget to call him 'sir.' And for Christ sake, don't move when he swings, 'cause he'll blame you for all the bad shots. Okay?"

"Okay."

"When you get done, say, 'It was a pleasure to caddy for you, sir.'"

"Okay."

"You hitchhike down at the turn; someone will stop; the lot's full of cars. I'll see you later. Don't let him bother you, understand?"

"Yeah."

"Well, I have to go now; my foursome's already out," I said.

On the way up the walk, I could see the benches were full of caddies. Jimmy came up to tell me that my foursome was gone. "Who'd Rinky give him?" he asked.

"M.B. Stratten. Ain't that a shaft?"

"Yeah. A fucking six-hour ride with a quarter tip, and he bitches all around the course."

"Rinky pisses me off, you know? He could've given him somebody halfway decent instead of Stratten."

"Yeah. You can bet he'll see the course, though." Jimmy laughed a little.

"Yeah. The woods, too."

As I was going up, I saw Duke and Basil together. Duke looked all torn up. His lip was cut. Basil was still shaking, like he saw God, man. I looked over to them as I walked. They just looked down and didn't say anything.

Romeo was further up. When he saw me he said, "Hey, why don't you leave that retarded fucker home? There ain't enough good loops now without you bringing zombies around."

"Hey, Romeo, why don't you go get a job like other old men? What are you now? Twenty-two? Twenty-three? And you still come out here mooching loops and skinning farmers."

Everybody laughed, because what I said was true. He was just too dumb and lazy to work.

"Aw, fuck you," he said. "Why don't you get a job yourself?"

"Because I'm not old enough, that's why. Least I'm not a phony dude all dressed up with fifty cents in his pocket. How're you gonna be a big stud up the corner tonight now that Rigley tore up your tailor-made pants, Romeo?"

Everybody was howling again; I got him good that time.

"Listen, prick, you're gonna get your ass kicked when I see you down at the turn." He stood up. Man, it would have really made me feel good to rip that fucker up.

"Come on, asshole. I'll finish what Rigley started."

He looked like he was gonna come on, but then he stopped and sat down. "I'll get you later," he said. "You just be watching for me."

"Why, you chicken son of a bitch. I'm ready any time. You better watch out for Rigley, though; he's like an elephant; he never forgets."

"Yeah, dumb like one, too," he said.

Everyone was laughing again, some at me, some at Romeo.

The Old Man was born in Scotland and had golfing in his blood. That day he shot a seventy, and he made it look easy, like all you have to do is whale the hell out of the ball. We got done early. All the members were out already, and there were still caddies in the yard, so I went home.

Rigley came over my house about nine o'clock that night. Man, was he happy! Two and a quarter, first time he ever made money like that in his life. He wanted to go out all the time from then on. I told him that I couldn't go out till Saturday because I had to go to school for an equipment check. Man, soon I'd be doing wind sprints and shit. He said he was going out himself.

Burt and I went up to school the next day. Man, you had to fight to get a good helmet. I got my lips puffed up a few times the year before because the helmet slipped down over my eyes and someone caught me with my chin up. It took most of the morning to get a suit.

We had a little touch football game in the afternoon. Sometimes the cheerleaders and majorettes would come by and watch us. I tried to look like a stud, but slow linemen don't come across like that. So the backfield guys always had first crack at the broads.

Burt and I did talk to a few. There was one dark-haired majorette that I liked, but she always dated older guys. Man, she was nice: clean and well stacked at the same time. Her girlfriend, a tiny little blonde cheerleader, dated Burt once. They talked to us about an hour. I couldn't help looking at the legs on the dark one. Man, I'd be talking and my goddamn eyes just couldn't control themselves. She caught me looking once, and just moved a little so she covered most of her legs. She did it cool, though.

When they left, we played for a while, then started home. It was a long walk, and the mill yard was hot and smelly because the creek was so still. Burt turned off for his house and ran home.

It would be good to get back to school again; I missed Burt. He was the only guy I could talk things over with. He liked girls and I didn't feel funny talking about them to him. He liked cars and sports, too. I mean he wasn't a hood like most of the guys out the golf course. He even liked to get good grades, so we'd study for our algebra tests together. Yeah, it would be nice to get back; I was getting tired of summer.

Rigley came over about seven and told me he sat there all day and didn't get out. He said he talked to some kids from the North Side, and they were nice. Pauly let him pick up pennies when they pitched, then he bought him some pop and crackers. He liked Paul. Jimmy talked to him for a while, too, and tried to show him how to play poker so he wouldn't get skinned again.

Duke and Romeo left him alone, he said. Basil wasn't even there; he was probably still scared from the day before. Rigley wasn't going out Friday, either. He had to cut the grass.

"You ready to go Saturday?" I asked.

"You think we'll get out?"

"Man, everybody gets out on Saturday. Mixed day, lots of doctors. They even bring their kids out to swim and play tennis."

"What time we going?"

"Early. Maybe we should get there at seven. He might put us out together if there's an early foursome."

"Yeah. That'd be nice. Okay, I'll be over here at six."

"No, come at six thirty. My dad'll take us out."

We got there at seven Saturday morning. A lot of kids were already there; everybody had the same idea, I guess. It was going to be a scorcher, but we all seemed to feel good. Some guys were playing Ping-Pong already; Ralph was setting out bags; things were hopping early. Rinky came down and called me.

"Morelli…" I couldn't figure out why he wanted to see me so early. "I thought you told me that big kid knew how to caddy?" he said, kind of pissed.

"He does. I told him all about it."

"Well, you're not a very good teacher. You know he got a 'Poor' on his card?"

"Shit! What for?"

"Stratten says he cost him his match."

"Hey, man, Stratten never won a match in his life."

"Don't get cocky, Sandy. The kid lost three balls."

"Where? In the woods on seven and fifteen, right? Rinky, you know what kind of guy Stratten is—"

"That's enough! I'm telling you the kid didn't do the job."

"Aw, fuck! You gave him the biggest hacker and prick out here for his first loop."

"Who should I give him, the Old Man? You know I can't give him a good golfer."

"Why did you give him a bastard, then? There are nice hackers out here."

"Look, I'm trying to run the yard. I don't have time to choose a nice guy every time I give your boy a loop. If he can't caddy, what the hell's he out here for?"

We were going 'round and around again. Finally I changed my tune. "He's been out once, so now give him a lady. The kid'll learn, Rinky. He wants to work; he wants to be good. And nobody's good at first."

"We'll see," he said. "By the way, the Old Man wants you for that eight o'clock foursome with Trask and Birmy and some guest, so go get his bag." He walked away.

"He'll do a good job for you," I said as he was walking. He didn't answer.

Trask was an old timer. Nice guy. They all liked to play early on weekends before it got crowded and all the broads came out. We went right out. The Old Man seemed pissed or tired or something, like he wasn't awake yet. It sometimes took him nine holes to warm up. It was neat coming in before noon; I wanted to sneak out and go home. Maybe go swimming.

The first nine went fast. The ball would get all messed up in the wet grass and I'd have to wash it every hole. The Old Man bitched about the grass, the balls, his clubs, everything but me.

It was getting hot, too. On fifteen, the Old Man looked tired. He was having a lousy day; double bogied fourteen, and couldn't putt worth a damn. He was gonna have to par out to break eighty.

Trask was pissed about something, too. Birmingham and the guest kept bitching about Washington, D.C. It was too damned hot for those old guys, but they still kept playing. Then to top it all off, Trask hit his tee shot in the lake on eighteen. As we walked across the bridge, I was really glad it was over. It was so hot I almost felt like jumping in that shitty lake myself.

"Tell Pete I'm gonna handle the tee at noon," the Old Man said. "Get the list for the matches and bring it down there to me. He's probably still in the clubhouse."

I went up to the booth, got paid, and started carrying his bag down to the shop. As I came around the putting green, I could see all the caddies lined up and Pete and Rinky standing in the middle of the walk talking to Rigley. When he saw me, Pete waved for me to come over. "Take him home," he said. "And don't bring him out here anymore."

"Why?" I asked. Rigely was over sitting on a bench by then; just Rinky, Pete, and I were talking.

"Because he's scaring the members, that's why," said Pete.

"I gave him Ann Horton, Sandy," Rinky said. "She got as far as the first tee, then sent him back. She told me he looks funny, and she was afraid of him."

"Aw, hell. What could he do in a foursome in broad daylight?"

"Just keep him out of here, that's all," Pete said. "I'm getting tired of both of you. I heard about his fight yesterday. Do you know if he'd have hurt one of those kids the club might have been liable?"

"They cheated him," I said. "And did you know that one of those 'kids' is more than twenty-one years old?" I was really getting pissed at Pete.

"He's too goddamn dumb to know whether he's been cheated or not. Didn't he also get a 'poor' on his card the other day? Just keep him out, that's all."

He started to walk away and I grabbed his arm to say something more. That's all I did, just touched his arm, but the bastard put on a big act.

"Get your goddamn hands off me," he shouted. The whole fucking yard came up to look; the bench of caddies was right in front of us, too.

"What are you getting so pissed about? I didn't do anything." I said.

"Don't you ever lay a hand on me again, kid!" he said, still loud as hell.

"All I wanted to do was ask you to give him another chance," I said as calm as I could.

"I settled that," he said. "And one more word and you go with him, too. I don't care if you are Christie's caddy."

Then I blew my stack. "What is this shit?" I said to Rinky. "You cook all this up with him?" I said, pointing to Pete.

"No," he said, "but I think he should go, too."

Then Pete said the wrong thing again. "The kid's a mental retard; we can't trust him around the women."

I really shot my wad then. "The women! The women? You're the one they can't trust around the women, you oily bastard. How many members' wives do you fuck up here every summer? But that's okay, isn't it?"

That was it, man. "Get out of here!" he screamed.

"Sandy, are you nuts?" Rinky said. "Shut the hell up."

A lot of members were watching, too. There must have been a hundred people around us. Ann Horton was there, too.

Just then the Old Man came through the crowd. "What's going on?" he said in a low, mean voice.

Pete answered first. "That big retarded fellow over there frightened Mrs. Horton, and yesterday he beat up some caddies half his size."

"Like hell he did, Pete. Tell him the whole story," I said.

"Shut up!" said the Old Man. He was boiling. He didn't like scenes like that on his course.

"Look, Mr. Christie—" I started to explain.

"Shut up, I said," he yelled again. It was bad news, man; all those members, all those caddies, and all of us arguing on the walk. The Old Man was having a nightmare.

Pete started again. "We want that retarded one to go home, and this one here," he said, pointing to me, "keeps causing trouble."

"Trouble?" I screamed. "Just because I tried to talk sense to you?"

Christie looked around. We were surrounded, and more and more people were coming over to watch. "Damn you, Sandy. Get back to the yard!" he said.

"Aw, hell!" I said, really pissed. "I'm through shutting up." I pointed to Ann Horton. "Look at him, Mrs. Horton. Does he look like a maniac? Who the hell do you need to carry your clubs? An Eagle Scout?"

She just stared at me, smiling, but really pissed. One of the members shouted, "Why don't you just leave, you hoodlum!"

This time I talked to all of them. Hell, I knew I couldn't come back anyway. "You people are so rich you don't even care about a poor bastard who all he wants to do is carry your clubs and take your lousy goddamn two-and-a-quarter, huh?"

"Out!" said the Old Man. "You'll never set foot out here again as long as you live. If you're not out in five minutes, I'll call the police."

"Come on," I said to Rigley. The whole group was quiet. I felt pissed and yet felt embarrassed, like I did something wrong. I blew my cool, I guess. Maybe that was it. Maybe because I swore at them; I don't know. How in the hell could I be right and they be wrong and yet feel so shitty? Those people could do that; they could make you feel like trash just by looking at you, like they always expect you to act lowdown and crude, like the whole world was made up of caddies and club members…like some people belong in the clubhouse and some belong in the yard.

Christie walked back into the crowd, shaking his head and talking to some members. The caddies liked the show, as long as it wasn't any of them who got thrown out.

"I ain't goin'," Rigley said.

"What do you mean you ain't going? Who the hell do you think this blowout was for? Me?" Man, he was so dumb sometimes!

"But my old lady's gonna be pissed if I go home without a loop. She's tired makin' lunches for no money."

"Come on, goddammit!" I yelled.

"All right," he grumbled, disgusted with me.

As we were going down the walk everyone was staring at us. Rinky was trying to get all the caddies back into the yard. As I rounded the corner, there was Romeo, same cool clothes, same pissed-off look, like he was better than you. "Well, you and your zombie really fucked up now, Kid," he said, smiling a little bit.

Man, I never wanted to kill anybody more than I did right then. I moved toward him and he got scared; that smile came off his face right away quick. I was going to bust him one to top off my caddy career at Indian Valley.

"That's enough," Rinky shouted. "Didn't you just cause enough trouble?"

I stopped for a second and looked at Rinky, then back at Romeo. He was shaking a little, and Rinky looked like he needed a physic. It just wasn't going to do me any good to rap Romeo; he would still be a cheap, hustling son of a bitch, and Rinky would still play Superman with the caddies. Nothing would change; I just wouldn't be there anymore. The Old Man would get a new caddy, and they wouldn't even remember my name next summer.

"Aw, fuck both of you," I said, and started walking again.

"You know, Sandy, I'm disappointed in you; I thought you had more brains than that," Rinky said.

"Yeah, well, I'm disappointed in you, too, Rinky. I thought you had more balls than that."

"Your big mouth got you into this mess, not me."

"Rinky, one word from you and that argument might have turned out different. But no, you were more worried about Pete being pissed at you. Well, just remember one thing: you were shitting on this kid, and when the time came to make it right, you didn't have any balls.

"And I'll tell you something else: all of a sudden this place stinks. Those snooty members, these grubby caddies, the whole fucking setup. I'm just glad I'm leaving."

I could tell by the look on his face that I got to him. He knew I was right. I just kept walking and Rigley kept following. When I got to the gate, I don't know why, but I looked back one last time at the shop, the yard, and the clubhouse. I never realized how much of the place you could see from the gate. It was pretty with the lake and the trees on number eighteen, and the first tee off in the distance. I liked the course. It was green and fresh and wet in the morning; I'd miss that.

Rinky was still there watching me; everyone else was gone then. "You know you're fighting a losing battle with that kid, Sandy," he said, sort of quiet, not like he usually talked. I turned around and closed the gate behind me.

At first my mother was mad because of the trouble out the course. My dad just nodded when I told him about what they did to Rigley. They got over it when I started cutting lawns. Besides, football practice was starting in three weeks anyway. Rigley helped me with the lawns. I did all the cutting; he did all the raking, because I hated that. We split the money and Rigley's mom didn't bitch much, though she still said we could have made more money out the golf course.

When we didn't work, Rigley and I rode our bikes all around the city. There was a spring on the East Side where we'd go to rest. It was cool under the trees and the water was cold. Rigley's mother used to send him there to fill up big bottles of water. She said that the water was better for her bowels than city water, whatever that meant. Anyway, we'd hit every corner of the East Side before we stopped for water. It used to take all day.

When football practice started, I spent a lot of time with Burt. The trees around the school were starting to turn, the buckeye trees especially. More and more kids were around the school then. The band had practice every day; the kids that worked summers at the school were there. It wasn't long before school started...school and football and cheerleaders and majorettes and dances and leaf burnings, pretty trees, rallies, bonfires, and nice weather.

Saturday nights were great; Sundays were quiet. I used to go to church, watch a football game, and maybe go to a show that night. It always seemed kind of lonely on Sunday; everyone in my house seemed to feel it, too. I guess everyone was thinking about getting up for work the next day. I never thought much about it, except during football season, when it seemed all I did was go to school, practice, and sleep. Sometimes, especially when the days were gloomy, I could feel that winter was coming soon.

Burt got into more games than I did, but neither of us made a letter. It looked like we'd make first string our senior year, though.

When football season was over, I got a job as a carryout boy in a Kroger store. It was good money, but in winter I froze my ass off carrying out groceries in cold weather. Later I became a produce boy and didn't have to go out as much. I was busy all the time, though; I worked four nights a week.

Burt and I doubled to the Touchdown Frolic dance. Burt fixed me up with a girl, and he took the little blond cheerleader, Patty. At first I tried to get a date with the dark-haired majorette, but she already had a date. It was tough asking her. It was one thing bullshitting with her while playing tag football with all kinds of other guys around and everybody talking at once; but it was another thing talking to her alone in the halls, face to face. Man, I was tongue tied! Nothing I wanted to say came out right. She smiled like she understood, maybe like guys always talked that way to her. No, she already had a date, but thanks, maybe some other time. Burt said she was dating a pre-law student in college. Well, anyway, she dated flashier guys than second-string linemen.

The girl Burt fixed me up with was called Marcia. I knew who she was, but never really talked to her; she was a brain. That night she really looked nice when I picked her up. She wore glasses and had short blond hair and her skin was real light. You couldn't talk any shit to her like you could to other girls; she wasn't on the make.

Burt drove his dad's car. We danced all night to the slow ones. The room was dark except for the big Chinese lanterns that hung across the dance floor in rows. All along the edge of the floor there were tables lit by candlelight. It was really nice. So was Marcia.

She looked beautiful, too. I noticed how nice her skin was. Man, when I danced, and her cheek brushed up against mine, it was soft. I wasn't used to girls, and it sure was nice holding someone soft. She talked nice, too, no bullshit, no phoniness. She was friendly and relaxed.

After intermission the band started making us march to the Mexican hat dance, and the bunny hop. I went wild then. Burt and

I had the whole place laughing at us. Marcia liked it, too. I liked to hear her laugh. It was quiet, not a crazy giggle.

After the dance, we went to Castorina's for a fine meal. We all had lobster, except Patty; she had a steak. Man, I could have lived like that forever; it seemed like nothing would ever bother me that night.

Father Conrad called me to ask if I'd like to be in the Christmas procession at St. Andrew's midnight mass. I told him I couldn't practice much, because of my job, but he said that was okay.

Practice was a wild time. It seemed like when you were in church at night, with no one there but school kids rehearsing for a Solemn High Mass and procession, everything was funny. One loud sneeze from anybody was enough to crack all of us up. I carried the censer, so I didn't have to spend a lot of time on the altar, except during the procession and the parts of the mass when the priest incensed the altar. Then I went right back to the sacristy.

There were about a hundred kids in the procession between the choir and the acolytes and the altar boys. It was a blast; I laughed so much my sides hurt. We had some real clowns in the procession.

Two nights before Christmas, I had to go down to help clean the church. Jimmy Beltram and Johnny Altino always worked the church during Christmas vacation. They were seminarians, two of the wildest asses I ever met. They tormented Father Conrad—let air out of his tires, hid his chalice, did everything to drive him nuts. There were also some kids from Italy there, Johnny's cousins, I think. None of them spoke English, but they were all funny as hell.

"Hey, Sandy, what're you doing here?" said Johnny.

"Ah, Conrad found out I wasn't working tonight, so he nailed me to help you out. Rigley's coming down, too."

I still saw Rigley once in a while, especially during school vacations. He was a senior and couldn't wait to get out of school. He came in a few minutes. "Hi, Sandy," he said. "Who are all these guys?"

"Some are Johnny's cousins."

"They dagos too? I can't understand them."

"Yeah."

We started sweeping the church, and it was a bitch. It was hard to sweep under the pews and kneelers because you couldn't see. We worked our asses off. Rigley cleaned all the old candles out of the rack; Johnny ran the waxer and Jimmy buffed the floor.

Outside it was dark, and the lights in the church weren't bright enough. No matter how you looked at it; it was spooky inside. The statues looked like they were alive. Shadows seemed to move around the altar, especially when the sanctuary lights flickered. Rigley came over after a while.

"Hey, Sandy, I don't like this place."

"Why?" I knew what he meant.

"You think there are any ghosts in here?"

"No, man, those are just statues and shadows. Go on with the candles. You almost done?"

"I got some more to do."

"Okay. Hey, want to get some ice cream at the Isaly store later?"

He was still worried. "Do saints appear to people in here?" He looked around like he thought people were watching him. Just then Jimmy let out a blast on the organ that scared the hell out of us.

Rigley started screaming, "Sandy, Sandy, Sandy!"

"What the hell's wrong with you, Jimmy?" I called up to him. He was in the balcony in the back of the church. "Man, you're making me swear in church."

"Hey, you guys, you want to hear some rock and roll?" he shouted.

"Knock it off, Jimmy," I said. Well, he just started in playing "Blue Suede Shoes." It seemed funny to hear that kind of stuff played in church. We all started laughing, but it bothered me a little bit. Somehow it seemed different than laughing during practice.

Just then the lights went out, Jimmy was playing the organ in a pitch-black church. And it was Johnny with the lights. The Italian kids were screaming, too. Rigley went ape, running in the aisle, falling down, screaming. Man, the noise was wild.

"Turn those goddamn lights on, Johnny!" I shouted.

The lights went on and the organ stopped. Rigley was climbing over a pew. It looked funny as hell.

"Hey, Jim, let's cut it out, okay?" I said. Man, the lights went out again, the organ started, Johnny started laughing like a ghost, and Rigley started screaming. "Blue Suede Shoes," man. It was hard to believe those two would be priests.

Since the Italian kids saw how scared Rigley was, they started to tease him by making all kinds of weird sounds in the dark. Rigley laughed some times, too. It was as though he wasn't sure if it was all scary or just funny. For a half hour the lights and organ went on and off. I was trying to sweep, but what the hell, I thought it was fun, too.

I told Rigley and the Italian kids to start taking the trash and stuff downstairs, and to bring up some new candles. Johnny and Jim finally quit pissing around and started helping again. I stayed upstairs and pushed the candle racks back in place and swept up all the old wax.

It was a beautiful old church, but it was better in the morning when the sun came through the stained windows and colored the whole place. I used to like to be there early in the morning. It was quiet; the priests said Mass and only a few old ladies came. At times like that I felt God was there, but he sure wasn't there at night.

Downstairs I heard noise, stuff falling, crashing; Rigley was screaming again. I kept sweeping. Then I heard like a goddamn avalanche. I ran down the aisle to behind the altar. The place was like an old castle from the movies: dark passages, loud strange noises, everything. I knew where the steps were, so I felt the wall on either side, the passage was narrow enough. Then I had to practically crawl down the steps it was so dark. Man, Conrad would have gone ape if he knew those assholes were destroying the church. To them it was like the funhouse in the park. The bastards had gotten to the light downstairs, too.

They could have made Dracula movies in the basement, there was so much shit down there: huge piles of boxes in the middle of the room, statues that looked like they were alive, some lying on the floor, so that if you walked up to one in the dark and lit a light, you'd see those glass eyes staring up at you as if they were alive. Some were covered with white sheets so they looked like ghosts. I never liked to go down there alone; the place had all kinds of scary rooms, too, so you never knew what the hell was waiting for you inside a door.

The dago kids were laughing like ghosts because they heard Baltram and Altino doing it.

"Hey, you guys, that's enough," I shouted.

Nothing. Just maniac screams and everybody calling Rigley. "Rigley, I'm a ghost, a devil, and I'm gonna kill youuuuuu!" That goddamn Altino. I couldn't hear Rigley anymore. All I heard were those other assholes.

"Baltram and Altino, quit fucking around!" Hell, even when I tried to watch my language someone was always pissing me off. "Rigley! Rigley! Where the hell are you?"

No answer. Man, the noise was driving me nuts.

"Jim and John, I'm gonna beat your asses. Turn on those fucking lights."

Same stuff. I started making my way through the dark, bitching and swearing. The lights never came on.

Then I remembered I had some matches in my pocket from the candle rack. I lit one, and just as it went on I saw Altino. He started running, but I tripped him just as the light went out. He was skinny, so I grabbed his neck and held on. "Now, fucker, you take me to those lights. Where are they?"

"Hey, let me go. I didn't do anything, you big animal!"

Man, I shook that son of a bitch like he was a rag doll. "Listen to me, asshole; enough is enough. Get those lights on before I break your neck."

Finally he realized I meant it. "Okay, I'll take you; they're over here. Just let go of my neck."

"You fucking lunatic, how'd you ever get into a seminary? You run away from me and I'll kill you. Understand?"

I kept calling Rigley, but I never got an answer. "Where'd he go, Altino, you wise little bastard?"

"I don't know. What are you asking me for? Maybe he went back upstairs."

I called again and Altino moved away. I caught the fucker with a kick right in the ass. He pissed and moaned, but I still had hold of him. We reached the cupboard where the switchbox was. I lit a match and put two lights on. Everyone else got quiet. The switches were only for lights in the main room; the smaller ones were still dark. You had to turn a separate switch for each one.

I kept calling Rigley, and he still never answered. "See, you bastard," I said to Altino, "when you don't know when to stop?"

"We were just playing, Sandy. Maybe he's upstairs. Really." He sounded a little worried himself then. John and the dagos finally came over to us.

"You guys see if any of those lights are on in the other rooms," I said. "Then see if he's in one of them."

Mike, one of the Italian kids, came with me. We went in one room and I lit a match, but the room was almost empty except for some canvas on the floor. The whole place was filthy with dust and soot.

I lit a match in the middle of the next room. Mike screamed, "Jesu Cristo! Jesu Cristo!" I looked up and saw a statue of St. John Berchmans staring down at me. It scared me, too, for a minute. Mike was gone; I could still hear him screaming Jesus Christ in Italian.

The room was loaded with boxes all covered with paper and sheets. "Rigley?" I said. He didn't answer, but I heard something, so I knew he was in the room. I lit another match and started walking around the boxes. I came to two huge crates with a space between them. I lit another match and looked into the space. There he was, just like a little kid hiding from somebody. He was crying.

"Rigley?" I said. He looked at me like he didn't know me. By that time Jimmy and John were behind me. I stepped toward him and offered my hand. He made a funny noise and jerked away.

"What's wrong, Rigley?" I asked softly. He still didn't answer. I moved toward him talking low. I had to keep lighting matches so he could see me, too. "It's okay, man. It's me, Sandy."

He blinked. "Sandy?"

"Yeah. Come on out, okay?" I was almost whispering. No one else made a sound either. He took my hand and I burned my fingers with the match as it went out. He made a noise and squeezed my hand, then tried to pull away. I held on and kept talking. "The light's on out here. It's okay."

I told Jimmy to get a candle from the side altar to light our way up the steps. He looked at me like he wasn't sure I meant it; then he went.

The Italian kids were whispering to each other. Neither Johnny nor I said anything. Rigley just stood there in the center of the room. "What are they saying?" he asked me.

"Nothing. They're just in a hurry to go upstairs."

I sat him down in a pew and talked to him. He seemed better. He used my handkerchief to wipe his tears. "Were you really that scared?" I said.

"Yeah. I thought I was dying."

"But you knew I was here, right? Those guys were just playing."

"I was still scared. I saw ghosts. And saints walking up and making faces at me. They were screaming. I tried to run, but I fell. They kept looking down at me, making faces."

"No, man. You heard those guys." I pointed to the others.

"No, not them. I know where they were hiding. These were real ghosts; they didn't speak dago or nothing."

He meant it. He really thought he saw ghosts.

Baltram brought our coats. "You guys ready? I have to fill the cruets and put them in the ice box. And Johnny has to set out vestments for early mass. Wait for us outside; we'll only be about five minutes."

So all the rest of us walked out the front door. Man, we took one look and couldn't believe it. The must have been four inches of snow on the ground. It was the wet, heavy stuff that stayed on the telephone wires and the rooftops. It was snowing huge flakes, making the city beautiful. There was no noise; everything was white and quiet. Once in a while a car would go up or down, but the road was slippery, and they skidded all over the place.

Johnny and Jim were taking a lot longer than five minutes. The snow was nice packing, and some of Mike's brothers started throwing it around. One kid, George, was playing tough, though. He got hit with a little snow and started getting mad. I think he was one of those guys that always had to get even with everybody. Anyway, he was making hard snowballs and throwing them hard, and before you know it, there was a real battle in front of the church. Man, dago snow was flying everywhere.

"Mike!" I called. He came over and I told him in Italian that we were getting cold and were going to start walking. They could catch up with us when Johnny and Jim came out.

As we were talking, someone hit me with a snowball right in the chest.

"Watch what the fuck you're doing!" I yelled. Christ, I didn't want Rigley to flip out again. "Let's go, Rigley," I said.

We started walking and another snowball hit Rigley. "Hey, you motherfucking dagos! Don't do that no more!" he screamed.

Then fucking hard-ass George hit one of his brothers right in the face and ran behind us. Two of them started after him, but the bastard was using us as a shield.

"Get out of here, George," I said. He acted like he didn't hear me. He was giggling. "Cut it out, fucker," I said. He grabbed my arm to keep from slipping and spun me around. My shoes wouldn't stay put. I almost did a split. "Motherfucker, George!"

They were all after him then. Rigley was trying to get out of the way, and George was dodging snowballs behind him. As George pushed Rigley to block off a snowball, Rigley slipped and stooped over. One of the snowballs hit him right in the ear.

He let out a scream and started crying again. Out loud, like a baby. Then he went down on his knees. I tried to pull him up, but he kept slipping, throwing himself around like a maniac. Finally, when I got him up, he started running after George. They all ran like hell up the street, scattered on both sides. When he knew he couldn't catch them, he stopped, threw his arms around like he was punching someone with all his might. He was swinging and throwing himself around and screaming. All I could do was watch. I didn't know what else to do. I never saw anything like that before. He started jumping up and down in one place, still swinging.

"Rigley! Rigley!"

He was going nuts. He started across the street, running again. But his shoes couldn't make it and he fell. In the mist, I could see a car coming down Sloan Street. I tried to get him up again, but he stayed down, crying.

"Come on, Rigley. Come on, okay?" I don't even know if he knew I was there beside him. And I couldn't get him up; he was like a bear. The car was getting closer, going slow; I knew it wasn't going to turn off.

"Come on, for Christ sake, Rigley, there's a car coming!"

"Leave me alone!" he screamed.

I shook him by the shoulder. "Goddammit, there's a car coming!"

"No. I ain't leaving. Fuck it."

I dragged him. Goddamn shoes of mine—one time I really needed boots and I didn't have them. He fought against me, but I got behind him and pulled his shoulders. The snow was blowing so much I could hardly see; all I could make out were two headlights coming closer. I fell down trying to drag him, so I crawled and pulled. When we got over to the curb, he wanted to go back out in the street.

"Goddammit, Rigley, what's the matter with you?" He was still crying like a baby, but I wouldn't let him move. The car went past.

He kept crying for a while, but I still held his shoulders and wouldn't let him up. Johnny and Jim came over, but I waved them on. "He's okay now," I said. "We'll walk up the hill later. I'm gonna take him home."

We stayed there for about ten minutes and I held him just like a little baby. Finally he got quiet.

"Why wasn't I like you, Sandy?" he whispered.

"What?" I said.

"Why am I a retard? Why can't I be just like you?" He started crying again. "Why can't I be just like other people?"

"Man, you're okay. There's nothing wrong with you."

"Yes there is. I'm retarded, and people are always laughing at me."

"Aw, what do they know? Fuck people! I don't laugh at you, do I?"

"You're different. But everybody else does, and I hate it."

"Look. You can walk, you can talk, you can work, you have friends. People like you, man."

He let me help him up.

"You okay? Can you walk?"

"Yeah."

I brushed some of the snow off his hair and around his neck, and wiped his face with my handkerchief. We were both soaked with snow. Another car went by; it sure was quiet out. I thought someone would hear us outside, but maybe they thought we were just playing around in the snow.

We walked slow, all the way up the hill. He'd stop every once in a while and I'd say, "Come on," and he'd walk some more. I was sweating; steam was coming from my face, and his too.

"We ain't the same, you and me. Nobody has to take care of you. You don't forget things like me," he said.

I really didn't know what to tell him. "You're okay; you're okay," I kept saying.

"I ain't okay," he said, his voice cracking up again. "I ain't never gonna grow up; I'm gonna stay just like this. Even little kids do things better than me, and I'm a dummy to them, too. Oh, Sandy, I ain't never gonna grow up!"

I had to try something different. "Look, do you believe in God or not?"

"Yeah, but he don't help me none."

"If you believe in him, then he'll help you. I'll help you, too. But first you gotta take care of yourself. Understand?"

"Yeah."

"Sure?"

"Yeah."

"After midnight mass you come over my house, okay? My mom says you should come eat with us."

"My mom won't let me come," he said.

"Try anyway. After Christmas, I'll call you and we'll go to a show. All right?"

"All right."

When we got to his house I said, "Take a bath and wash off all the snow and stuff. Then go right to bed, okay?"

"Yeah...see you."

I waited for him as he walked up on his porch to go in. He never looked back. His old man opened the door and started bitching about his coat being wet. Then he slapped him on the side of the head and closed the door.

The next year, in June, Rigley graduated and I moved. It was the same old story; I was busy with school, and work, and later, spring football practice, and never really saw him much until summer.

I remember, though, how excited he was the night he graduated. I went back to Thornhill to see him. He wore a suit for the first time, and looked real nice. Some kids from Thornhill came over in a car to pick him up and take him to the parties.

A few weeks later he got a job as a clean-up man in a Christ Mission store, making sixty cents an hour.

Me? Well, even though our new house was on the other side of Youngstown, I was still going to finish my senior year at Liguori High. I was glad, too; it would have been tough making all new friends in another school that last year. I spent a lot of time down on the East Side anyway; Burt and Rigley and Marcia all lived there.

That day I moved, Rigley told me I'd forget all about him, and then he'd have no best friend anymore. I promised him that as soon as I got a car, I'd see him once a week all through the summer.

The car was a 1953 Ford hardtop with fake leather seats and a stick shift, really clean after I put a lot of work into it. It was nice just to get in and go whenever you wanted to see someone.

The first time I stopped to show it to Rigley, he wasn't home. The next time I got a chance, I stopped again, and he was just leaving.

"Hey," I said, pulling up alongside as he walked down the street.

"Oh, hi, Sandy," he said.

"Where are you going? Get in; I'll take you," I said.

"No. I'll walk," he said.

"Come on. What's the sense of walking?"

"No. I can walk."

"But where the hell are you going?" I said.

He looked confused, like he didn't want to tell me something, yet didn't know how to not do it. I knew that look. "Come on in here, Rigley!" I said as he kept walking.

"Oh, all right." He got in, but he was disgusted.

"Let's go to the Isaly; I'll buy you a sundae," I said.

"No, I don't have time."

"Rigley, where the hell are you going?"

"Okay, I'll have a sundae, but I can't stay too long, okay?"

"Well…Yeah, okay." It was the first time he ever tried to give me the brush.

He liked chocolate sundaes, so I ordered him one. We sat there waiting for a few minutes. He was changing, I thought. I noticed that he had some scars on his face I'd never seen before, and that he always seemed to need a haircut and a bath. And his breath always smelled. And then, that night, he was quiet and nervous, and kept looking at the clock.

"You gonna talk to me or something?" I asked.

"Yeah, I will."

"Aren't you gonna tell me where you're going?"

"My girlfriend's house," he said without looking up from his ice cream.

"You have a girlfriend?" I asked, trying not to sound too surprised. It was hard to believe.

"Yeah. I go see her every night."

"What's her name?"

"I don't know."

"What?"

"I don't know, I said."

"What do you mean? How could you have a girlfriend and not know her name?"

"That's right. You have girlfriends; why can't I have one?"

"You can have one; I didn't say that. But how could you forget her name?"

"I can't say it, that's why. I always forget."

"What's her first name?"

"Macie."

"Macie? And her last name? Try to say it."

"Dr…uh…Drz. No. I can't say it. What the hell do you want to know for? It's a secret."

"You want me to take you to her house? Does she live far?"

"No, she lives close."

"I'll take you anyhow. I don't have anything else to do." I was dying to know who she was.

"I told you, I'll go myself!"

"Okay…Okay," I said quietly. "You don't have to get mad about it."

"They never put enough nuts on this ice cream," he said. "Harold is a stingy son of a bitch."

When we were done, we went out and I waited to see what he would do. He started up the street. "I'll see you," he said.

I didn't answer. He walked a little way, then turned to look back at me. "Okay," he said, "you just leave me off where I tell you; all right?"

"Come on," I said. He seemed to relax a little then. He even told me he liked my car. We talked about what he had been doing, and he told me about his raise, all the way up to eighty cents an hour. I teased him a little about making big money. Sometimes it seemed like he wasn't paying any attention to where we were going.

"When should I turn?" I asked.

"Oh…Up at the next corner."

"Then where?"

"Then you go down two streets."

"Is that it, then?" I asked.

"No, then you turn again."

We were driving quite a way. "Hey, I thought you said she didn't live far?" I said.

"We're almost there…Okay, stop at the corner."

"Where's her house?"

"It's across the field."

"Well, let me drive you around."

"No, that's okay. This is the best way." Then he got out of the car. "I'll walk over myself…the back way. See you."

I didn't understand the whole damned thing. I don't know, maybe he was ashamed. Hell, you could never figure out what he was thinking anyway. I went over to pick up Burt.

I made it down to see Rigley quite a few times that summer. Sometimes he was there and we had a sundae; sometimes he wasn't home. His mother said he was gone every night.

When I caught him home, I'd try to find out what he was doing. He never would say. We'd go over to the Isaly, and then I'd take him up to his girl's house; that was it. He still said he couldn't pronounce her name.

One time, toward the end of the summer, he finally told me. Her name was Macie Dawkins. I couldn't get anything else out of him. He said she went to Thornhill High School. When I saw Burt, I asked him about it. He could never understand why I came over his house so late just because I stopped to see Rigley. He never said much, but I'm sure he thought I was a little crazy.

"What's her name?" Burt said.

"Macie Dawkins. Do you know her?" He didn't answer; he just huffed a little, kind of disgusted.

"Well, do you?"

"Yeah."

"Yeah, what?"

"So does every guy at Thornhill. She lives up by my house."

"No, man," I said, "this broad lives over near Guerin Woods."

"If she's the Macie Dawkins that goes to Thornhill, she lives near my house."

"Man, I've been taking him over there all summer and she sure as hell doesn't live near you."

"Then her name ain't Macie Dawkins," he said. He used to get irritated with me when he thought I was being dumb.

"Okay, okay. What's this Macie broad like; the one you know?" I said.

"She's a whore, man. She's fucked every man at Thornhill three times, nigger, PR, and white."

"Bullshit. He wouldn't go with a broad like that."

"You suppose he's getting laid?" he said. Then he laughed after he said it.

"Nah. He couldn't handle a hard broad like that. She'd cut his balls off. What would she want with him anyway?"

"I don't know." He shook his head. "But she's mean and nasty. A real dog."

One time during football season, we had an open weekend, no game scheduled. Thornhill always had a good team, so we went over to watch one of their games. We sat in the student section because Burt knew most of them. They all lived near him. We had a ball yelling and bitching for the other team. Everybody knew we went to St. Alphonsus, so they didn't do anything to us. We made so much noise, they thought we were funny. It was a good time.

At halftime, Burt said, "Hey."

"What?"

"Look down there. See that broad with the blond hair?"

"Where? Down by the fence talking to Skinny Tom?"

"Yeah. What do you think of her?" he said.

"Not my type, but she's just his speed. Two pigs."

"Well, that's your Macie Dawkins."

"What? You kidding me?"

"No, man. That's the one."

"Is she Tom's girl?"

"I don't think so. Even he ain't that hard up."

"Was she sitting with him?"

"No, he was walking by and she started talking to him."

"Hey, when he goes, I'm gonna go talk to her. Save my seat."

"Man, you're really crazy! What do you want with a broad like that? She's crude; you wouldn't even know how to talk to her."

"Just save my seat, okay?"

Tom went by, and she stayed by the fence, talking to some girls. I had to elbow my way down the steps to the walkway.

"Macie?" I said.

"Hey, I don't know you." Man, Burt was right; up close she looked hard as nails, and almost as tall as me. She was smiling anyway.

"My name's Sandy Morelli."

"Sandy? Ain't that a girl's name? You a fag or something?"

"Would I be talking to you if I was a fag?" I said.

"What school do you go to?" she said. I don't think she trusted me.

"Liguori."

"Oh, one of them Catholic boys, huh? You rich?"

"Yeah. I'm a millionaire."

She laughed at that. Man, she didn't even seem human compared to Marcia.

"What kind of car do you drive?" she said.

"Fifty-three Ford," I said.

"Is it nice?"

"Not bad. It gets me around."

"Will you take me in it?"

"Sure."

"Bullshit!" she said. "What do you want, man, a blow job?"

92

"No," I said, "just some talk."

She still couldn't figure what my program was. "You know Burt Mueller?" I asked.

"Yeah, he lives by me. Do you play football, too?"

"Yeah."

"What position?"

"Guard."

"First string?"

"Yeah."

People were coming back with coffee and hot dogs and pop and kept bumping into us. The band was playing too loud, and I felt like an ass talking shit to a dumb broad.

"You know a kid named Rigley?"

"Why'd you ask that?"

"Just curious, that's all," I said. She didn't believe me. "Well, he's my friend."

"You a friend of that creep?"

"Yeah. I used to live by him."

"What's his program anyway?" she said.

"What do you mean?"

"What the hell's he always hanging around the Isaly for?" she said.

"What Isaly? The one on Sloan Street?"

"No, dumb ass, the one on Ayers Road."

"He never hangs out there," I said, not really sure.

"The hell he doesn't; he's there every fucking night."

"You sure?"

"Yeah, I'm sure. I work there, don't I? He's weird, man. He comes in every night to buy a sundae, then takes so long to eat it, it turns to soup. And he keeps looking at me all the time. Scares the shit out of me."

The whole thing sounded unreal, like we were talking about someone else named Rigley. "How long has he been doing that?" I said, changing the tone of my voice.

"The whole goddamn summer. Ever since Skinny Tom brought him up."

"Tom?"

"Yeah. I think he hangs around Tom and his boys."

"Where do you live anyhow, somewhere near Guerin Woods?" I asked.

"Hell no. I live right near the Isaly on Huron Street. Hey, you know what that son of a bitch does? He eats his sundae for two hours, then goes out front to sit on the wall. When I come out at eleven, he jumps off the wall and walks right in front of me and says, 'Hi,' real short and sweet; 'Hi,' so you can barely hear him. He's really a squirrel, man." Then she laughed. What a mean, lousy bitch.

"Does he ever bother you? You know...."

"No. One night he followed me home, but I told him to fuck off, so now he just goes down the street. Still he makes me nervous; he's like a Frankenstein."

"Now look...don't get mad...but, well, do you think maybe he thinks you're his girlfriend?"

"Me? That fucking creep? You're pissing me off, you know, buddy?"

"And you don't hang around Guerin Woods, right?"

"I'm getting tired of this, man."

"Just a few more questions, okay?"

"No. Get out of here."

"Come on, Burt said you were nice, and easy to talk to."

"You ain't no lawyer, man. You ask too many questions."

"Does he come up every night?"

"Every goddamn night; just like clockwork."

"What time does he come?"

"Usually about six o'clock. Once in a while he comes late; he must work or something."

"Yeah? How often?"

"About...I don't know, maybe once a week."

"What time does he come then?"

"Like nine thirty maybe."

That was it, man. I could see the whole picture. God! Poor Rigley. "Hey, thanks a lot," I said.

"That's all? Thanks a lot? What is all this shit about a ride in your car anyway?"

"I told you. Rigley's my friend, and I was curious about what he did at night."

"He drives me crazy; that's what he does," she said.

"Well, he won't hurt you anyway. I know him."

"He better not, or I'll have Tom kill him."

"Look, Macie, uh, the half's almost starting. I gotta get back to my seat."

"Hey, whyn't you come out the Blue Star tonight? Maybe we can dance?"

"I can't. Football curfew."

"Don't come in then; I'll come out to your car. The lot's real dark and I can get some whiskey."

"Nah, man. Whiskey would kill me."

"Man, I could throw you some good moves. Maybe you are a fag. Anybody that's a friend to that big ape has to be a fag."

"See you," I said.

"Fuck you, big shot!" she said. Then she went back to her girlfriends.

I walked back up to my seat feeling sick. "God, Burt, Rigley made the whole thing up. That fucking broad hates him."

The next Wednesday night I was off, so I went down to Rigley's. We did the same old thing: had a sundae, then drove up Garfield

Street like we always did. But instead of turning toward Guerin Woods, I kept going, and turned down Ayers Road. He didn't say anything. I stopped in front of the Isaly. I didn't say anything either. We sat there for about five minutes. I was looking at him and he was sitting there with his head down and his hands in his lap.

"Why did you lie to me all this time?" I asked quietly.

"I didn't lie," he said.

"She doesn't live out in the Woods; she lives right down the street, doesn't she?"

"Yeah," he said. Big tears started rolling slowly down his face. I gave him my handkerchief.

"Nobody lives out there, huh?" I said.

"No, I was just pretending. I didn't mean to lie, Sandy. But then I started being afraid to tell you."

"Why?"

"'Cause maybe you'd tell her about me and she wouldn't be my girl anymore. Maybe you'd even make her your girlfriend."

"Hell, I wouldn't do that. Did I ever treat you like that?" He didn't answer. "Did you come over here right after I'd drop you off out the Woods?"

"Yeah. It took a long time, but I did it."

"But why? Christ, why didn't you just tell me? Why'd we do this all summer?" I was trying to keep from getting hot; I just couldn't believe what happened.

"You kept telling me to come in your car. I didn't want to. I told you, but you kept asking me, and I thought you'd be mad."

"Rigley, she isn't your girl."

"She is, goddammit. She is. She is..."

"Okay, okay. Don't get mad," I said. We were quiet for a while, then I started again. "Rigley, now listen to me. You can get into trouble—"

"Shut up! Don't tell me that! I didn't do nothing. She's just my girl, that's all."

I wasn't reaching him, and my voice kept getting louder. "Rigley, that broad and those guys you hang around with are no good. Don't you understand? They're gonna hurt you some day."

"That's what you say. But they treat me nice." He got out of the car and headed for the Isaly.

"Hey, man, come over here," I said. "Don't be mad. I was just—"

"They're my friends now. You done moved too far away." Then he went inside.

I sat there for a few minutes, not knowing what to do. Then that seemed like the only answer: Don't do anything. I drove back to Marcia's house.

That Christmas, I practiced for midnight mass down at St. Andrew's again. After practice I met with Burt at the Isaly on Sloan Street, near the church. There was a whole gang of guys there: Will and his boys, Pauly, Jimmy Ryan, O'Brian, and Sam; just everybody. We were older then and didn't fight and bitch as much as before. Maybe we were just growing up.

"Hey, Sandy, you finally made first string, huh?"

"Yeah, Will. Class will tell," I said.

"Wait till Liguori plays Thornhill next year," he said. "There's some sophomore kid that's twice as big as anybody you got. He's gonna clean up on your line."

"Yeah, but maybe he's dumb, Will, like all those lineman from Thornhill."

Everybody laughed. We went in and had a sundae, then got coffee and came back outside. Everybody liked to stay outside even though it was cold as hell; you could see a lot more from the corner. The coffee was steaming, and we talked about girls and getting jobs when we got out of school.

Just then a car went by. It was a big Lincoln, black and shiny. He blew the horn real loud and kept on going.

"Who was that?" I asked.

"That was Skinny Tom," said Sam.

"Where the hell did he get a car like that?" I said.

"Man, he picks up Bug slips. He's a hood. He got thrown out of Thornhill, so he became a racky," said O'Brien.

"Wasn't that the kid you used to take care of, Sandy?" said Will.

"Where?" I asked.

"In the car with Tom, man," he said.

"You mean Rigley?"

"Yeah, that's him. The big retarded one."

"Does he still hang around with Skinny Tom?" I asked all of them.

"Are you kidding?" said Sam. "They love it."

"What do you mean, Sam?" I said. I knew he wasn't saying what he meant. They all looked like they all knew something I didn't.

"Come on, man, don't tell me you don't know about that kid and Tom's boys," said O'Brien.

"Shut up, O'Brien," said Burt, really nasty.

"Huh? What the hell's going on, Burt?"

"Tell him, Burt," said O'Brien. "He'll find out sooner or later."

"No. Just shut the fuck up," said Burt. "Let's go, Sandy." He turned my shoulder toward my car and started walking. But I turned back.

"Come on, O'Brien; tell me," I said.

"Man, he blows everyone in that car once a night," he said.

"You bastard, O'Brien," said Burt. "He's lying, Sandy. What the fuck does he know?"

"That true, Sam?" I asked.

"Yeah, Sandy. I saw him one night behind the school. O'Brien did too. It was sickening. I felt sorry for the poor bastard."

I felt like someone just hit me with a hammer. My eyes went glassy for a minute, like I could have cried. "Burt," I said, "did you know that?"

"Yeah, man," he said softly, "that's the word out."

"He's more messed up than that, Sandy," said Sam.

"Yeah," said Jimmy. "I picked him up one day as he was walking home from town and he told me he was the 'Holy Spirit.' Everybody knows he goes to Mass and communion five times a Sunday."

"Yeah, man, you never see him much anymore, Sandy. He really went downhill, real fucked up in the head," said Sam.

We left soon after that. Before I got into my car, Burt said, "I'm sorry, man. I know it's bad, but what can you do? You're never gonna change that kid."

I thought for a second before I started the car. "Yeah," I said.

Part III: Wyandotte Hospital

It was like the grounds of a huge estate: a long road winding through dense thickets of trees that opened onto clear acres of manicured green. On the left as I drove I could see a small lake, and swans, some black, some white, pushing languidly through the still water. The late sun colored the whole world green and gold. Everything was misty and quiet.

It was strange. The sounds of the town didn't seem to intrude beyond the trees and bushes that rimmed the hospital, as though the real world stopped outside and Wyandotte were a kind of island retreat.

I parked in a small blacktop lot in front of a Victorian mansion long since converted into an office building. A steep flight of steps led up to the porch. The entrance was a giant double screen door at the rear of it.

There was an old man sitting by the door smoking a cigar and reading a folded newspaper. He looked up as I climbed the steps.

"What can I do for you?" he said around the cigar clenched in his teeth.

"Can you tell me where Mr. Hostetter's office is?" I asked.

"Ray's office is on the second floor of this building. But he's not there; he's over at the House."

"House?"

"Yeah. See that building over there?" He motioned to a building across a small street from the main office building.

"Yeah."

"They call that the House. He said he was gonna be there a few hours. You have an appointment?"

"Yeah, for eight o'clock. Okay, I'll go over there. Thanks."

"My name's Charlie," he said. "You gonna work here?"

"Maybe. I'm going for an interview now. My name's Sandy," I said, offering my hand. He took it.

"Sandy what?"

"Morelli."

"Morelli? Italian kid, huh?"

"Yeah." I was always a little uncomfortable when anyone said that.

"Well, you look like a pretty good chap. Hope you get your job."

"Thanks. See you."

The House was a small Greek-style temple. It had Doric columns on a small portico, a huge domed roof, and a square base. It was compact, almost as though someone had bigger plans for it but ran out of material. Charlie told me to walk around front because the entrance facing the incoming drive was always sealed.

The street was a couple hundred feet long. I walked down and turned the corner. There was another portico, only this one was enclosed, so that in a few steps you'd come to eight large doors, four sets of doubles, made of small-paned glass set into varnished wood. Inside, there was a small vestibule, and about twelve feet further was another set of doors that let into a small auditorium.

At the entrance I turned around, and for the first time saw the whole hospital. There were about twenty huge houses spaced evenly around a giant oval whose major axis was about an eighth of a mile in length. The houses were old, probably built before the turn of the century, and each was buttressed by banisters and open porches. The grass of the oval was dark green, and in the sunlight sprinklers mushroomed rainbows as they cooled the earth from the day's heat.

I knocked on the doors and waited, then turned again to see if there were any signs of life. Some people were sitting on porches; some were looking out upstairs windows in houses across the oval. Chainlink fencing stretched across every upstairs window that I could see. I knocked again. A small, blond, crew-cut, athletic-looking man came through the inner doors and walked toward me, smiling.

"Hello. Are you Alessandro?" he said as he opened one of the glass paned doors.

"Yeah. Sandy Morelli." I extended my hand and he grabbed it firmly.

"Ray Hostetter here," he said. "Did Charlie tell you where I was?"

"Yeah. He said you'd be here for a while, so I decided to come on over."

"Good. I'm glad you could make it tonight. This is really the best time to ever talk to anybody around here. Well, come on in; these are the Recreation Therapy offices."

We walked into the office through the same kinds of double doors, small-paned rectangles from top to bottom. The office was strewn with junk: ashtrays full of butts; stacks of dusty records piled on one of two office-sized, wooden desks; and canvas bags full of baseball gloves and balls and bats and other equipment.

The whole building really seemed Victorian from the inside. Everything made of wood, massive and dark-stained. In the corner beside the stack of records was a hand-crank, upright Victrola.

"Did you have any trouble finding the place?"

"There was a lot of traffic on the freeway coming up, but once I got into town, I found it easily."

"Where'd you say you lived?"

"Columbus."

"Oh, yeah. We used to play in St. John's Arena when our high school team won the regionals." He was looking at my application casually. "English bachelor's and Special Ed master's, huh? That's an odd combination."

"Well, I enjoy it. And I get a chance to do both at school...sometimes together."

"How old are you?"

"Twenty-seven."

"Where were you stationed in the army?"

"Vietnam for two years; then one year in the States."

"Ever deal with mentally ill people?"

"One year with emotionally disturbed children." I was being given the third degree, and started shifting in my seat as he probed. Somehow I thought I wasn't what he wanted for the job.

"How long have you taught at McKinley?"

"Two years."

"Why'd you apply here?"

"Well, I had some recreation therapy courses in my master's program. And after working with kids, I wanted to try working with adults."

"We've got both here," he said, "only the kids are teenagers. Cigarette?" He extended a pack toward me.

"Yeah. Thanks."

He took a drag, blew his smoke at the floor, then sat still for a few seconds, looking at me. "Ever play baseball?"

"Not on an official team, but I played a lot when I was young."

"Like to play cards?"

"Yeah."

"Good," he said, still looking down at my application, as if to find something he didn't like or some reason not to hire me.

I watched him as he read. I hadn't seen a real crew cut in a long time. His legs were short, but he had a long muscular trunk, a small straight nose, and blue eyes—a nice looking guy. "Craver talk to you yet?"

"You mean the head of Personnel?"

"Yeah."

"Well, after I applied, he called me. Told me to set up an interview with you. He said you did the hiring in Recreation."

"Craver's a nice old guy. He's one PhD that knows his ass from up."

"He sounded nice on the phone," I said.

"Do you live at home? Oh, no, you were born in Youngstown, right?"

"Yeah. I share an apartment with another teacher."

"Male or female?"

"Male, unfortunately."

He chuckled, then lit another cigarette. Maybe he's nervous, too, I thought.

"Like teaching?"

"Yeah."

"You get both degrees at Ohio State, huh?"

"Yeah."

"Like football?"

"Crazy about it."

He chuckled again, a soft nervous chuckle.

He started talking about the hospital and the patients. There were two parts: Entry and the City. Entry was a large, modern receiving hospital at the far corner of the grounds where new patients were admitted. Most were under sedation or on tranquilizers and restricted to one floor of the hospital. The City was the oval, the convalescent part of the hospital. Most patients were free to roam the grounds around the City from eight o'clock in the morning until eight at night.

There were two buildings on the inner side of the oval: one was the patient recreation center, the other the patient dining hall. The corridor between the two buildings was a little store where patients and staff could buy cigarettes, soft drinks, snacks, and a few cosmetics. The whole complex was directly across from the House, separated by a two-lane drive that circumscribed the green of the oval within the array of houses.

Hostetter talked nearly two hours, about himself, about his philosophy of rehabilitation, and a little about the job I wanted. It was dark outside, and the light in the office was dim above us.

"Any other questions?" he asked finally.

"I can't think of any now, but I'm sure a lot will come to me five minutes after I leave here."

He smiled, then stretched out his hand. "You'll do," he said.

"Why, hell, thanks a lot," I said, pumping his hand. "When do I start?"

"Can you be up here Monday?"

"Yes," I answered.

"Good. The orientation class starts Tuesday and ends Friday. Everybody has to take it, so you'll be paid to be a student next week. It'll give you a chance to get the feel of the place."

"Okay."

"Let's go see your room."

To the right of the vestibule, running alongside the office, was a small corridor, and at the end of it, steps that led to the apartment upstairs. When we entered, the first thing I could see was a bay window overlooking the oval, covering half the length of the far wall.

On the left, near the entrance, was the bedroom alcove where a brass double bed nestled a few feet away from a window that would catch the morning light. The alcove was partitioned off by a huge bookcase that also formed a wall to the living room. The left wall had a stone fireplace with two bookcases on either side, extensions of the mantle, and covered by glass doors. All the bookcases were loaded with old books.

Again on the right, up near the doorway, was a small hall that led to the bathroom. Beyond that, built into the wall, was a huge empty china closet.

There was a couch, two upholstered chairs with ottomans, and a table. Everything was clean and lovely.

"Housekeeping takes care of this for you. They come in every day to clean. If you ever need anything, let them know."

"This is really a nice place," I said.

"The chief of staff used to let guests stay here before they added new rooms down at Entry. If ever a doctor or VIP from the state board came up, this was one of the suites he stayed in. It's usually empty now, except when a supervisor needs a room."

"What time does work start Monday?" I said.

"Whenever you get here; just get yourself moved in so you can start the orientation class Tuesday. You know about the hours you work, don't you? Monday, Wednesday, and Friday till nine at night?"

"Dr. Craver just told me I'd work most evenings."

"It's not so bad; if you have something to do, you can take some time off. We don't punch clocks around here. Tuesday nights especially; there's nothing for RT to do. There's a movie, and the medical and house staff get the patients in and out of the auditorium. RT stays out of that."

"I'll have to get used to the town, too," I said, almost to myself.

"Yeah, you have to get out of the hospital once in a while or you'll end up a patient, too. There's pressure out here sometimes."

I didn't say anything else. I had a long drive to Columbus ahead of me and didn't want to start him talking again. We walked back down to the vestibule.

"Well, take it easy. Have a good weekend," he said. "I won't be here next week, but Wes Arnold will; he'll start you off right. Get him to help you if you need anything. I'll see you the following week after you're all moved in and ready for work."

Outside the House, the oval was lit by old-fashioned street lanterns, and under them you'd half expect to see a coach and four come clopping around the other side. It looked like a small Dickens village in the darkness.

———— ∞ ————

The following Monday, I was fingerprinted and sent to work. I drove my car alongside the House and unloaded some boxes up to the apartment. Housekeeping had done a nice job. They had old-fashioned doilies on the end tables and the mantle. Old fashioned. I had to stop using the words. Anyway, they made the place look like someone lived there. They even had tie-back curtains on the bay window and the window by the bed. The best word was cozy, cozy with a modern touch: a nice TV, nice books, nice small kitchen. Man, I was a VIP.

It didn't take me long to set up house. I didn't take many dress clothes: one sport jacket and a couple pairs of good slacks. The rest were jeans, khakis, and knit jerseys. That done, I became Supervisor I in a Victorian-era mental hospital. It was good getting out of Columbus.

Across the vestibule from my office was another one identical to mine, with several smaller desks of dark wood, more weathered but still nice. It was the RT staff room.

A black man was sitting at one of the desks. I pushed the glass doors apart and walked in.

"Hi, I'm Sandy Morelli," I said.

He seemed to shake my hand reluctantly. "You the new supervisor?" he asked. His voice was soft and deep.

"Yeah. Ray said you'd be around today. I'm glad I caught you before you went to work."

"I am at work," he said coolly.

"Oh, yeah. I was thinking of an actual session," I said, feeling dumb for saying what I did. "What are you doing?"

He sighed, then took me over to show me the closet full of forms the department used. He had been filling out an evaluation form when I interrupted him. He talked slowly, without animation.

He was in his late thirties or early forties, thickly muscled and lean. He had dark brown skin and long, sinewy arms. His hair was short and thinning across the crown of his head, and his nose was flat, with a scar running diagonally across the front of it. It looked like it had been a real mess at one time. His lips were not very thick and he had a small moustache spread around the corners of his mouth.

I listened, then asked if he could show me the RT facilities. He looked disgusted. "Well, maybe later. Right now I have a lot of evaluations to do."

"Okay, I'll look around a little. See you later."

I took a walk around the oval. The cottages, as they were called, were given numbers for men and letters for women. There wasn't much going on, it seemed.

As I approached Entry, I could smell the cafeteria food cooking. In the back of the building there was an ambulance dock, where patients could be picked up and delivered. I walked in through the ground-floor entrance and went up to the main lobby. It looked the same as any other hospital: a small gift shop, an information desk beside the front entrance, and couches and chairs along the walls.

On the way back to the City I passed the pond. There were lily pads, rushes, and cattails, and some large goldfish besides the swans. It was a pretty place.

I went back to the staff room. "Wes, where's the payroll office?"

He looked up at me with that same pissed-off expression. "Over in the Ad building on the third floor."

"Thanks," I said.

I had some forms to fill out, and it ended up taking me more than an hour. When I got back to the House, Wes was gone, so I went to supper. The staff cafeteria was behind the rec center; it was large and clean, and the food was good. Dining alone never gave me an appetite, though; I always needed conversation with my meals.

Many of the staffers came in at five o'clock, and a long line formed as people slowly slid their trays past the food. Most were nurses and ward attendants, all dressed in white. Occasionally a person in civilian clothes stood out; they seemed to be from a residual office staff that worked late into the evening. Only the RTs wore casual clothes and tennis shoes.

People weren't especially friendly. They clustered in small groups at seemingly preassigned tables.

When I went back to the office, Wes was still gone. The rest of the staff was at a seminar in Bowling Green, so I was alone again. I bought a newspaper from the snack shop and then went up to make coffee in the tiny kitchen across the hall from my room. I looked out the window from time to time as I read. The patients were lined up trying to get into the mess hall. I watched them for a while. Apart from the obviously retarded and mongoloid, you'd never know that the line was made up of mental patients.

The paper wasn't interesting. Too many things were on my mind; I was restless, curious; everything was new. Hell, I needed someone to talk to. I went out to see if Wes was back. This time he was talking to a patient in the staff office.

I waited until he was done by killing some time looking around the auditorium. There were hundreds of folding chairs set up, with an aisle between them. It was an old building; the walls were drab, and the gilt-scalloped borders dirty enough to look shabby. The stage was backed by faded red velvet curtains. The dome was about forty feet in diameter and echoed when you stood under it.

When I went out, Wes was alone, writing. I was irritated, because he knew I was waiting outside and he never ventured out to see me. It occurred to me that I was being avoided. I walked into the office. "Wes?"

He didn't look up. "Yeah?"

"Are we going to make that tour?" He pushed away from the desk, still not looking up. Then he raised his eyes to look at me and spoke deliberately, emphasizing his disgust.

"I told you, man: I'll let you know when I can make it."

"Yeah, well, I thought—"

"You'll see the place soon enough anyway. You've got all summer."

"Yeah," I said, "I guess I will."

I started to walk out, but hesitated at the doors. The whole thing was starting off bad. I was new, and sort of disoriented, and getting shit on by a guy I was supposed to be supervising. Same old crap, I thought. Some guy who knows where they keep the forks and spoons and where the johns are is playing a big wheel. Goddamn. Things never change. I turned back to him.

"Hey, man?" I said. He looked up with the same sullen expression. "What the hell's your program? I mean, what are you so pissed about all the time? I come in here with straight questions and all you do is try to gag me."

He looked surprised. "I'm too busy to orient new summer help, man. It's not my job."

"Well, what the hell is your job? Sitting her writing papers and ignoring me, right?"

"You starved for affection?"

"Not from you, man. But what the hell's so hard about showing me around?"

"Nothing, except I'm tired of you big-stick RTs coming in here and laying your college education all around like cow shit all over the place."

"Yeah? Well, let me tell you something. I don't need any education to spot a prick when I see one."

He started to move toward me but had the instinct to hold back. "So I'm a prick, huh? Well, College Boy, I've seen your kind before. You guys come down here every summer and pin on a supervisor's badge and start telling us what RT is really all about. But the sad thing is, you're all full of shit, and wouldn't know how to help a patient if he told you."

"Did you ever think that I might want to learn something from you?"

"Sure I did. And wild bears don't shit in the woods either."

"Man, you have a hard-on for the world," I said. "I just thought we might work together a little better than this, that's all."

I left him standing there and went outside. The snack shop was closed, so I walked off grounds to the Tinkerbell, a small bar across from the hospital, for some cigarettes. When I got back, the sun had gone down and it was dark. I went back into the House; Wes was still there; I kept walking.

"Sandy." He was standing at the office door. "I think I was wrong about you," he said.

"Maybe so, Wes," I said wearily. "I'll see you tomorrow, okay?"

He nodded.

I read for a little while in my room, then fell asleep. I was tired after all.

⊸∞⊶

The next morning, I made coffee and stood by the stove in the kitchen, still not awake. I had left the door open to the hallway. Wes appeared with a white bag in his hand.

"Any coffee?" he asked.

"Yeah, lots. Come on in." He seemed friendly and smiling, almost as though the previous day had never happened.

"I had a few donuts and I thought we could make a deal for coffee." He spread the bag on the table.

"Hey, man, you didn't have to do that," I said.

"You buy next week," he said, sloughing me off.

"It's hot as hell out there, huh?"

"Yeah. It's like this sometimes in June. You're gonna die at orientation."

"Yeah, I'll sweat like hell."

He was quiet for a few seconds, then he said, "You were in 'Nam?"

"Yeah."

"What'd you see?"

I snorted. "A year and a half in the States and the same in Khe Sanh. How about you?"

"Started in Korea; did lot of US time, then ended with a belly-full of Operation Hastings in Dong Ha in '66. Lost some good friends. Retired after twenty in '71."

"Yeah, me too, friends…in '68. A devil dog, huh?"

He nodded. "Glad it's over…but we should have won."

We changed the subject and never talked about it again. Neither one of us had gotten over it yet, both the war and waking up every morning wondering if it would be our last day of life. And then the scorn of so many righteous people when we got back home. So we talked about what I'd go through at orientation class.

The donuts were fresh and warm. His rank was RT II, and he'd be up for RT III in October. That was as far as he could go without a college degree, and he seemed a little bitter about it.

"Well, I'd better get going," he said.

"Where to?"

"On Tuesday I go up to Cottage Erie to play cards and set up some games. I come out early to get all the stuff set up, then sometimes I take off during the movie at night. Sheila and Mrs. Smith go down to Cottage Jackson to do the same thing this afternoon."

"Why don't the patients come down to the center?"

"Those are the lock-up cottages, man. You got old people, suicidals, cutthroats, retarded…really a mixed group. Some are being 'observed' pending trial."

"Oh."

"Look, I'm gonna be around tonight; maybe we can shoot some pool?"

"Sounds good, Wes."

The class had about twenty people in it: orderlies, ward attendants, all types of technicians and therapists, anyone having to do with patient care. There were two old nurses who would conduct orientation. One was named Davis and the other named Wilkinson. All morning they lectured about Wyandotte State Hospital, its philosophy, and the kinds of patients there.

In the afternoon we saw movies on how to handle emergencies, like what to do when a patient has a seizure. It was a long day and I labored through it, hot and exhausted at the end. I had much of it in my master's work, had even seen two of the films, so I was bored.

I ate supper with two men in the class. Well, I sat at their table anyway; neither of them talked much. Then I went to my room to take a shower. The cool water on my skin made me feel more alive than I'd felt all day. Later, I lay there on the bed in my shorts, read the paper, and smoked cigarettes. It was strange being there. Other than work, there just wasn't much to do. Already it seemed like I'd be lonely.

I turned on the TV and watched some news; turned it off and smoked another cigarette. If Wes didn't get back, I'd take a ride to see the town.

Someone knocked. I couldn't hear him come down the corridor; the carpet from my room went into the hall and down the stairs, and muffled footsteps into silence.

"That you, Wes? Come on in," I yelled as I pulled up my slacks.

"Ready for some pool, man?"

"Christ, I'm ready for anything. I don't know what to do with myself."

"You won't say that when the new summer program starts."

"What's that?"

"Man, we're gonna have indoor and outdoor recreation down at Entry and up here both. And it's all gonna go till nine o'clock."

"Anything's better than this; I'm going crazy."

He looked at me and took a drag from his cigarette and smiled.

"Bad choice of words, huh?" I said sheepishly.

He nodded. "Come on, Crazy, I'm gonna skin you at pool."

The rec center was a room about seventy-five feet square. Along one side were Ping-Pong tables, along another side, a shuffleboard game. A couple dozen card tables were set up in the center of the room. At the two far corners there were open spaces: one in front of the lavatories, the other near a jukebox—a little room to dance. Between the two open areas was a large semicircular counter, where refreshments were served and where patients got the cards, games, and Ping-Pong equipment they needed.

We played pool and Wes killed me. But soon we had an easy thing going, and I began to like him. He was interesting to talk to; he'd been to Germany, Italy, Panama, and Vietnam, and liked the service a lot more than I did.

Once in a while he'd lapse into the black jargon I'd hear him use with the black patients. We swapped whorehouse stories and laughed a lot. It felt good to laugh. I had been tense and uncomfortable all through orientation that day. Now I was starting to unwind.

"White Boy, I'm gonna learn you how to shoot pool. You might even turn good."

"Know what I like about you, Wes, aside from the fact that you're sorry you pissed me off yesterday?"

He laughed.

"You didn't say, 'Morelli? That's an Italian name, isn't it?'"

"You get that a lot?"

"Not as much as before, but I still get it. But I think I've blown some good jobs by giving a smartass answer to that question."

"Hey, man, at least they have to ask you! For me it's right on my face—right here." He tugged at his cheek.

It was a nice, pleasant night. We walked around and played some Ping-Pong. After he showed me the rec room down at Entry, I drove him home.

He didn't want to live at the hospital, though he could have. His life was too wild, he said. He didn't drive. After smashing up a car in the marines he hadn't driven since; he didn't even have a license. Every day he took a bus to and from work.

The next day, I was up early again. All I wanted was coffee; it was going to be hot and muggy and cloudy. The orientation classroom wasn't air conditioned, and a few small fans wouldn't help much in that kind of weather. The drone would just make it easier to fall asleep.

I got there early, too. One of the instructors was standing out in the hallway as I walked down the steps to the class. The room was in the basement of the nurse quarters. She was talking to two other people—orderlies, I think. They had been working a few weeks before the orientation session began. It was held only once a month.

I was sitting in the back of the classroom, at the last row of desks, watching the room gradually fill up. Some of the people had not been to yesterday's class.

Then I saw her: the most beautiful creature I'd ever seen in my life. There were two doors into the room; she came in the back door, stopped, surveyed the class, glanced at me because I was directly in her line of sight, then walked up front and took a seat. Her hair was red, maroon sunlight, which fell just below the nape of her neck. In front it was short, and feathered around her forehead. Man, where in the world did she come from? I could see her clearly from where I sat. She had a short, one-piece, powder-blue dress on, and white sandals, the kind that were just soles and a few thin straps.

God, was I ready for someone like that! What a winner this orientation class was going to be. Someone else came in and sat in my line of sight just as the instructor entered the room.

We met the chief psychiatrist, who spoke in a tedious half-whisper for almost an hour, lacing his talk with allusions to Freud, James, and Skinner. Everyone in the class seemed to be dying.

When we broke for lunch, the redhead went out the front door and down the long end of the hall. I went over to the cafeteria and started eating alone until two orderlies in the class came over and sat down. They worked down at Entry and were bored with orientation, too.

One guy, Roy, said the most important thing for him to remember was to lock the doors. Lock to open; lock behind you; lock to go to the john. Lock, lock, lock. It made sense, they said, but it was hard remembering it enough to become second nature. I became conscious of the ring of keys in my pocket. Lock, lock, lock.

After lunch we sat through three chaplains, one director of nursing, one head of Occupational Therapy, one head of the Bureau of Vocational Rehabilitation, one head payroll clerk, and finally one Dr. Edward Stiner, the head of Social Services, which was the counseling and psychological treatment unit. He was a guy with long hair and a moustache, an "intense young man," I think most people would call him. Full of commitment and righteous indignation at the iniquities of society. He wore a wide bowtie, a pin-striped yellow shirt, and plaid pants, and he talked about his own background—he was my age and already a wheel—and the new programs he had instituted.

Then he introduced the red-haired madonna in the class as "Miss Covington," a new member of his department. She was on a summer fellowship to complete her bachelor's degree. He made her stand up when he introduced her; the first good thing he'd done all afternoon. Man, she was fine.

She had a few freckles around her nose, but she wasn't pale like most redheads I'd ever known. Her skin was gold, like she'd been swimming every day, and soft looking.

Once in a while, they'd exchange a knowing look as though Stiner spoke two languages, one to those of us in the class, a vulgate, and another, more classical, to her.

I disliked the bastard already. As much because he had the red-haired broad in his department as for my instinctive dislike of pompous, self-important movers of men and heart-to-heart talkers.

When he was done, he and the redhead walked out quickly and were gone. I didn't do much about getting out quick. I was hot and sweaty and bored again, and couldn't wait to start meeting some patients.

When I got to the cafeteria, Wes was waiting for me. "How you doing, White Eyes?"

"Fine, Spook."

He guffawed. I had caught him off guard, but I was glad he laughed. We were becoming friends.

"Man, Wes, I saw a vision today."

"A what?" he said quizzically.

"A girl, man. With the most beautiful body I've ever seen. Man, her tits were just like little footballs, standing straight out. And her legs...pillars to heaven..."

He snorted. "Out of sight, man. You have one hell of a way of describing a babe. Was she in the class?"

"Yeah, she works in Social Service."

"Aw, shit."

"What?"

"Man, Social Service is a pain in the ass. They fuck up more patients than any other group out here."

"How do they do that?"

"By acting like the whole world works at their pace, that's how. They forget that their real job is to get the patients the hell out of here and whole again. Stiner and a few of those faggy guys keep running studies and having meetings, and starting new programs—which end up like all the other old programs. Meantime, the patients are rotting out here. Then they hire these kids out of college who don't know dick about the real world, and who act like patients are tape recorders, like you can turn 'em on and off any time you want. The whole place sucks. Wait till you have to go down and deal with them arrogant bastards; you'll understand."

"What's Stiner like?

"Like he looks, man. A fast starter, a baby PhD who's gonna wake up in twenty years maybe...gonna wake up and realize all his life he's been fucking playing doctor and never got to the heart of one patient he's ever seen. Unless he becomes too much of a honcho to see patients anymore, which might be the best thing anyway."

"That's sad, Wes."

He nodded.

"You should see this broad, though. She's a dark redhead. You ever see one like that?"

"She really that good, man? Or are you just horny?"

I shrugged. "Wait till you see her. Then tell me what you think."

That night I left the hospital and went to a movie. It was lousy, but I stayed through it. Then I went to a carryout and bought some cokes, and a few paperbacks to read, though there were dozens of books back at the apartment I hadn't even looked at. Then I stopped for a beer at a place called the Workingman's Night Club. It was an old beer garden, like the ones I knew in Youngstown long ago. The jukebox had vintage Frank Sinatra and Nat King Cole records, and some big-band standards. I had a beer and talked with some old guy about whether Cleveland had a chance for the pennant.

The next day was hot and sunny and humid, a big day. We were going on tour, finally getting out of that damned classroom. Red was there again, in a dazzling blue, one-piece outfit that looked a little like a pair of shorts, though it was a dress. She had her hair in two short ponytails. From the back she looked like a little girl, until you noticed her legs. Man, her legs looked firm; they were developed all the way down to the ankles, nothing skinny, just lithe and lovely muscles.

After hearing from a few more VIPs, we started on our tour: today the physical plant and supportive facilities; tomorrow, patients. One more day and it would all be over.

We walked as a group, but I always lagged behind, occasionally getting a glimpse of Red. She was about five four or five five, small-waisted and graceful, like a dancer. From far away she seemed taller than she really was.

I wondered if she realized what a blessing it was to be born with a body like that. No, I guessed not; she had never earned it, the body or the face. She walked around like she was glad to have it, thanks, but hell, it was better on her than on someone else anyway. What an awesome ass for a snooty broad.

The farms that bordered the hospital on two sides belonged to Wyandotte, and the hospital used most of the produce in its own kitchens. Patients worked the fields, but they had to be from the City, not from Entry. They looked hot and tired, but they waved as we passed. The fields were green and well-tended; it was a pretty-good looking farm.

Then we saw the laundry. The patients who staffed most of it seemed more used to the hellish heat than we were. I was sweating like hell. Soaked. And steam was coming out of everywhere. When we went to the pressing room, the hot steam irons just made it worse.

I asked the guide a question. "Where do the patients' clothes get pressed? Isn't this all hospital white?"

"Well, you have to remember that we have twelve hundred patients out here. We just don't have enough facilities and personnel to press their clothes all the time; we're too busy with staff uniforms and bedding. I can guarantee you that the clothes are clean, though," she said.

Everbody was shifting back and forth. I was picking a bad time to ask questions. "How long do patients work out here every day?" I said.

"They work four hours, and get fifty cents an hour," said the guide, who seemed to be getting irritated. She looked at our leader, Mrs. Davis, who was wilting herself. Davis started for the door on cue, and everyone in our group made a run for it. The red-haired madonna got caught behind, and suddenly I was beside her.

"Would you like to work here?" I asked as we walked.

She gave me a strange look. "No...I wouldn't," she said coolly.

"My name's Sandy Morelli; what's yours?" I said as we moved out into open air again. As hot as I was, it seemed cool against my face.

"Sandra Covington," she said. "That's an Italian name isn't it?"

Better believe it, baby, I thought. I muttered a yes and didn't say anything more. She kept walking, unconcerned.

But as she walked in front of me I thought of her face again. Her eyes were hazel, a mysterious pale green, and she had long, dark lashes. Fantastic. Her nose was small and straight, like those of the girls in makeup ads. But her face didn't have that gaunt professional look; there was a ripeness about her body. Maybe the word was healthy. Man, she looked healthy.

That afternoon we toured the warehouse. Mrs. Davis deferred to the warehouse superintendent; he became our leader, and she became one of the pack. He was a large man, about six two and weighing two fifty or so, and had thin blond hair. Behind brown horn rims he wore a hawkish, tough expression and spoke in a deep voice, seeming always to be suppressing a great huff at having to show us his domain.

The place was immaculate; cartons were stacked in neat rows and piled atop wooden pallets that kept them off the floor. Huge drums of cooking oil and flour were arranged along one wall, with enough room behind them to drive a forklift. The man ran a hell of a warehouse.

He then led us to the clothing supply room. Patients worked throughout the building, and they worked silently, probably because they feared the superintendent.

He told us how the clothing shop was a real problem to manage, and how he had a hard time making it break even. "Some of these staff people order dress clothes, like this is a store, and even specify styles and colors. You can't do that out here; we just don't have a budget for that sort of thing. When I get orders like that, or when one department is ordering too much, I scale it down. I buy what I can get, and they take it and like it. These clothes here"—he pointed to a shelf of denim overalls—"are good enough. They wear better and they keep people warm."

I didn't like him. He was efficient, but humorless and unfeeling. The thought of having to reckon with him in deciding patient rehabilitation had me sneering in disgust.

"I have a question," I said. "Can you countermand a doctor's or supervisor's orders for clothes and supplies?"

"That's right," he said coolly. "If they think they can run this warehouse any better, they're welcome to try. Any other questions?"

"Yeah, I have another one," I said. "What if a patient's mental well-being is dependent on some nice clothes?"

He flashed an annoyed glance at me. "This is not a store, as I said before." He spoke always to the group; never to me. He projected his voice like a sergeant at map demonstrations. "If their families can afford it, fine. But my job isn't to make people look good."

Phallic bastard. I tried to throw a little more shit into the game. "But don't you think that everyone dressing in these overalls would have a depressing effect on patients?"

Man, he didn't like being needled like that. "I leave all the psychology to the doctors. I'm just trying to run a warehouse, and I do the best I can."

I backed off, and the class started moving out. I followed along, still fascinated by the neatness of the place. Sandra Covington walked up ahead. The humidity was eighty-six percent and we still had an hour movie ahead of us.

We made a side trip down to Entry to go through the offices and the counseling center at Social Service. It was located on the second floor of the hospital. All the staff was at a meeting; only the secretary was in. The place was nice—small offices, modern furniture, color coordinated with carpeting and drapes, and air conditioning.

Then we went through surgery, the laboratories, and one of the patient wings.

On the way back to our classroom at the nurses' quarters, I was sweating and miserable. I didn't dress in really casual clothes for orientation, but I should have.

We had a ten-minute break before the movie started, so I went to the nurses' lounge for a Coke. Sandra was at the machine. She turned to see who it was that came up behind her.

"Hello," I said.

"Hi."

She turned back to get her pop. She got it and stepped away. As my cup filled up I watched her settle onto a couch in the lounge. I sat in a stuffed chair on the other side of the room. There were too many people milling around; it was a bad place to try to talk to her. She seemed quiet and self-possessed. You could tell by the way she moved it that she was proud of her body. She knew I was watching her, and ignored me by reading a magazine. Her hands and feet were slender and flawless; her nails were painted with clear enamel.

She glanced at her watch. I was trying to figure her out. Maybe it was the clothes, I don't know; I just got the feeling that she moved through her life effortlessly, and never really got tired or distressed. She looked like money.

After the movie I was one of the first ones out of the room. Sandra was on her way down the same hall. "Goodnight," I said as she passed me.

"Goodnight," she said, smiling.

As I reached the door, she was walking down the drive between the House and the Ad Building. A guy with long blond hair was waiting in an MG roadster convertible. She got in, and he drove away.

The cool air in the House felt good. Wes was in the office. "What a piece of ass she'd be, Wes."

"But how do you know, man? Sometimes those knockout broads aren't any good in the sack. They're so busy worrying about their bodies, they don't have time to be a good piece of ass."

"It's funny, you know. I'm still trying to figure out if she really is a snob or just shy. She never says much to anybody, but she never has that pissed-off look either…But she sure got out of there fast after class. Some blond dude was waiting for her in an MG."

"Hell, man, if she works in SS you're never gonna see her again after orientation anyway; you're gonna be up to your ass in volleyballs every night."

"SS people never get up here, huh?"

"Very little. They stay down at Entry, where it's cool. Most of them are afraid of real people; patients walking around loose make them nervous."

The next morning was Friday, and at eight in the morning it was seventy-five degrees out and humid as hell. What a break, a heat wave all week.

As I entered one entrance to the nurses' quarters, Sandra was coming down the hall from the other door. I nodded to her and she smiled. She was wearing a loose, short dress that reminded me of a pajama top. But she sure as hell looked good in it. She sat in the front row again and I sat back by the fan, sweating like hell already.

The district fire chief gave us yet another lecture on fire safety. After he left, the maintenance foreman took us out behind the building to demonstrate how to use a fire extinguisher. We formed a large circle around him. His young assistant was with him. He looked like he was in his early twenties, and had a sullen, glum look, and never took his eyes off Sandra.

"Could I have one of you volunteer?" the foreman asked. No one moved. He asked again. Again no response. So I stepped into the center of the group. He moved me into position and made me hold the can in my hands. He started telling how we should be careful to have the nozzle ready before we try to use it. "Turn it over," he said.

I did. And the fucking thing was loaded and open, and the shit inside went all over my shirt and down the front of my slacks. I was furious; the bastards set me up, and then both got a big charge out of seeing me all wet. Everyone in the group seemed mildly amused, and relieved that they hadn't volunteered.

"You didn't tell me the goddamn thing was open," I snapped to the foreman.

"I was explaining how you should be very careful in turning it over," he said, grinning.

"Yeah, well, your explanation came a little bit late," I muttered.

He turned to the group again. "Now let me show you how to do this the right way," he said, still very smug and amused.

It took everything I had in me not to smack his fucking assistant, who enjoyed the joke just a little too much. I walked to the rear of the group, and was bending over, wiping the stuff off my pants with my handkerchief, when I felt someone watching me. It was Sandra. But I was too pissed to feel polite or horny. And I wasn't sure if she felt sorry for me, and resented what that wise ass of a foreman did, or if she enjoyed my looking like a fool who had just pissed his pants.

I looked down and kept wiping. When I was done, I left the group and walked up to the office. They were going to Occupational Therapy next, and then to RT. If it weren't for the tour of the cottages, I'd have just stayed at RT, then left for Columbus early.

"What the hell happened to you?" said Wes.

"That cocksucker maintenance man..." I said.

"Shit!" He snapped his fingers. "Shit. I meant to tell you about that son of a bitch. Goddamn, how could I forget that? He gets his rocks off that way, man...every orientation."

"Look at this fucking shirt," I said, fuming.

He chuckled, then started to laugh out loud. I did too, but I was still pissed.

"Hey, man, go change. If they went to OT, they'll be through here next."

"Yeah. You're the tour guide, huh?"

I took a quick shower to get the smell of chemicals off me. When I went back outside, Wes was showing everyone the stage. As he talked I joined the group, still smarting. Then he showed them a large closet full of games and card decks.

As some of the group looked through the games, he caught my eye. He nodded at Sandra approvingly, then rolled his eyes like Birmingham in a Charly Chan movie. As soon as he was through, we went to lunch.

"Man, I didn't think she looked like that," he said. "You got good taste for a wop."

"I told you, man."

"She looks pretty high class, though. What's her name again?"

"Sandra Covington."

"I'll bet she's Dr. Covington's daughter."

"Who's that?" I asked.

"He's a doctor in town who comes out here to do volunteer surgery. Big man. Carries a heavy stick, and always gets his name in the paper."

"Find out for me, will you?"

"You gonna be in town this weekend?" he asked.

"No. I'm heading back to Columbus for some things I have to bring back up here…and some sportin' life."

"You have a girl down there?"

"I see one now and then; she's working on a PhD at Ohio State. It's not serious, but I like her…We have good times together."

He told me a little about his ex-wife, how they lived it up for a few years and blew money left and right. Then one day the money was gone, and when they really took a good look at each other, they knew it was all they had going for them. He seemed pained by what happened. He offered me a cigarette, and I lit up. He was a decent guy who had some painful memories to live with.

In the afternoon we toured the City. It was sweltering, and I was defeated before we started out. As we entered the cottages, the smell of too many bodies in the heat struck us in waves, almost overwhelming us.

The patients were tired and wasted, seeming bored to the point of forgetting they were ever good for something outside Wyandotte. The women were the most pathetic. Some were so old and gnarled that they seemed dead already. They just sat and stared. The heat didn't intrude upon their private emptiness. There was an old woman who, the guide told us, sat in a chair all day and pulled each hair of her head out one by one, even her eyebrows. She was totally bald except for some short new growth of hair that soon she would pull out.

Mrs. Davis led us to the men's cottage then. They, too, were listless and miserable. Most stared at us as we walked through their house. Our leader told us that most of the younger patients worked during the day, so that was why we saw so many senile, retarded, and deranged. About a dozen men were sitting in a screened porch on the side of the cottage in the shade. There was a young man lying totally naked on a bench near the screen. He was on his back, with his knees drawn up to his chest and clamped tight against him by his arms. His eyes were closed, but he was not asleep. Whenever anyone dressed him, he took the clothes back off. The other patients ignored him as though he were dressed.

I was sick. From the heat, from the smell, and from the grotesque ugliness of humanity cramped onto long benches and old chairs in buildings built before most of them were born.

I looked at Sandra. The veneer of self-possession looked marred. She saw me watching her, then looked away. I recalled the old women we had just seen. Some must have been attractive once, must have been as vibrant and promising as Sandra was now. I looked at her again and felt the ache of imagining her deformed into one of them. What kind of torment would it take to do that to her?

The last two cottages were the lock-up wards for men and women. Cottage Jackson was the women's ward, and it was more a walk through hell than through a hospital. Women shrieked and moaned and paced the floor. We saw padded cells, and women in restraints, strapped down so they wouldn't kill themselves by bludgeoning their heads on the walls.

We saw women giggling at us and making faces. Some cursed us, and others stared through us. You could sense the violence within many of them; it seemed to rumble through the heat like distant thunder. This was the movie version of mental illness: rage, wild-eyed madness, and whining, screaming, senseless laughing. Strange that so many laughed rather than cried.

The men's cottage was named Erie. Not all of them were so sick. Many had been confined for observation by court order. Sometimes you could see the sickness in their faces more than in their overt actions.

Even the way they dressed added to our depression. The women wore loose, wrinkled, ill-fitting dresses; the men, overalls. Everything seemed at least one size too big. How could somebody let that warehouseman dress them like prisoners?

I followed Sandra up the stairs in Erie. She suddenly glanced back, looking into my eyes, silently allowing me to see her heartfelt revulsion of these scenes at Wyandotte. The stench and the heat had touched her.

We waited in the stairwell until the door at the top of the stairs was opened by the attendant from the inside. I was soaked with sweat, and ever feeling normal again seemed like a dream.

Above Sandra's lip there was some sign of moisture; the hair around her forehead and around her ears was damp, and her skin didn't have the glow it had that morning. He legs and feet were smudged by the dirt of the cottages and the dust outside.

The men upstairs seemed more lethargic than the others we had seen; they huddled near each window for air. Attic fans were not enough.

"Sandy!"

Sandra turned, startled, and looked at me.

"Sandy!"

I turned too, somehow confused and frightened by my own name.

"Don't you remember me?"

"My God! My God! Rigley!"

Our group broke suddenly broke apart; one woman screamed. Some of the patients were scared too. Before I realized what was happening, Rigley had swung me around by the shoulders, and had thrown his arms around me in a hug.

The ward attendant came running out of the back dormitory room. An orderly came from the lavatory. They tried to grab him.

"Wait. It's okay; it's okay," I shouted. They stopped. The whole place was quiet and still. "It's okay. I know him; we're friends," I said weakly.

"I was just gonna say hello," Rigley added. "I got friends too. Look at him."

Mrs. Davis was pale and flustered. Something had happened to change the script she had run through countless times before, and she didn't know how to deal with it. Her instinct was to leave. She told the orderly to unlock the door immediately.

"You gonna go already, Sandy?" Rigley said.

"Yeah, but I'll be back. I work here now, so I can see you soon, okay?"

"Yeah." He was smiling like a child.

The patients surrounded us. We were something new to break up their day. They gawked like children, credulous and curious. Mrs. Davis was almost in a panic to get downstairs. I waved at Rigley and followed, the last one out.

Outside, the class gathered on the oval, looking at me as though I were some strange new animal in their midst. Sandra was watching too, but never said a word.

My mind was numb. I was hot, depressed, and shocked by the hospital. Mrs. Davis wished us good luck, and then dismissed us. I walked wearily back to the House, took a shower, and headed for Columbus.

Wyandotte Hospital. I was a stranger among twelve hundred names and faces, and had to learn them all. At first I was uneasy walking among people condemned to the City; I imagined being jumped on and strangled, or stabbed. But gradually my fears dissipated, and I relaxed.

Anyway, my job as supervisor was to watch and listen—always listen. I had to walk from place to place. Anywhere RT was going on, I had to be looking in. The patients were supposed to know me, and confide in me if they felt at ease. Catharsis. How easy it all sounded.

I wasn't accepted so easily, though. People felt I was a different kind of RT; I came and went too much. At first their attitude was the same as mine, apprehensive and untrusting. But slowly they lost their fear of me. When I'd approach one of them, he'd react openly, if not warmly. Trust later grew to mutual affection, and I became one of them, sometimes even forgetting that I was in a mental hospital, and reacting to people the way I always did, yet with a subdural awareness that I was there for a purpose.

I had to keep a log, and write my behavioral evaluations on patients for RT. Often I found myself listening over and over again to the same stories from the same person, trying to find in them a key to his psyche.

We were the most successful therapy staff, and Wes was the master. He had a tired, experienced assurance that the patients seemed to know he had earned a hard and bitter way. He spoke softly and distinctly, his eyes once in a while betraying a look of loneliness and pain, long endured and never really eradicated from his heart. So they felt that he was one of them, and might ease them on their way out of Wyandotte.

Sheila and Mrs. Smith had the same effect. More than anything else, they were friends, not counselors or psychiatrists, just good friends. And to them the patients often volunteered feelings and insights that the heart-to-heart people could scarcely unravel in countless hours in the office.

There were daily Evaluation Committee meetings chaired by Dr. Craver, where therapists from the different departments discussed individual patients from their own vantage points. I sat in on the meetings whenever I was told to. Hostetter was the official representative of RT, and I just observed quietly. But as time passed, I grew more and more eager to speak, and when Hostetter wasn't there I spoke my mind.

I began to learn why Wes disliked him...began, too, to see the effect of his personality on RT. His ego was too much in the way of any therapy. He was, of course, clean-cut, smiling, and energetic—an Eagle Scout—the kind of person I never was, yet always envied. But somehow he needed more from the patients than he could give them in return.

They cheered him. He was the best Ping-Pong and badminton player, a good pinochle player, and a first-class pool player. And a shortstop...a good shortstop...a perennial shortstop...fielding soft-balls with one bare hand for miraculous throws to first...swaggering, exhorting, and chattering...yet unfulfilled.

The enmity between us grew slowly. He was a man's man, which none of the men working with him ever really trusted...drinking beer over at the Tinkerbell, winning at pool and gin rummy, and being admired for his skill. I was the ornamental RT; he was *Mr. RT*, the guy who had to win, had to be young, had to be liked, and who never really had much time for the patients. So in almost every-thing, it was Director against Supervisor I, and seven weeks left of summer.

One day Hostetter called me into his office in the Ad Building. He said that Social Service sometimes interviews patients from the City who were either old or in lockup. He said he had promised them that if I wasn't busy, I'd help them out by escorting a few patients down to SS, since I often went back and forth during the day. Then he gave me the name of an old man in Cottage J.

I picked him up on the second floor of the cottage. That familiar odor of too many people in close quarters hit me again. I was anxious to get him out. His name was Dan, and he was seventy- nine years old, bald, and toothless. He was a tall man who walked in slow, minc-ing steps, and I had to help him down the stairs. He was senile, I thought; what the hell did they want with him?

It took almost fifteen minutes to get down to Entry. Dan talked about the heat, and something about working on a farm. He seemed more attuned to the past, as though fragments of it always inter-spersed themselves into his perceptions of present reality. And he couldn't tell now from yesterday, so he chose those moments he liked best, and they became the world he lived in.

When we walked into the SS office, I could see several smaller offices, cubicles really, with doors with large glass windows in them, closed to keep the noise out. The secretary told me that the counselors were busy and that I should have a seat. Her manner irritated me, and all of a sudden I wondered if Hostetter had gotten me caught in something I'd live to regret.

"Miss, I'm just supposed to deliver these patients."

"Well, who's going to bring them back?" she said, smiling to herself at my absurdity.

"I don't know; I guess one of you will have to do it."

"One of us?" She was still smiling.

"I don't care who it is, really, but RTs don't have time to wait around here while you complete your interviews."

"Well, I don't know who's going to do it. Our schedule is too full to—"

"What's wrong, Cathy?" It was Sandra Covington.

"This gentleman says he's not going to wait for that patient. He wants to leave."

"Who's going to come and get him?" Sandra said to me.

"No one from RT," I said. She looked me over. I was wearing cotton slacks, a crew-necked jersey, and tennis shoes, not really standard hospital issue.

"What do you mean, 'no one'? How's he going to get back?"

About that time I was getting pissed. "Look, Miss Covington, personally I don't give a damn how you get him back, but as long as he's in your custody, you'd better see that he gets there safely."

She glared at me a few seconds. "Maybe if I called the RT supervisor, you'd be a little more agreeable..."

"Yeah, well, I don't think so, because I'm the RT supervisor."

They both looked at me like I was a barbarian in the sanctuary.

"Where's your name tag?" she said.

"I didn't get it yet. Where's yours?"

She didn't answer. She turned to Old Dan who was sitting in her office, and then back to me. She was uncertain about her next move. "I don't know…Dr. Stiner's not going to like this."

"Look, I'm telling you: I'll be glad to bring patients down to you whenever I can, because I come down here at least once a day. But I can't just wait around here until you're done with them. Stiner has to find some way to get them back again."

"That will waste too much time for us," she said coldly, looking at the floor. "Can't you leave your games long enough to help us with a patient? This is more important than recreation."

"The word is therapy, Miss Covington. Got that? Therapy. And I know it's hard to imagine, but it just might be as important as the work done in this office."

"I doubt that."

"What can you possibly ask a senile, arthritic old man who's been out here a third of his life that's going to do him any good?"

"Dr. Stiner's gathering data for a longitudinal study," she said.

"So this isn't about Dan at all, is it? It's about this office. But aren't you supposed to be clinicians? How do you have time to do elaborate studies on old men?"

"You just don't understand," she said.

"I understand that there are patients who should be counseled out of here, and you can't be doing that if you're busy doing longitudinal studies on terminal residents."

She and the secretary both walked away. They were through arguing.

"Miss Covington?" I said.

She knew the question wasn't settled. "I'll take them back myself," she said, never turning around.

What a great place, a haughty secretary and an arrogant little chick.

I saw Rigley as much as I could. The Tuesday after orientation, I went to see him. It was like seeing a ghost. I still couldn't believe he was there. I asked Wes about him. Everybody knew him, he said. He had been there about four years.

"You're the RT supervisor; you can take him out on leave from the cottage. Go get him," he said. That was how it started. It was movie day, and the RTs didn't do much in the afternoon, so I was free.

I went upstairs to the second floor of Erie and knocked. Nothing happened. I knocked again...and waited. Nothing. I knocked again. I knew there had to be someone there, but I went downstairs to check with the attendant anyway. He said they were up there. So back up I went. Knocked. Waited. Nothing again. Then I really started pounding.

"Who is it?" I heard a low, growling voice say.

"The RT supervisor. I've come for a patient."

"Use your key!"

"I don't have a key!" Man, the whole world was full of assholes.

"Then you can't come in. How do I know you're the supervisor?"

"I tell you I'm the supervisor. Are you gonna open this door or not?"

"No. Go away!"

"Goddammit, open this door or I'll kick it down." I started pounding again.

Finally he opened it. He was a huge, grizzly, ugly man with small eyes and thick round glasses, and he was scowling. "What the fuck do you want?" he said.

"I told you I wanted a patient. Why didn't you open this door?"

"You didn't have no key. I did it this time, but next time you ain't getting in."

I moved toward him and he stiffened. I never knew I could hate someone so quickly. Then I stopped. Some patients were standing around us grinning, waiting for a fight.

"I'm gonna get a key, bastard. Now give me Rigley Potter." The guy was going to be trouble for me forever, man.

Rigley came out dressed in overalls. He brightened when he saw me. "Come on," I said. "We're going outside."

"Yeah? Oh boy! Now?"

"Let's go." Before I walked outside, I sneered at the attendant. He still wore that dim, vicious look.

Rigley stepped out on the porch and took a deep, exhilarating breath. "Come on," I said. We started walking around the oval. He was silent. I could have asked a million questions, but I didn't.

"I ain't seen you in a long time, Sandy," he said finally.

"Ten years almost."

"That's a long time, huh?"

"How have you been, Rigley?"

He started telling me about himself as we walked slowly toward the House. Once in a while, he'd pause to question me. "You got a wife, Sandy?"

"No."

"How come? You're pretty old now. My sister got four little kids."

"I don't know. Never met anyone just right, I guess."

"You still like me, Sandy?"

"Sure. We've been friends a long time, haven't we?"

"But I was mad at you once't. You had all them new friends and girls and such. Alls I had was Skinny Tom, that mean ol' son of a bitch."

"Well, we're still buddies now. Don't worry about that stuff."

"How come you never came to see me all them years?"

"I don't know…"

It was a question I could never answer, even to myself. I meant to go see him so many times, but after Ohio State, and the service, whenever I hit Youngstown I was busy. He was out of the way, too, and seeing him again…I don't know…it would have been a big thing. I felt guilty, and just couldn't walk in on him, just like that. So I waited for the right time, that special time, and it never came.

"Ah, man, we get older, you know? First it was the army, then college; then I didn't live in Youngstown anymore. Sometimes it's easy to forget even special friends like you."

He looked down at the ground and shook his head, and made a clicking sound through his teeth the way he always did. It was like he understood what I was saying, and it made some sense, yet beneath it all he knew it really didn't. His world—no, my world never made sense.

He was crying. I turned him toward me but he pulled away.

"Hey," I said, "don't cry now. We're back together again."

"But it ain't the same no more. Look at me, big and fat…can't even ride a bike. We're like old people now, Sandy. Like old John with the chicken coop. There ain't no creek no more; there ain't no place to go anymore…aw…"

He shook his head again. We were both quiet for a few minutes. Then I spoke.

"Rigley?"

"What?"

"We're not little kids anymore, but still we can be friends."

"You gonna go away again?"

"Yeah, at the end of the summer."

"Then I don't wanna be no friends."

"But why not? Look, we can be men friends, not kid friends. And I won't ever stay away from you like I did before. Honest."

He looked down at me. "Promise? Best friends again like before?"

"I promise. Best friends."

He smiled.

"We gonna shake hands?" I said.

His face lit up in a broad, happy grin. He shook my hand and started doing a little strut step. "Wowee! I got my best friend again."

"Okay, come on now. Tell me all about yourself."

"Yeah, I got a lot to tell you."

Park benches lined the wide walk leading to the House. We settled into one of them as he rambled on about himself. I watched him as I listened. What a difference ten years had made. Rigley was the same child, inwardly, he always was. But outwardly, where he was once tall and ungainly, he was now massive and lumbering, his lips scarred, and his teeth broken and jagged in front. There were scars all over his face, smaller ones mostly, but a large stitched scar over his right eyebrow. His hair was cut short and fell flat forward. His shoes were huge high tops, like the old steel toes my father wore to the mill. He smelled of sweat and bad breath, and his speech was unsteady and slurred. Yeah, ten years was a long time.

As the summer passed, he would recall old times for me, and we'd laugh at the foolish things we did as children. Every movie day, the same thing: walk the grounds, then sit on the benches near the House, waiting for the movie to end.

One day, about midsummer, as he talked, I was facing west, leaning my chin on the back of the bench and listening. Down the oval I could see Sandra walking a woman up to Cottage Nine. As Rigley talked, I watched her come toward us. She was escorting another terminal resident.

Sandra's legs grew more golden every time I saw them. I undressed her in my imagination. What would it be like to run my tongue all over that belly? God! She wore sandals again, and the same kind of short dress, only another color, white. She walked like a European woman, like the Italian women I used to know in Youngstown, with a kind of deliberate grace that kept her body always erect as she moved. I caught a glimpse of her eyes, the flashing green under dark auburn lashes.

Rigley was telling me about Skinny Tom dying in an auto accident. For a moment, I lost Sandra. Death is one part of childhood that never fits right into your memories.

"Hi, Miss…Cov…"

"Hi, Rigley," she said, not looking at me. They passed us slowly. I couldn't take my eyes off her, but I didn't speak. Cottage Nine was two doors away from the House, around the oval.

Rigley said, "What's her name, Sandy? I can't say it."

"Covington."

He tried it once again. "Cov…"

"Covington," I said slowly. After a few times he had it right, and kept repeating it to himself.

"I'm gonna say it when she comes back," he said. "Covington."

She came out of the cottage quickly and started down our way. I think she would have crossed to the other side, but there was no walk. She knew I was studying her as she continued toward us, but I didn't care.

When she was in front of us, Rigley said, "Hi, Miss Covington."

She said, "Hi," and passed us quickly, lowering her eyes.

When she was about ten steps behind us, I turned and called to her. "Miss Covington?"

She turned around warily, expecting something nasty from me. "Yes?"

"Welcome to where the real people are," I said, smiling.

She sniffed and turned quickly. Maybe I shouldn't have said it, I thought, but what the hell, she wasn't behind a desk in the SS office, she was in my territory.

Rigley and I talked another hour, until the movie left out. His parents were both dead, and his sister still lived in Youngstown. He came to Wyandotte a year after his mother died.

"Do you know why you're in Erie, Rigley?" I asked.

"I don't know...can't remember. Maybe just 'cause I got 'vulsions in my head."

"What?"

"You know, 'vulsions...falling down and spitting and such like that."

"You take convulsions?"

"Yeah."

"Very often?"

"Nah. Sometimes only. They ain't too bad. I just get sleepy after." Then his mind went back to Sandra. "I like her; she talks nice to me. Always asking how I feel..."

"That's good," I said.

"Maybe I should make her my girlfriend."

"Okay." I remembered those terrible times another girlfriend once caused us.

"You won't take her away, will you?" he said.

"No," I sighed. "Not hardly. I don't think she likes me."

I had told him I'd see him maybe three or four days a week, depending on what I had to do on Fridays. He didn't understand it all, and always went back reluctantly, with my promise that I'd see him soon again.

———∞∞∞———

The first week of July we got three student RTs, two girls and one boy, all having completed freshman year in psychology. The girls were young and pretty, one blonde and one dark-haired. The blonde, Karen, was tall, and had a slender body, almost no waist, and nice, small, firm breasts. The other girl, Diane, had black, shiny straight hair that was down to the middle of her back, parted above her forehead. She was almost chubby, but not quite. Her face was beautiful, and her ass was the kind that waved at you when she walked away.

The guy was tall and blond, a foppish bullshitter full of jargon coming through on an affected Princeton accent. But he was a nice kid with a good heart, and in a week or so eased out of his pose and began to grow on us. Anyway, we found them to be gentle and concerned, giving everything they had to help the patients.

The three of them and Wes and I handled all the outside RT activities. Mrs. Smith and Sheila were a little old for all the jumping and sweating, so they worked the cottages and the golden agers. There were times when they weren't with us all week except on Friday nights, when the whole RT staff assembled for the card party, and Monday nights for the softball games.

So the outside team, as we called ourselves, really began to enjoy being together. RT was not just fun for the patients, it was fun for us. And at the end of each day, we were tired and sweaty and had spent our energies to do some good. Sleeping was always easy.

I even began to enjoy being the RT supervisor. Sometimes I was able to take end-runs around bureaucrats in the hospital to get our department some new equipment, or to change our procedures a little. The inside-outside teams were my idea, and they worked.

I had the feeling that if anyone was doing good at Wyandotte, it was RT. We helped draw people out of themselves, and that, somehow, was good for all of us. It was only when I went to the evaluation meetings that I realized how halting and sluggish our pace really was. The same names came up for consideration again and again, and each time something new deferred a recommendation for release. We were strangling in our own rhetoric. After I spoke against our pace at a few meetings, Hostetter found things for me to do and went alone. I seldom went back to them for the rest of the summer. They all had a good thing going: all jobs were circumscribed and intact. No one got hot, or even upset. Language was cool, and softly spoken, and rashness frowned upon, especially in regard to discharging people from the hospital.

A few times a week I still brought patients down to SS—and saw Sandra most of the time. Well, I looked at her anyway. We never talked. And yet I was always disappointed when I went down there and didn't see her in her little office. It was always worth a trip just to see that face. Hell, I was falling in love with someone who hated me.

One day in July I decided to try to speak to her. It was a good time, late Friday afternoon, payday, and the office was empty except for Sandra. I marveled at the way she worked. It was more than a job to her; she cared, enough so that I'd see her there sometimes hours after everyone else had gone.

As I ushered the patient into the office, the door of Sandra's cubicle was open. She saw us and came out, smiling to the woman I brought and calling her by name, and, as always, ignoring me. When she turned away, I spoke...very timidly. Courage, Morelli.

"Sandra?"

She showed the same uneasy surprise as the day I talked to her up at the House, and this time I used her first name.

"Can I talk to you about something?"

I looked serious and conciliatory, so she said, "Just a minute," and put the patient in her office and closed the door. She came back to me, not knowing whether I was going to be nice or going to start another bitter fencing match with her.

"Why don't we stop this?" I said.

"Stop what?" she said reflexively, her eyes searching my face for any glimmer of insincerity that would have ruined the moment.

"You know what I mean," I said.

She turned her head aside and put her fingers to her forehead as though she had a headache, or was absently brushing her hair away from her eyes.

"Yes, I know what you mean," she sighed. I had caught her when she was tired, and in a mood for peace.

"This delivery system has worked out okay, hasn't it?" I said.

"Yes, it's okay. I don't mind it."

I smiled then. "I won't bait you anymore—even when you're in my territory."

She smiled, too. God what a face. She lowered her head, but turned to me again.

"We do have to work together. I guess we can be civil."

"No more remarks about SS," I pledged.

Finally she trusted me enough to relax a little. "Me too. No more RT putdowns."

"Okay," I said.

"One more thing," she said. "Will you call me Sandy? Everyone else does."

"How will I know if I'm talking to you or to myself then?"

Her eyes twinkled at that little bit of foolishness, as if at first it made some sense. Then her face brightened and she gave a small tinkling laugh that I'd carry with me like perfume when I left.

"So long," I said. "See you next week with a new contingent."

"Yes. Next week."

⸎

There was something about Rigley that was bothering me. There were too many holes in his story of the past ten years. I told Wes I still didn't know what really happened to him. "You ever have anything to do with him?" I asked.

"Not much. He never came to open house when he could; he'd just walk around the City. Since he's been in Erie he doesn't do much but sit. Can't get him to play anything when I'm up there."

"Man, that's a shitty thing to do—keep him in Erie because of convulsions. Why the hell don't they just give him medication? He shouldn't have to be locked up for it; hell, he could have one up there."

"Yeah, it's sickening. But it's the doctors' fault. Locking people up is one way of neutralizing them. Least you know where they are, then."

"You know, Wes, at those evaluation meetings, I get the feeling that hardly anybody ever gets moved out."

"Man, the City gets to be a way of life. Look at little Eddie Rothman; they should have got him out two years ago, but he's still here playing Ping-Pong and fucking around. And one of these days he's not gonna be able to face that outside world anymore. Then you got a terminal resident on your hands that nobody's doing shit for, and he ain't even twenty-five years old."

"But isn't anybody doing anything?"

"Man, we got nineteen doctors out here and we should have more than twice that many, and I'll kiss your ass if you show me more than five real psychiatrists in the bunch. But I'll show you queers, alcoholics, drug addicts, quacks—anybody who can't make big bread on the outside. Only one worth a damn is Ramirez, and he's getting out soon as he can."

"Man, that's frightening, Wes."

"Nobody knows the shit going on out here, man."

"I'm gonna go down and look at Rigley's file. Think they'll give it to me?"

"You're the RT supervisor, ain't you, White Eyes?"

Down the hall from the Social Service office there was a large room with row after row of steel shelves. On them were files of every person ever to be in Wyandotte. Along one wall, there were carrels where you could read. When I asked for Rigley's file, the girl at the desk glanced at my name tag, then got it for me without a word.

The file was huge, about an inch and a half thick. There were physical profiles, blood pressures, urine analyses, electrocardiograms, and electroencephalograms. All the psychiatric material was at the end, but I still paged slowly through the mass of documents. I read a report from St. Rita's Hospital in Youngstown. "Petit mal seizures evidenced in post-pubertal adolescence. Passenger in automobile accident at age nineteen, hairline skull fracture. Incidence of seizures increased—gran mal. EEG indicated progressive deterioration."

I read a story he hadn't told me completely. A coroner's report listed two deaths in Rigley's accident, Harold Ramos and Thomas A. Miller. Jesus Christ, Skinny Tom!

Then I got to the psychiatric profile, and it read like a series of bad short stories, telling as much about the interviewers as it did about Rigley. The reports were typewritten, verbatim accounts of interviews, and the summary conclusions of the counselors.

Over a four-year stay, he had about a dozen interviews. I read the first carefully. It was full of fashionable psychological cant, and through it all Rigley was evasive and uncommunicative. The report ended with the interviewer's comments: "Rigley Potter is a huge, corpulent man with a rather small head, which gives him a grotesque look…He exhibits withdrawing behavior and seems hostile toward the interviewer…"

I read through the rest quickly, and could hardly stand it. No one seemed aware of the previous interviews. They commented on his physique, his body odor, his scars, and his poor speech, but few of them ever touched the real Rigley. Occasional flashes of insight were buried in almost two inches of verbal garbage. And with each interview, Rigley became more and more remote. Then lost.

I suddenly realized who had done the final interview. There, on the last page: Sandra Covington. And then I read more carefully, not only to learn about Rigley but to see what I could learn about Sandy. Rigley responded to her, but she asked the wrong questions, somehow missing the childhood anguish he felt at seeing everyone grow up different.

> Mr. Potter is a giant, gnome-like creature with the mind of a child. He is pathetically secretive and hostile; psycho-social aggressive tendencies were evident throughout the interview. He exhibits obvious latent, if not overt, homosexual tendencies, which can begin to explain his behavior set.
>
> Evidently, Mr. Potter's family had a matriarchal structure, with Mr. Potter and his sister competing for the mother's affections. Potter displays a profound hostility toward his sister.

Jesus Christ. I paged back through the file to a series of letters from his sister:

Dear Dr. Huffman,
My husbands working now again. We don't have much but we can take care of him now, my kids like him too. Rigley

don't hurt nobody and it ain't rite that he has to stay there all the time. Please Dr. Huffman I can come an get him maybe for a little while then I'll bring him back.

Mrs. Dina Howard

The other letters were the same, simple and pathetic, but full of love for Rigley. How in the hell could Sandy miss those? No wonder the poor bastard never got out of Cottage Erie.

I looked at the clock. It was twenty after five, my lunch hour almost over. I carried the file down to Social Service. The outer door was locked, but through the door to Sandy's office I could see her at her desk. When I knocked, she came out to open it, and she was smiling.

"Hi," she said inquisitively as she opened the door.

I wasn't smiling. "I'd like to talk to you about Rigley Potter. Do you have time?"

"Yes…a little," she said, leading me to her office. "What about him?"

"I just read his file—and your report on his interview."

"And?"

"And it's wrong, most of it."

She stiffened a little. I think we both knew what was coming.

"What makes you so sure that I'm wrong?" she said.

"I've known him all my life and he just isn't like you say."

She pushed herself away from her desk and was quiet for a moment. On the wall, to her right, was a large poster of a young man and woman naked and embracing in a clear stream of water. The title of it was "New Love." Below that were pictures of children from Vietnam, a peace symbol made of vines entwined around small white flowers, some greeting cards, and a picture of a dove.

"I write what I gather from the interview," she sighed.

"But you didn't gather enough," I said.

"You always have these judgments ready to pass at a moment's notice, don't you?"

"Did you read all the other interviews?"

"No. I wasn't supposed to. Dr. Stiner said he wanted fresh impressions."

"What good are fresh impressions if they're wrong?"

"Now just a minute. Are you really conceited enough to believe that? Wrong? What gives you such fabulous intuition?"

"Because I'm his friend, and I know him."

"And that's enough to make you an expert, is it?"

"More of one than you about Rigley," I said, being remarkably cool so far.

"And where did you get your psychological training?" she said.

"Don't pull that on me, Sandy. I wasn't 'trained' in psychology, but I know enough to recognize jargon and clichés substituting for insight when I see them."

Man, she was burning. But fuck it. Rigley was up in Erie because of the shit that went into that file.

"Maybe you don't know enough to realize what you don't understand," she said.

"How about talking about what I do understand? How about some facts? Are you such a snob that I can't even tell you facts? If you want to put all that ad hoc bullshit into your report, that's harmful enough, but at least you could have your facts straight."

"Harmful because I give a sincere judgment of his behavior? You're really something, you know that?"

"Well, let me tell you just a few things you might have missed. Do you know that he realizes he's retarded? Now how do you think it affects his responses to those interviews? Don't you suppose it becomes a worthless ritual to him?

"And let me tell you a few more. His family wasn't matriarchal at all. His mother was a witless, pill-popping hypochondriac who never should have had kids in the first place. And his father was a monster wino whose only exercise was working Rigley over five days a week. But hell, you never had a clue about that."

"This isn't getting us anywhere," she said.

"You can change it," I said.

"I don't want to change it."

"But Christ, Sandy, it's wrong. Don't you understand?"

"Don't you understand that mental illness isn't diagnosed like appendicitis? We need every little bit of information we can get—we're not all as omniscient as you. And though you don't agree, those interviews add up to something valuable."

"Shit!" I said as I got up out of my seat. We were both nearly shouting. She looked a little scared. "Rigley's been up there in Cottage Erie for years because people like you write all that thoughtless crap in his file. It's not just your impressions; if that were all, it'd be okay. But other people read that stuff. And there's nothing in there to really give him a break."

"A board of psychiatrists confined him to Erie, not I."

"Aw, save the bullshit, Sandy! What the hell do you care about Rigley? You have a nice cushy job, and every night you ride out of here with your sunshine superman in his MG. Why don't you come up to the City sometime and just relax with these people—no soft rugs, no air conditioned office, no arrogant secretaries—where you can see what those crummy reports of yours really do?

"I think you're afraid, Miss Covington. I think you're hiding behind that goddamn desk."

"Well, I don't care what you think. I do my job…and that doesn't include arguing with you an hour after everyone else is gone. And not only that. I didn't ask you into my private life. Understand? It's none of your business."

I pounded the desk like a wild man. "Dammit! What you do is my business as long as it helps keep Rigley locked in that stinking cottage."

I scared her finally. Maybe she suddenly realized that we were alone and I was able to hurt her if I wanted to. She grabbed her purse. "That's enough. We've got nothing more to say to you each other."

"Don't forget to tell Superman how by being stubborn you helped keep a harmless epileptic locked up. Tell him that while you roll the hell out of here in his sports car."

Her eyes clouded; there were tears in them she was trying not to show. She whirled, opened the door, and left me in the office alone.

That night, over at the Tinkerbell, I told Wes what happened. He nodded in agreement.

"Man, that's all those doctors need is an asshole group like SS to cover for them. They'd fuck up the whole world between them if we'd let 'em. You know, they act like OT and RT aren't even here."

"I was so pissed at her, Wes. She wasn't even listening to me… and I was yelling."

Wes smiled wickedly, then chuckled. "You know, man, you've been here almost two months, and you been battling that little broad all the way."

"It's goddamn frustrating, Wes. The thing is, she's got balls; she works hard; she's smart; and she doesn't want to hear any shit from anybody. And yet…she's only a small cog in a big problem."

"A street kid like you shouldn't let that get to you," he said.

"Aw, the whole place sucks, Wes. Those three kids in our department are doing more good than that whole SS office. You should've see them with the golden agers today. What a bullshitter Jerry is. He had about fifteen of those old broads in a circle teaching him how to knit. They just sat there talking up a storm. It was beautiful.

"And you know how Carly Thompson likes to grab-ass the broads? Man, he was hopping today, and Kari and Diane were always one step ahead of him. You know, it's too bad Sandy can't see what good RTs can really do."

"Yeah. We're lucky; we got us three naturals." He was quiet for a moment. "You know, White Eyes, just 'cause you always fight, that don't mean you ain't liking her."

"Come on. I'll beat you in pool," I said.

"No kidding now."

"Hey, man, did you see that Greek god with the long flowing gold hair and the sports car? That's her speed, Wes. I couldn't touch that kid."

"Let me ask you something: when you two have these fights, does she feel bad about it?"

I thought for a minute. "You know, I think she really is trying to do good."

He was just looking at me with a smug expression.

"That's supposed to mean she likes me, huh?"

"You said it; I didn't."

"Get your cue stick, man."

———⋘———

It was almost August, and I had five more weeks to work. Wes and I were close friends; Hostetter and I were becoming more and more estranged, and he was leaving us alone. The old-time clerks and orderlies told us RT hadn't been as smooth running and happy in years. Whenever I stopped up in the cottages to see Sheila and Mrs. Smith, they were efficient and content. It always seemed more like a ladies' sewing circle than a therapy session.

"You know, everybody ought to work out here a while, Wes," I told him one night. "Sometimes I think there are more real people out here than I meet outside."

"Funny, huh? Crazy as they are, they're more real. I guess sooner or later they sense we're trying to help...to accept them for what they are."

"I'm beginning to think the really sick ones are out there, Wes. These people in Wyandotte are victims. The real screwballs are the ones who drove them in here."

On Wednesday night we had open house at the rec center. Most of the ambulatory patients showed up. The outside team was there because it was a good chance to mix casually with the patients. We played cards and Ping-Pong and pool; the only thing we didn't do was dance with them. Some patients just sat around talking, and some played the jukebox and listened to music, oldies and soul.

Wednesday, August 8, was a warm night. I had played pool and gotten skinned by one of the older patients, had played Ping-Pong and couldn't hit the edge of the table all night. Then one guy by the name of Don Kelly came up to me and started talking. He asked where I was from and I told him. Then he started talking about hunting. He seemed glad I didn't know much about it, so then he could proceed to explain it all at great length. I thought he had an Appalachian drawl, like he was from Kentucky or West Virginia. But then he started telling me how he used to hunt in the Rockies and in Texas. His favorite rifle was a thirty-ought-six. He killed bighorn sheep, bears, and coyotes. He loved to hunt. In his pocket he had a copy of a rifle magazine. He pointed out the weakness of each gun, and how out West some of them weren't worth a damn and some were.

We talked for an hour. Maybe I should say I listened for an hour. He was a small man, really shy, but intensely interested in what he was saying.

Wes came over to join us. He had been cleaned off the pool table too. Kelly left us in a few minutes, promising to show me more about guns the next day. As soon as he got out of Wyandotte, he was going to show me his gun collection and then take me on a trip out West to do some "real huntin', not that sissy bullshit squirrel and bunny stuff."

As he walked away Wes asked me, his eyes following Kelly, "Well, did you learn all about hunting big game out West?"

"Yeah. He seems to be a hell of a man with a gun."

"He's never been out of Ohio," he said sardonically.

"Are you kidding?"

"I tell you, he's a farm kid from down near Cincinnati. Read his file."

"Have you read it?"

"Yep. I doubt if he's ever shot a gun either. Everything he knows is from hunting magazines. All of it's a fantasy."

"God, he was so convincing," I said in wonderment.

"Yeah, man. He gets to every RT sooner or later and snows the hell out of them. Watch tomorrow, now: he'll avoid you like a plague for fear you'll ask him some questions he can't handle. See, he found a city boy that didn't know much about hunting and he gave you his pitch. He never realized you learned about guns in 'Nam. If you would have come on like a hunter, he'd have walked away quick. You know he's never been in the army either?"

"Jesus, what an imagination."

"That's all he's got: imagination. You take away those hunting magazines and he wouldn't know how to cope with the world. Read his file; it's a real education if you can wade through all the SS bullshit."

I took a drag on my cigarette. We were leaning up against the counter just watching everybody enjoying themselves. It was a nice crowd. Someone asked for a pinochle deck, so I went behind the counter to get one. Wes stayed out front. I went down on my knees to fish for a new deck in the large storage box.

"Speaking of SS, look here, White Boy," Wes said.

"What'd you say?"

I stood up and he nodded toward the main door of the center. Sandy had just walked in. She stood there for a moment, looking for a familiar face. She hadn't seen us yet. A few women patients walked up to her and started talking. A few of the young guys were already eyeing her, trying to figure out if she was a patient, and fair game, or not.

"Look at that face, Wes," I said. "A broad with a body like that have any right to have that face?"

She was wearing sandals, another short little dress, and those little ponytails. As we watched her for a few minutes, Jerry came over to us; he had seen her too. "My God," he said, "do you see that?"

"I do," said Wes. "So does Sandy here; right, boy?"

"Yeah. I see her," I said.

"Well, man, what are you waiting for? She ain't up here to see me. Go ahead, before those studs on the pool table start fighting over her."

She was still talking as I went over to her. Our eyes met for what seemed a long moment. My heart was doing double time. "Hi," I said.

"Hi." She was embarrassed and uneasy. "I decided to come up to see what RT was all about...the way you said I should."

The others left us alone. It was awkward. I knew everybody was watching us and so did she.

"Come on; I'll introduce you," I said. I touched her elbow gently to urge her through the tables that seemed to be strewn all over. First I introduced her to Jerry and Karen and Diane. Then finally to Wes.

"Hello, Miss Covington, I've heard a lot about you." The bastard was grinning.

"Hi, Wes. Sandy told me you were the world's greatest RT," she said, smiling as though sensing that Wes and I were trying to gag each other. I think Wes blushed a little.

"Oh, he doesn't have much to compare me with," he said.

I walked her around the center, introducing her to the patients she didn't know. When we were done, I said, "Do you want to circulate by yourself now?"

"All right. Should I play any games?"

"Yes, if you want to; I think they'd like it. Uh…I wouldn't dance with them; we usually don't. And…" I hesitated for a second. "You'll probably get propositioned a few times."

"Really? How should—"

"Just say no very simply, and they won't bother you anymore."

"Will I cause trouble since I'm a stranger?"

"You're not a stranger to me," I said, not really wanting to sound like we had something going. Hell, I was nervous. "Go ahead; it'll be okay."

She was soon in a card game. Then one of the guys got her to the Ping-Pong table. Then she played pool. I was aware of almost every move she made, though I tried to act nonchalant. As I watched, I concluded that she was friendly, but not really gregarious; sometimes she even seemed shy. All of a sudden I liked that. Somehow, being that beautiful, yet being shy. I liked that.

Diane came up to me with a pout on her face. "Sandy, get her out of here; none of the patients are paying attention to us." She was half serious, but smiling.

"Man, you're beautiful, Diane. Anyone ever tell you that?" I made a mock attempt to grab her. She looked at Sandy, then back at me. "She won't hurt you," I said seriously. She shrugged then walked away.

The night was pleasant; a little warm, but a breeze was blowing. At nine o'clock the patients started drifting out. Wes locked the back door and I helped him cover the pool tables.

"Go ahead, man. I'll close up. The kids can straighten up the tables."

I walked toward the front. Sandy was waiting. "Do you have a ride home?" I asked, thinking of Superman.

"Yes, my car's in the front lot."

"Oh...I'll walk you out, okay?"

"Okay."

We left the center and walked down the drive between the House and the Ad building. The main lot was in a grove of trees beyond the Ad. For some reason we didn't say a word until we were out front. Almost all the cars were gone. Hers was at the far end of the lot near the street outside the hospital.

"Why'd you come tonight?" I asked.

"To see RT," she said. She didn't look at me to answer. After a pause, she said, "And to see you."

To see me? Hell, she really said it; she came to see me. "What for?" I said stupidly, before I could make my brain catch up with my mouth.

"I don't really know," she said. "I guess I wanted to talk about my report...If I knew I had anything to do with Rigley being locked up..."

"Look, before you go any further, I'd like you to know that I shouldn't have said those things to you. I'm sorry."

"Did you believe them?" she said.

"Not the part about you not caring. I didn't believe that."

The lights in the lampposts were starting to brighten as it grew dark. In her eyes I could see their reflections, smothered and shaded by those great dark lashes. You didn't look at her eyes, you looked into them, and I had never been close enough before.

"Every time I've seen you, I've fought with you," she said. "We're both trying to do what's right, and yet we have all this conflict. It's crazy."

"Maybe we shouldn't talk about conflict," I said. She made no move to get into her car. In the distance, I could see Wes getting into Jerry's car with him, and driving away, not even acknowledging us. We were all alone in the big lot.

"Will you come back again?" I asked.

"I don't know; I really don't have anything to..." She hesitated and looked up at me. "Should I?"

"Yeah, I think you should," I said. "Look, Friday night's payday and..."

I caught myself. I couldn't be having the same effect on her as she was on me. Slow down, Morelli; remember Superman? I changed the subject.

"This is a nice little car; I like VWs."

"It's my parents', but my sister and I share it. What were you saying about Friday night?"

"Well, every payday, the RTs, the ones you saw tonight, go over to Bernie's and have some beer. I thought maybe you'd like to come with us."

"Well..." She hesitated again. I probably had just made an ass out of myself.

"If you have another commitment, that's okay," I said, just trying to let her off the hook so she could let me down easily. "I just thought...well, I'm sure you'd like it."

"I think I would too." She was deciding, man. "All right. I'll come."

"Good. I'm glad. We have a card party at the rec center on Friday nights, and after that I escort the golden agers to the back cottages. If you come to the House a little after nine, maybe we can go in my car."

"The House?"

"Yeah. You know, the movie theater. That's where the RT offices are...and my apartment."

"Do you stay here all the time?"

"Yep. Except on a few weekends."

"Where do you go then?"

"Columbus, mostly. Twice I went to Youngstown." She looked puzzled. "I was born in Youngstown," I said. "My family's there. But I teach in Columbus."

"Do you live alone down there?"

"No. A friend and I share a townhouse. He's a teacher too. How about you? You live in town, right?"

"Yes, I live with my parents."

"Where'd you go to school?"

"St. Mary's, in Indiana," she said. "How about you?"

"Ohio State."

"Did you play football?" she asked, smiling. A thousand twinkles of light played around that smile. Her lips were glistening and full.

"Not well enough or fast enough or big enough," I said, smiling too. "But sometimes they even let non-athletes graduate."

She laughed. The Volkswagon was a red convertible, and as she leaned against it, I could see the red of her hair seem to glow in contrast.

We talked a little longer—about her graduating in September, and about her plans to stay in Social Service.

"Well, I'd better be going; we've been talking a long time."

"It doesn't seem like it," I said.

She opened the door and sat in the car. "I'll see you Friday night," she said.

"Okay...Sandy?" She looked up, searching my eyes for a second. "Thanks for coming tonight."

Whenever I had free time, I'd go up to Erie and get Rigley. Those weekends I stayed at Wyandotte, we got a chance to be together a lot, just like old times.

There was a grove of trees behind one of the geriatric cottages. Under them were park benches in a semicircle where we could sit in the shade. The grove was on a small knoll that sloped gently down into about three acres of green, where we sometimes held badminton and croquet matches. Beyond the green were the cornfields of the hospital farm. From our vantage point, it looked like the hospital had cut a wedge into the fields. The corn was high, and ripening quickly in the August heat. We faced west from the knoll, where sundowns were pretty and gold on the trees, skirting the tips of the corn in the last farewell of evening. Going down the slope to the green were steps made out of old railroad ties. Rigley liked to sit on them and talk to me.

By then I knew from his file that the last ten years had not been empty. As he and I had grown apart, the despair I felt for him had been prophetic. All the things he couldn't cope with: the adult world, people getting older, death...All of them had been milestones on his way to Wyandotte.

I watched him as he moved and talked. The slurred words, the haltings, the remembrances of years past as vividly as yesterday—it was like talking to an old man, a terminal resident.

"You 'member them times we used to go down the spring and get water, Sandy?" he asked.

"Yeah, that was good water, huh?"

"Yeah. 'Member my old lady used to make me go get it all the time?"

"How about your father? You remember much about him?"

"Sure, that goddamn son of a bitch. He used to give me and Dina some awful lickins. Hey, remember that big bike I had? It was bigger than yourn, huh? Man, it was hard to peddle up hills, but I sure liked comin' down Sloan Street faster'n hell."

"That was a twenty-eight; they don't make big bikes like that anymore, you know."

"That right? Maybe I still got it over Dina's house."

"Maybe."

"Hey, Sandy, you 'member them dago words I used to say?"

"Which ones? You never said any Italian words, did you?"

"Yeah. There was two. 'Member the time I broke that little tree and you got mad at me?"

"Man, you're going back a long time, Rigley."

"That tree was an Italian word. What was it?"

I scratched my head. I hadn't thought of that story for ages. "Hell, what was the name of that?" I said aloud to myself. "Ah...I can't think of it...it was just on the tip of my tongue..."

"We used to go up to Council Park on our bikes, and you used to buy me sundaes, huh?"

"*Dracaena Marginata*! That was it," I said.

"Yeah, that's it. Tell me again so's I can say it. I ain't just no little kid now; I'll show 'em back in Erie; they won't think I'm so dumb when I tell them I know dago words. Come on, say it."

"Okay. You say it after me."

"Dra."   "Dra."

"See."   "See."

"Na."   "Na."

"Say that," I said.

"Dra...nesu."

"No, I'll say it again: Dra...caena."

"Dra-cae-na."

"Yeah, that's it. Okay, now say the last part."

Just then, as we were sitting on the steps of Wyandotte, I could have closed my eyes and gone back twenty years, as though we did all that yesterday. He took a long time and slurred it around, but he got most of it.

"That sounds okay, Rigley."

"Wait till I tell my friends back at the cottage. They ain't good friends as you, but some talk nice to me and listen to my stories before they go to sleep. I'm gonna tell them about that little tree."

"That's nice of you to tell them," I said, blowing smoke more slowly.

When it was time to go back, I'd take him over to the little kitchen behind the counter in the rec center and make him some punch. We had tons of mix there for card parties and open house. I told him I made up a special flavor just for him and he liked that. He'd drink several glasses. It went on like that all summer.

<hr>

The day after Sandy first came to the rec center, Thursday, it rained like hell, and the oval was soggy. Wes opened up the center, since we couldn't hold RT outside. I decided to go up to Erie to get Rigley.

When I got to the second floor and opened the door, I didn't see him. "Where's Rigley?" I asked the attendant.

"He can't come out tonight. Doctor's orders," he growled.

"What do you mean, 'doctor's orders'?" I said.

"He had a little seizure today," he said casually, "so he ain't able to get no special treatment from you."

Man, it never took more than a cross look from him to make me want to go for his throat. "Where is he now, down at Entry?" I said.

"No. Back in his bunk. But you ain't supposed to go back into the sleeping rooms."

"Get out of my way, fucker," I said through my teeth.

"I ain't authorized to let—"

"You shouldn't be authorized to even be here," I said as I walked past him.

The dorm was a huge room with four rows of beds in about sixty-foot length. Some patients were scattered on the bunks, resting. The beds were so close there was hardly room to walk between them. The room was dim, but in the shadows I could see the ugliness, the broken plaster and exposed pipes, and the institutional gray walls, covered with flaking paint.

"Where's Rigley?" I asked an attendant.

"Down the third row. That bunk near the end," he said in a high-pitched voice. "He's been sleeping for a long time."

Rigley was breathing steadily; mucus was running from his nose and mouth. I stumbled over his huge shoes beside the bed. I picked them up and could see how run down at the heels they were. I called him but he didn't answer. I shook him, but he was sleeping too soundly to wake up. And he was foul with sweat. I touched him behind the neck and could feel the matted wetness of his hair. There was another patient, two beds away, by the name of Keating, an alcoholic who had gone through the DTs so many times, his mind was a sodden shadow of what it once was.

"Where do they keep the towels, Paddy?" I asked.

"They's one under his bed," he answered.

I took it and shook it and started wiping his head. I strained to turn him over. He still had his pants on, and when I managed to get him around I could see the dark stain on his underside. The whole front of him was wet with urine. "My God, Rigley," I muttered to myself.

"He's pissed his pants, mister," Keating said.

"Yeah. Go call the attendant," I said.

"Why? He ain't gonna do nothing."

"Just go get him, okay?"

When he came up to me, the attendant was flushed with anger. "What the fuck do you want? I gotta watch the other rooms. I can't be coming in here all the time."

"He urinated all over himself," I said.

"So?"

Man, that was all I needed. I was ready to strangle him right then. "What do you mean, 'so'? Aren't you going to clean him up?"

"Me clean it up? You gotta be joking!"

"Just what the hell are you supposed to do for them?"

"Mister, I ain't no orderly, and I don't clean up piss off nobody."

"Then get an orderly," I snapped.

He and Keating both laughed. "Mister," he said, "ain't no orderly to get. And even if there was, he sure as hell wouldn't come up here just for this. You know how many people piss their pants in this hospital every night?"

We just stood there glaring at each other. He was smiling defiantly.

"Where's a basin and some soap and towels?" I said.

"What you gonna do?" he said anxiously.

"I'm gonna clean him myself. When was the last time he had a bath?"

"How the hell do I know? I told you: that ain't my job, man; that's an orderly's job."

"Where's the stuff?"

"I don't know."

"Listen, you bastard, get me a basin and some soap and water, or I'll call up that ward supervisor right now and have him transfer your ass to the fucking laundry."

I knew it was an empty threat, but he wasn't so sure, so I got my stuff. I also got clean overalls for Rigley, but decided to let him sleep in underwear in case he wet the bed again. Keating was still watching me with an amazed look on his face.

"What're you doin' this for? Ain't you the RT supervisor?"

"Yeah. Go get me some sheets for this bed...and get a rubber sheet for the bottom."

"He won't like that. He'll be mad if I ask him."

"Just do as I say. He'll give them to you."

I stripped the bed and then started washing him. His hair was easy to clean because it was short, but he was so huge I had trouble getting his clothes off. Keating took them to the hamper.

I was sweating like a pig myself. I was hot, and working hard. Rigley reeked of sweat and urine; he hadn't had a bath in weeks.

"You gonna wash his dick, mister?" Keating said.

"I'm gonna wash everything," I said, wincing at Paddy's crudeness.

"You queer, mister?" he said.

"Do you have to be queer to wash a poor bastard like this? Doesn't he stink enough for you? Shut up, Paddy."

165

Bad job. The smell of sweat, urine, and dried semen was lethal. But as I got to his legs, it was easier. I made the bed one half at a time, the army medic way, but then had a hell of a time getting his underwear on. He was a dead weight, and the strain made the sweat pour down my forehead into my eyes.

When I was done, Keating put the basin away for me. Rigley was going to sleep all night.

I sneered at the attendant as I walked past his desk. He was sitting there reading a magazine. "I'll be back tomorrow, pal—and there better not be anything wrong with Rigley," I said.

That night I stayed under the shower for a half hour just getting all the sweat off me, and trying to purge the smell of Erie out of my nostrils. As the water poured over me, I thought of Rigley. He was still getting a raw deal. Man, Wes was right. The bureaucracy cools it in air-conditioned offices while the patients go on sweating and stinking, sixty beds in a room.

I was out in the kitchen having coffee and a cigarette when Wes came in. "What the hell are you doing here so late?" I said.

"I had some evaluations to do before tomorrow's meeting, so I figured I'd stay around to get them done."

I poured his coffee and he motioned for a cigarette. I threw him one.

"How about taking me down to the liquor store tomorrow at suppertime?" he said.

"Yeah, let's go to the bank, too, huh? I want to cash my check if we're going out."

"What kind of scotch we gonna get?" he said.

"Anything, man, you're the expert."

"How's the sweet woman department, son? Green eyes's coming tomorrow, right?"

"Damn right. You think spooks are the only ones that get any action?"

"You ain't gonna get the action I get."

I chuckled. "No, I think you're right…but I don't see you sharing any of your good fortune, man."

"Aw, this one's private stock—like Chivas in the cupboard."

"Hurry up and drink your coffee so I can go to bed. Some of us have a lot of work to do tomorrow."

"Yeah. Supervising and walking around all day is a bitch, ain't it?"

I had bad dreams that night. I was due to go to Youngstown again. Maybe I'd stop and see Marcia and the boy.

———⁂———

I didn't see Sandy during the day on Friday. I looked in on Rigley, but he was still groggy, so I talked to him about an hour, then left. He told me the attendant's name was John Madden, and everybody up there hated him.

Rigley was moody, too, because I couldn't take him out. I told him I was going to Youngstown and that if he was better he could come with me to the softball game Monday night. That seemed to make him feel better. He liked to take swings at the ball while the teams were warming up.

The card parties were held every Friday night. Hostetter always showed up to play a starring role. We had tables all over the rec center. He came in and took a seat with a few of the younger patients. The studs never came for cards; the party was made up of adults, usually twenty-five or older. Still, he singled out the younger, most attractive patients to play with.

At the first party I attended, in June, I was escorting and passing out cards, so most of the games started without me. Many of the patients had their own foursomes. As I started walking around, I saw three old women just sitting at a table quietly watching everybody else. They needed a fourth player, and I was their man.

"Do you know how to play pinochle?" one of them asked.

"Well, I know some of the rules, but I'd need some coaching."

They glanced at each other, then brightened up. "Come on, then; we'll teach you."

And they started on me. The next week I was busy again, but since no one else ended up playing with them, they waited quietly for me, anxious to begin the second phase of my pinochle apprenticeship. They were patient, tolerant of my mistakes, chatty, and delightful. My partner was named Ruth, and occasionally we caught her dozing when it was her turn to bid. I became a regular member of the little group, and I enjoyed Friday nights more and more as the summer passed. It was a nice way to end the week.

I was fascinated by them. They seemed gentler and more refined than so many of the younger ones there. They spoke a brand of English you might expect to hear at afternoon high tea. They were fragile anachronisms, lost anywhere outside the City, used to being ignored or avoided, sitting there in big ill-fitting dresses, long since tired of dreaming, but still hoping that once in a while, someone would pay attention and be nice to them.

That Friday night in August, the party seemed too long. I made some bad bids, miscounted my melds, and often drummed the table absentmindedly. Ruth chided me. "My goodness, Sandy, what's come over you tonight?"

"I don't know, Ruth; I'm sorry."

"You look tired. You get yourself some rest this weekend. You've been working too hard."

"Yes, I will. Thank you."

Strange, I thought, a patient in a mental hospital sensitive enough to perceive anxiety in someone else, and to care enough to counsel him? It was as though my grandmother was coddling me again.

The party was livened by a lot of talk and laughter. My punch was, as usual, superb; Jerry called it mead of the gods. All I did was mix every flavor I could get my hands on, then charge it with a strong dose of lemon to make it tart. Everyone seemed to have a good time at the end of the evening. I was as nervous as a high school freshman on his first date.

Wes came over to talk to me just before I took the golden agers back. "Hey, man, I'm not gonna stay much later than eleven down at Bernie's. I have to be somewhere by midnight, and I grow weary of that heavy talk those kids lay out." He winked.

"Sure, man, have one for me, okay?"

"I ain't gonna put down much liquor tonight—got other things on my mind. Hey, don't forget we didn't plan the RT for next Thursday and Friday yet, and my man Hostetter's gonna want that report Monday afternoon for his meeting."

"We'll get it in. I have all of it done except for the motor skill evaluations. But I've got them in my notes. We'll be all set for the whole week."

"Right. See you later. Remember, when I give you the nod, I'm gone...Hey, White Eyes, you're goin' courtin' tonight. Goddamn respectable like."

I cursed him and started escorting the ladies back to their cottages. We said goodnight like old friends. Back at the center, I checked the lavatories and turned out the lights. Everything was locked except the front door. I turned the key and gave it a tug to see if it was secure. When I turned around, Sandy was standing across the street in front of the House. She wore yet a different pair of white heeled sandals, white slacks, and a little green knit top with a bare midriff. Christ, she was almost too much for a tired man to stand.

"Hi," I said. "I have to lock up the offices. Want to come in?"

"All right," she said, smiling, still looking a little nervous.

"That's a great outfit," I said, trying not to look too lecherous as I spoke.

"Why, thank you, sir," she said, and the whole world lit up with green stars from her eyes.

While I was locking up, she wandered around my office, going through the 78 records, scanning RT sheets, and trying on baseball gloves.

"Look, I have to wash up a little. Would you mind coming up to wait? It's a little more comfortable in there."

She nodded and I led her up to my apartment. "Oh, this is nice in here," she said as she entered the room. "You're very neat."

"No, I'm not. Housekeeping cleans it up. These women feel sorry for me because I have to live here alone. They even turn down the bed for me."

"What do you do in your spare time?" she asked.

"Oh, I smoke and read a lot; the paper, some books; listen to the stereo. See Rigley whenever I can."

"What do you read?"

"Most of the stuff I didn't have sense enough to read in college. How about a Coke? I'll just be a few minutes."

"Yes, I'd like one."

As I went across the hall to the kitchen to get ice, she looked at my books. When I walked back into the room, she was holding one in her hands. "Do you read Spanish?" she asked.

"Yeah. A lot better than I speak it."

"Is Lorca your favorite?"

"Yes."

"Which poem?" she said, holding the open book to her breast and smiling.

"Cancion' de Jinete."

"Cordoba?"

I nodded. She was delighted at my answer.

"Do you know it?" she said.

"Yes, I love it; it's probably my favorite."

"Say it."

"Will you help me? I'm not sure of all of it …

> Cordoba
> Lejana y sola…"

She looked at me, so I spoke another stanza.

> "Jaca negra, luna grande
> y aceitunas en mi alforja."

She went on with the rest until the lament, and then I joined her again.

> "Ay que camino tan largo!
> Ay mi jaca valerosa!"

As we spoke, her eyes peered into mine, trying to see what I was feeling. When the poem was over, she looked away and was quiet. I went into the bathroom to wash up and put on a clean jersey. She was still reading when I came out.

"Ready," I said.

She set the book aside and left the chair gracefully. Whenever she moved, it seemed as though she had done that last movement before, like a practiced grace that had become natural to her. Even when she sat, her body rested with the ease of feeling that it was the most natural, most inviting way to meet her environment.

"Kari and Diane were hoping you'd come tonight," I said. "They admire you; I think you're what they'd like to be some day."

"They flatter me too much. I'm not as successful as I might seem."

As we walked, she told me about patients she had seen during the day, and about the new staff changes being made in SS. Just small talk.

When I opened the door of my car for her, she stood beside me and waited. Somehow, as I stood erect after unlocking the door, I found myself so close to her face that I could almost feel her breath on my cheeks. It was too much, even for an instant, and something burst out of me.

I said, "Sandy, I've never seen anyone as beautiful as you in all my life."

It was hard to answer that, I knew. All she said was, "Thank you," awkwardly, as she got into the car.

When I got behind the wheel I said, "I didn't mean to embarrass you. It just came out. I guess I shouldn't have said it."

"No, it's all right…You never hesitate to say what you feel, do you?"

"I'm not always that honest. But with you it comes naturally. Either we're fighting and anything goes, or else I'm telling you how beautiful you are."

Bernie's was a couple notches above the Tinkerbell, a small neighborhood lounge with dark paneled walls and padded booths lit by tiny lamps. The booths were separated from the bar by a planter full of cacti and sempervivums and ferns. The waitresses had gotten to know us all summer, and knew what our payday nights were like, so they were friendly, and tended to us. The place never seemed crowded; everything was relaxed and subdued, especially the talk.

As we entered, Wes rolled his eyes when he saw the bare midriff. I smiled and licked my lips. Jerry just stared. We started drinking beer and talking about Wyandotte rumors and staff scandal. Kari and Diane wanted to know all about SS, so Sandy told them a little about what she did. Some of their freshman psych began to show in their questions to her. Heavy conversation. Wes winked at me. We started talking about patients Sandy and RT had in common. You could see the commitment in her eyes as she spoke.

Then we talked about Wes. I wanted him to squirm a little. It was great. Wicked corrupter of youth. Teaching us to drink scotch, and like it. He grimaced in mock anguish. I told the story of how Wes and I went to the liquor store for the first time. We got a tenth of Johnny Walker Red and ended up killing it over a couple of corned beef sandwiches and hot pickles from the Star Delicatessen. I always hated whiskey, but Wes, in his fatherly manner, explained how one had to come to an accord with something as chaste as good scotch. Which I did—willingly—and later made too many bad bids at the card table that Friday night.

We warmed up on the beer; I was glowing a little too much, I thought. We told jokes and lies, and were having a good time. At eleven thirty, Wes gave me a nod. The others begged him to stay, but I said nothing, so he got away.

So Sandy and I were left with three college freshmen, and the conversation grew ponderous: Vietnam, the election, war in general. From war we soon went to personal morality, then love and sex... from politics to elusive and basic drives.

I was horny. My tongue was slipping and I felt so much older than Kari and Diane and Jerry. I tried to stay out of it so I wouldn't sound pompous and make an ass of myself.

"What about you, Supe?" Jerry said.

"What about me?" I said uneasily.

"How do you feel about love and sex? Should they be separated?"

"I'm all for them."

"God, Sandy. What kind of answer is that?" Kari said.

"Look, I'm tired and half smashed, and I don't feel up to defending Judeo-Christian ethics, okay?"

"That's a copout," Diane said. "It's a moral question you have to face sometime."

"I've faced it. I'm older than you are, remember?"

"How'd you manage that?"

"All right. If it's going to hurt someone or exploit them, don't do it. Otherwise, enjoy yourself," I said.

"Maybe you don't know you're hurting someone. That's the problem," said Sandy.

"That's the best I could come up with...If you really try not to hurt someone, and mean it enough to stop if you realize you are... What more do you people want out of life?"

"Does love ever enter into it?" said Karen.

"I don't know much about love...But love...if you can find it... would be the solution to the problem, wouldn't it?"

"Oh, Christ, Sandy!" said Jerry, annoyed at my evasions.

"But doesn't it just happen to us—to the lucky ones? How many people do you know who thought they were in love and found out later it was a mirage? Hell, you tell me what it's all about." Man, I was sounding like a teacher again. I knew I should have shut up.

Sandy was quietly watching me as I was waxing philosophical. I didn't know if I sounded profound or just shallow and screwed up.

For a while, as the others talked, I just listened. I was right about Sandy; she was really rather quiet. She added short comments and asked some questions, but never really opened up.

The beer finally took its toll on Jerry and the girls. Karen left first. "Well, I'd better get going. I'm off to Cedar Point tomorrow, and I'll need a little sleep," she said. The others made their excuses and said goodnight. I ordered a cup of coffee, lit a cigarette, and blew the smoke slowly. I had the feeling of being alone with Sandy for the first time, maybe because we were out of Wyandotte. Neither of us spoke for a few minutes, but she watched me intently.

"Tell me about yourself," I said.

"There's not much to tell. I'm twenty-two years old, a doctor's kid, and in a few weeks I'll have a BA in psychology. I live with my parents, like Lorca, and until this summer I've been reasonably happy. How about you?"

"That's not enough about you," I said. "But, okay, I'll give the first installment. I'm twenty-seven years old, three years in the army, one in Vietnam, BA in English, masters in special ed. I was born in Youngstown, teach in Columbus, and like Lorca."

I gestured back to her. "Your turn."

She smiled and looked down at her drink.

"What about Superman?" I asked.

"I'm supposed to marry him," she said softly.

"Supposed to?" I caught the doubt in her answer.

"We just considered ourselves engaged this last year," she said.

"When will you be married?" I asked hesitantly, fearing any kind of definitive answer.

"I don't know," she sighed. "And that's the reason for the unhappy summer. It was supposed to be this fall, but we don't talk much about it anymore."

"What does he do?"

"He's in sales for Ashland Medical. Your turn; are you seeing anyone?"

"No one seriously," I said. "I date a girl who used to teach with me. She's back in Ohio State now. And there's a girl in Youngstown I used to date in high school. She's divorced and has a little boy. Whenever I'm home, I often stop in to see her."

"Did you see her when she was married?"

"No. I hadn't seen her since high school. But I met her last year at Christmas time when I was shopping in Youngstown. I took her out that New Year's Eve, and I've seen her ever since."

"Do you love her?"

I blew some smoke and was quiet for a few seconds. God, maybe I was sounding like a bad ass. "I don't think so, but I like her. She got a raw deal, you know. She married a football jock in college who was never good enough to make the pros. When he started to knocking her around, she left him." She kept looking at me. "Why did you come tonight?" I said.

"You asked me that before. I was invited, remember?"

"But what about Superman?"

"His name is Larry, and he's very nice." Her eyes flashed at me. "What about the girl in Youngstown?"

"All right," I said. "I'll answer honestly...if you do for me."

"I like that," she said seriously. "Let's be honest."

"Okay, you're first," I said. She smiled. "What about Larry who's so nice."

"I realized in the last six months that I don't love him. Once, I was sure I did. He's handsome and exciting; everything we did was fun..."

"But?"

"But I don't know. It was as though we always had to have fun... like we were trying to prove something..." She was looking down, twirling her glass in her hand. "What are those other girls like?"

"The one in Columbus, even if I don't see her for months, we can go out and still have a good time. I don't know if she has any kinds of feelings for me. I doubt it. She's just nice and clean and intelligent, and doesn't want to get tied down before she's found what she's looking for.

"The one in Youngstown's named Marcia. She's different: a little older than Barbara, more quiet and vulnerable...I'm a friend."

It was twelve thirty and I ordered more coffee. The warm glow from the beer was gone. I still couldn't believe she was sitting there across from me.

"This has been a miserable summer. All I want to do is be natural, and I can't even do that. Every time I've been with Larry, I've hated myself for pretending. And school—I'm so tired of school...." She hesitated for a moment, then looked down at her coffee. "Listen to me pouring out my heart to you," she said almost to herself, surprised at her own candor.

"Do you still see Larry?" I said.

"Not very often lately."

We drank more coffee and I played a song. Guitars. Beautiful.

"Sandy?" she said.

"Yes?"

"You think I'm beautiful...What if I weren't? I mean, would you have come down to the office that day to make peace with me?"

"Make peace maybe. I don't know about anything else. But don't you see? You're not a bunch of standard parts that someone wired together. There aren't any other ugly Sandys in the universe. And I don't have to imagine any. There's only you."

She was touching the knuckles of my hand with her index finger, tracing over the hills and valleys.

"And I've been falling in love with you all through the summer," I said.

She closed her eyes, and I thought she shuddered quietly, almost as though she'd hoped I wouldn't mean it.

"Look, I'm not sorry I said that. But I'll never say it again if you don't want me to."

She huffed. "I want you to...It's just that it happened so fast... Could it be real?"

"Hell, Sandy, life doesn't slow down just when we want it to. Maybe it's..."

"Maybe it's because we're lonely at the hospital," she said tremulously. "Maybe it's because I'm afraid of facing a house in the suburbs with Larry."

Her voice broke a little, and she stopped and looked out into the room, away from me. I played another song. "I'd better go," she said in the middle of it. "It's late."

On the way back to Wyandotte we talked about our families. She told me how her father had wanted her to be a surgeon, like him. We talked about my parents, and college, and teaching.

"Are you going to Youngstown tomorrow?" she asked.

"Yes."

"Will you see Marcia?"

"Maybe. What are you going to be doing?" I said.

"I'm going sailing with some friends."

"Will Larry be there?"

"Yes."

I stopped for gas. "I guess this isn't polite," I said, "but it's one way to talk to you a little longer."

She smiled, but didn't say a word at the gas station. Once we got going she spoke again.

"Have you ever made love to Marcia?" she said.

I looked at her. She was looking straight ahead, but turned toward me.

"Are we still being honest?" I asked. I wasn't expecting that kind of question.

"Always…okay?" she said.

"Okay…" I said uneasily. "Yes."

"And with Barbara?"

"I'm twenty-seven years old, Sandy," I said, somehow bothered by having to tell her.

"Have you?"

"Yes."

We rode for a while in silence. My turn. "How about you and Superman?"

She didn't answer for a minute. Then she said, "Yes."

It was getting breezy out. I found myself struggling with my own thoughts and not talking. Larry, goddamn Larry. Why was he ever born?

Finally she broke the silence, I'm sure painfully for her. "It only happened a few times, Sandy. I was in love with him."

"I didn't ask you that," I said.

"Were you thinking it?"

"Yes, I was thinking it," I sighed. "Is he the only one?"

"Yes. Would it matter?" she said stiffly.

"I think so."

More silence. "We sound like teenagers," she said as she looked out the window, away from me. "I shouldn't have started all this. I'm sorry."

I stopped beside the red VW in the parking lot at Wyandotte. The lamplight shined over my car and left us in darkness inside. We sat there in silence. I reached for her hands and turned her toward me. They were so soft I could feel the life throbbing in them.

"We don't have any time," she said. There were tears in her eyes.

"I have three weeks…to know whether Columbus is far enough away to forget you."

She was about to say something again. As she attempted to speak, I bent to kiss her hands where I held them. My lips stayed there, lost in their softness…as though I had never felt another girl's touch in my life. Then she drew near me, brushed my cheek with her lips, and let them rest against me for an instant.

When she drew away, I said, "Tuesday night's the dance, and they don't need me in RT, so I usually take Rigley out of Erie for a while. We go to the little grove of trees behind Cottage Thirteen. Will you come?"

"Yes, I'll come." Then she straightened without looking at me. "Is three weeks enough, Sandy?" she said softly.

"We have to take the chance, don't we?" I said. "Do you ever want to regret not knowing?"

She shook her head. Without a word she got into her car. I waved as she drove off.

Hostetter held softball games every Monday night; the City would play Entry in slow-pitch. He was player-coach. Position: shortstop.

The players from the City had grown into a real team through the summer. They all had regular positions, and some played well enough to compete in a bush league. Their best player was a big, powerful kid about six foot four who had arms long enough to whip the bat around like a propeller blade. He was a former Class B baseball player who had love and instinct for the game. He was freckle faced, auburn haired, and surly. I never did find out why he was at Wyandotte.

The Entry team's coach was Supervisor I—me. It was a team in only the vaguest sense of the word. Each Monday night I went up to the wards at Entry and asked who wanted to play ball. We seldom had the same players from week to week. Usually we had nine men and one or two substitutes, all of them on medication, and most having so little coordination that if a ground ball came their way, they often literally fell over trying to catch it. So my team was a motley assortment of non-regulars who sometimes had not played since childhood.

I made sure that Rigley came down to the field with me each Monday night. He was from the City, but he cheered for my team, and I needed all the help I could get. After the game, he would help me carry the bases, bats, balls, and gloves back into the Entry storeroom.

Our side was down the first-base line, where I paced all night long, chain-smoking cigarettes and chafing at Hostetter's smugness. The City side had a few bleachers, and they were usually full of women that Kari, Diane, Sheila, and Mrs. Smith escorted down and back.

The Monday after Sandy was with us down at Bernie's, Wes and Jerry were sitting sullen in my office. "Fuck," said Jerry. "Look at that sky. It's gonna rain as soon as we get down there."

"This is the boss's big scene, guys. Anything short of a hurricane, we play," I said.

"Man, this fucking softball is killing me," said Wes. "I'll take volleyball anytime; you get more patients into the game, and you have twice as much fun."

"Yeah, but Hostetter's not a volleyball player, Wes; softball's a big ego trip for him," said Jerry.

"Man, if it were even a contest, I wouldn't mind," I said. "But half those guys down there can barely walk. And the City team is damned near semipro...The whole thing sucks."

"Hostetter knows we hate this; that's why he twists our balls to go down there," Wes growled.

"Well, coach, are you ready?" said Jerry.

"Yeah. I guess so. Wes, how about bringing Rigley down? That way I can leave now to set up the Entry team."

"Okay, man. Jerry, get the boys out there to help you with the gloves and things, okay?"

Jerry left. The girls were already on their way to get the women patients. "Fuckin' gonna rain," Wes muttered. "Hey, there's the boss; we'd better get going."

I collected all the volunteers from Entry, and started a little field practice. Jerry was designated umpire, a job he detested.

My team was a surprise. Suddenly over the past month, a few patients had developed into regulars. And there was a new patient, a big, good-looking guy about my age who could really powder a ball. His name was Steve Williamson, and he was almost as good as Carpenter from the City, but far more intelligent and personable. Wes had told me that Carpenter was home on a one-week leave, so that made things a little more even. The sky was glowering and heavy with rain.

Pitchers were always my big trouble. We couldn't get a guy to throw it over the plate without giving up a slew of runs. The scores were always astounding: 22-3, 28-4, 26-6. And Entry always lost. Still, I would have liked to win one game, despite everything being rigged against us by Hostetter. I glared at him out there on the field, scooping up grounders, chattering, relaying to second, first, and home. He even had fans from the City to cheer him on.

In the first inning, Entry scored six runs. Steve Williamson blew a ball over the head of their left fielder and three runs scored at once. We were looking good. Hostetter's team scored two in the second and two in the third. In the fourth we scored seven runs and were ahead 13-4. Carpenter's leave was hurting them.

Then my pitcher called me over and told me he couldn't play anymore; he was getting dizzy. All I had left was a tall, lanky black guy by the name of LeRoy Harris, who seemed to move and talk in slow motion. I never could figure out if he had mind and body together. For weeks he had begged me to pitch him, but I always used him as an outfielder because he seemed so uncoordinated. But what the hell, I needed a pitcher, and maybe he could pitch the way he said he could. It wouldn't be the first time I was wrong about a patient.

Wes ran over to me; he was third-base coach for both teams. "You gonna put LeRoy in?"

"Sure, man. I'm gonna give one of your boys his big break."

"I don't know if he's gonna make it, Sandy. He looks stoned."

"I don't have much choice, Wes; I need a pitcher, and fuckhead over there won't quit till he's ahead, remember?"

It started sprinkling.

"Let's have a beer tonight, okay?" he said. "After this we're gonna need it."

Two outs; new pitcher. The batter hit a grounder to third and was out at first. Side retired. We made two more runs the next inning, and they were still behind 15-8.

LeRoy threw another goose egg and they knocked it a mile. Here it comes, I thought, Entry's doing its fifth-inning fade, and we're gonna get our asses beat again. Then someone grounded to LeRoy and he tried to get it. It hit him in the leg and dribbled off the mound. Third base, LeRoy, third base! LeRoy looked like he saw ten balls on the ground and was trying to grab every one of them. He finally just picked it up, and held it.

Jerry came over then. The rain was steady; all patients had gone back with the girls; Rigley, too. Two teams battling in a hurricane. Time out!

"My fucking mind boggles...boggles," he said. "We're playing baseball in the rain. Mind you, a tornado's coming to destroy us all, and we're fucking playing baseball in the rain."

Time in. Hostetter's team charging now. Score tied. Rain falling. My pitcher goes for a grounder and falls down. Runs score. Entry losing. Rain! Rain!

"Hey, Ray, how about it? We gonna quit or not?"

He smiled. I had lost again. "Yeah, okay. The field's getting a little soggy."

Wes and I sat morosely over beer at Bernie's and muttered curses about the rain, the game, and Hostetter. "He doesn't like you 'cause he sees you as a threat. We get along too well without him. See, he thought you were gonna come in here and fuck everything up so he could straighten it out and look like he earns his money. But you didn't do that."

"We did it, man. We work well together."

"How'd you make out Friday night?"

"Make out?"

"Did you get a chance to talk to her, asshole?" he said impatiently.

"Yeah."

"Man, the chick's in love with you."

"Think so, huh? What the hell do you know."

"Why did she come up to see you in the center, White Eyes? Man, the broad is loaded; she can have her cellar full of good-looking rich guys, but she gave it all up. You don't see that MG rolling out of here anymore, do you? You're the one, man."

"Me? I'm just horny for a classy piece of ass."

"Man, that's bullshit and you know it."

Tuesday night I went to get Rigley and we walked down to Cottage Thirteen. We sat on the steps and talked about the game; we hadn't talked much at all since his seizure.

Someone approached. Sandy in blue, blue culottes, blue sandals. The afternoon sun was shimmering on her hair. I turned as she sat beside us. "Hi," I said.

"Hi."

"Rigley, do you know this lady?"

"Yeah, I know her."

"What's her name?"

"Uh...Miss C-...I don't remember."

He was shy, and avoided her gaze even though she was smiling at him. She touched his arm gently, but he shrugged. The situation was different to him. He was used to seeing her behind a desk in SS, or walking by us as I taunted her.

"Rigley," she said.

He looked down the steps and tried to catch a fly. He ignored her for a moment, like a bashful child. Finally he answered. "What?"

"My name's Sandy, too," she said softly, still touching his arm.

He turned to her. "You got a boy's name?"

She was smiling. Nobody could stay unfriendly to that face. "No, my name's really Sandra, but everybody calls me Sandy."

"Just like you, Sandy," he said to me.

"No, man, my name's Alessandro."

Sandy looked at me. "You know, I never knew your real name."

"Aren't you glad?" I said.

"No, I like it; it's musical."

"How come you never told me your real name, Sandy?" said Rigley.

"It was too hard to say," I said. "Sandy is easier."

"That a dago word?" he said.

"Uh, yeah, I guess it is."

He turned to Sandy. "I know dago words, too," he said. "Don't I, Sandy?"

"You do?" I said.

"Yeah. You know the ones you showed me how to say?"

"Oh, yeah."

"What is it?" said Sandy to me. Her eyes were dancing; she was delighted with Rigley's childlike simplicity.

"*Dracaena marginata*."

"What?" she drawled off her tongue.

"*Dracaena marginata*. It's the name of a tropical plant."

"Is it Italian?" she said.

"Every foreign word is a dago word," I said.

"Oh." She turned to Rigley. "Want to play badminton with me?"

"Yeah. I'm a good player, but I'll play easy 'cause you're a girl... so's I won't hurt you. Huh, Sandy?"

"Yeah," I said. He had already started for the net with a racket. "You don't know what you're getting into," I told Sandy.

"Oh, it'll be fun," she said.

"You'll be tired."

"That's okay,"

She took off her sandals and wiggled her toes in the grass. Her feet were graceful, perfect extremities of her golden body.

When they started playing, Rigley smashed the shuttlecock with all his might. No finesse, man. He had Sandy running all over. Once in a while, when he'd hit a high one, she'd jump to hit it, and I'd behold the grace of her legs in mid-flight.

But Rigley never tired, and she did. We walked along the cornfield so the two of them could cool off. Sandy was sweating. Then we headed back to the rec center.

"Chef Morelli's gonna mix up some of the world's finest punch. How 'bout it, Rigley?"

"Yeah, make that blue one, okay?"

I went behind the counter and wrung out two cold water towels and handed one to each of them. Even when Sandy sweated her hair seemed to arrange itself. She wiped her face. Rigley wanted to play Ping-Pong, but I told him we had to be getting back. The punch pacified him.

Sandy was carrying her sandals, so before we left, she sat down to put them on. I almost volunteered to do it for her, but there was no way I could do it and control myself, so I just watched.

As I locked the back door, Rigley said, "Sandy, why'd you give me a bath?"

"Who told you that?"

"Some of the guys in Erie were making fun of me. Don't do it no more, huh?"

"I won't," I said.

We took him back, then Sandy and I walked across the oval to the House. It was nine o'clock, but the movie was still on, so instead of going in we started walking toward her car out front.

"Come on," she said, grabbing my arm, "let's walk around the lake."

It was beautiful; the sun was down and the lamplight was turning the little park into a misty fairyland. For a while she walked beside me without speaking; then she sat on a bench near the swans.

"When did you give him a bath?" she said.

"Last week."

"Why did you do it?"

"He needed it."

"I know that, but that's not the reason. Supervisors just don't go around giving baths in Cottage Erie…Sandy?"

"He had a seizure last Thursday afternoon and I didn't know it. When I went up there that night to get him, I found him all drugged up and sleeping in his bunk. That bastard attendant let him stay there in that miserable room with all his clothes on." My voice was getting louder, and I found myself snarling just at the thought of the ward attendant. "When I went in to get him, he was soaked in his own sweat and urine. No one cared if he just rotted there, so I gave him a bath and changed his clothes and his bed."

She started walking further around the lake. We could hear movement in the water, some swans near the rushes.

"How long have you known him?" she asked.

"All my life."

"Was he always like this?"

"No. He got worse as he grew older. The seizures are causing brain damage, I think. His speech is worse than it was."

"Did you always do things for him?"

"We were children together. He's part of my life."

"He worships you," she said, "like a little boy does a big brother."

"You know, he never wants anything except that I talk to him and keep him company. How often do you matter to someone that way in life?"

As we walked around the lake, we could see the lot was empty except for Sandy's car. I sat on a bench just in the shadows of one of the lights along the pathway. She stood in front of me, looking down. "I have to go away this weekend," she said hesitantly.

"What? Aw, Christ, Sandy!"

She sat down beside me and started to explain patiently, as though I were a child. "I promised Jill I'd take her back to school Saturday."

"Hell," I muttered.

"There's more too. Want to hear it?"

"I know, you eloped with Superman last night."

She giggled and gently punched my arm.

"What's the news?"

"I have to be in Columbus until Wednesday next week. All of SS is going."

"Great…just beautiful."

"I'll miss you," she said softly, turning my face toward hers.

"Well, I won't miss you," I said.

"Now you're being petulant," she scolded.

"I've been waiting for this weekend."

"So have I, but I forgot that I had promised her. She has a lot to take down. Besides, I have to arrange some things about my own graduation."

"But we hardly have two weeks left," I said.

"You said three weeks would be enough."

"Not three weeks minus five days. Damn, Sandy!"

"Will you really miss me?" she said. Her eyes were sparkling, and she was teasing me, because she knew I'd be miserable.

"Hell no. I'm going out partying—drinking, fornication, and debauchery."

"Sandy?"

"What? More good news?" It wasn't easy to sulk when she was smiling at me.

"Will you promise me something?"

"Sure; name it. We losers cop pleas to anything, right?"

"Will you not go to Youngstown or Columbus this weekend?"

"Well, hell, Sandra, that's no problem. I can get laid up here—"

She put her hand over my mouth. I kissed it.

"Please?" she said. "It means a lot to me." Her eyes were looking straight up into mine and I could feel the warmth of her breath against my face. "Please?"

I nodded. She kissed me on the lips for the first time, and it was warm and soft, like I had never been kissed before, like I had never held another girl in my arms before.

She ran toward my car, and when I caught up with her, she was breathless. I kissed her again, longer, and held her for moment, feeling the smallness and warmth of her against my body.

"I'll see you Thursday night at the grove, okay?" she said.

"Yeah." I didn't want her to go, the night would never be bearable while I wanted her like I did.

"Want to have lunch with me tomorrow?" she said.

"I can't; I have to go to the evaluation meeting for the straw boss."

"Call me tomorrow after work, okay?"

"Okay."

I was having coffee in the kitchen the next morning, hating the taste of my cigarette. Wes came in. "Hello, White Eyes," he said, pouring himself some coffee. "Want a donut?"

"No. Hey, Wes, how about taking me to one of your spook joints Saturday night and getting me smashed?"

"Well, hey, Woppo, now you're talking. Ol' Wes can do that, he can. Uh...you want a little bit of sister action? I can line you up with a real fox."

"No, man. Just put me to bed when I'm out."

"What happened to that Columbus-Youngstown run, kid?"

"It ain't running this weekend."

"And you don't want me to line you up with some ass, huh? Maybe all that shit about you dagos all being fags is really true."

"Oh, get fucked, Negro. Where was all that black sister ass early in the summer when I was slamming my cock in the dresser drawer every night?"

"Goddamn, you're in love, Alessandro," he said seriously, almost to himself.

"You gonna just sit here and eat fucking donuts all morning or are you gonna go to work?"

He blew smoke in my face. "You sleep at my place Saturday."

———※———

Sandy was waiting for us when Rigley and I walked around the side of Cottage Thirteen. She was confident and smiling, never nervous anymore, as though my heart was in her pocket to reach in and touch whenever she wanted to. She was in white, and teasing—part child, part woman, radiant and happy.

"Hi, Rigley," she said, "who's your friend?"

"This here's Sandy," he said seriously. That changed her expression a moment. She liked to tease me, but not by using Rigley; he was too credulous and honest.

"Oh, I know him, silly," she said, brushing his shoulder with her hand. "Rigley? When you were little boys, was Sandy bad?"

"Yeah, sometimes his mom an' grandma used to beat his ass."

"Was he ugly, too?"

"Yeah, a little bit," he said. He had caught on, too, and knew it was "get Morelli" time. "Hey Sandy, want to hear about this here Sandy's pants? Some guys pantsed him out in Council Park and he had to hide all day in the bushes. Then that night he had to sneak home without no pants." Rigley was giggling himself; Sandy was wide-eyed and delighted.

"Hey, Rigley," I said, "we're supposed to be buddies. How come you're telling her all my secrets? Now she's gonna tease me."

"No, she ain't."

"Oh, yes I am," she said. "How'd it happen, Sandy?" Her nose wrinkled when she laughed. I had never seen her laughing so easily before.

"I don't remember," I said in mock seriousness.

She threw some grass at me. "Yes you do; come on now."

"I told you; it all slipped my mind." I couldn't keep the smile from playing 'round my lips. Rigley was having fun watching me squirm.

"Sandee…" she drawled the last syllable of my name out softly.

"Some guys and I were throwing rocks at each other in the park, and hiding behind trees and bushes. I accidentally hit a car of some older guys we used to know. They used to hang out at a dairy store in the neighborhood. They all came out of the car like wild men and caught me. Then they took me up to the other side of the park and took my pants off. Okay?"

"But what did they do with your pants?" It seemed like a funny fairy tale to her.

"They threw them away! We never played polite games like you rich kids."

We talked more nonsense for a while. Even Rigley was at ease with her now.

"Why don't you two play badminton?" she said. "I'll watch this time."

I groaned.

"Make him play with you, Rigley," she insisted.

"Come on, Sandy. I'll play easy with you," he said.

"All right," I said. "Only don't hit the birdies so hard, okay?"

"Okay," he said.

It was a reenactment of the other night. Rigley would blast the shuttlecock as hard as he could, and I would run all over, sweating like hell, trying to get it. We played for nearly a half hour, and I was tiring, but he wouldn't let up. Suddenly, as Rigley hit a high one toward me and I was just about to swat it, another shuttlecock hit me above the ear in the back of my head. I turned around, startled.

Sandy was standing behind me. "Oops," she said, running away.

I started after her, but she had taken her sandals off to stay ahead of me. We had run almost to the edge of the cornfield in a large semicircle before I was able to tackle her from behind. She fell, laughing, crawling, trying to get away. She kept calling Rigley for help, but I held her fast. The squirming stopped only when she realized that my hands were all over her. I was facing the cornfield, resting my head against the magical smoothness of her legs.

In a second, the feel of her, her voice—everything—changed, and she grew still. "Sandy?" she said quietly.

I could sense the fear in her voice. As I turned to look up, all I could see was Rigley, face down on the ground beneath the badminton net. God, I thought, as I ran toward him, not again, not tonight. I grabbed his shoulders and tried to steady his head. He kept shaking, but I managed to get the wooden stick between his teeth. We all carried them clipped to our belts in case of a seizure of one of the patients. Red mucus streamed from his mouth and nose; his eyes rolled back in stupor.

"Sandy, get away," I said. As I held him I could hear the gas rasping from his body and the small spot of urine growing larger and larger in front of his jeans. "Go get Wes in the office," I said. "Tell him to call the night nurse and the truck."

She had been kneeling beside me, frightened by the violence of Rigley's convulsions. She hesitated.

"Go on, Sandy!"

Suddenly she stood up, regained her composure, then ran around the corner cottage toward the House.

In a few minutes, Wes came running. He knelt beside me and felt Rigley's head. The seizure was over. "Goddamn, man, this is bad, huh?" he said.

"Yeah. I never saw it coming either," I said. Sandy was kneeling beside me.

The ambulance pulled between the cottages and Leo came running with Mrs. Allen, who also felt Rigley's head. He was still in my arms, blinking his eyes, trying to focus on someone. She took a vial of sodium amytal, filled a syringe, and put it to his arm. "This will help him a little," she said.

"He just had one last week," I said.

"I know," she said. "For a while he's okay, then in a short time he has several. Let's get him up, Leo."

Wes and I helped Leo get him on the gurney and into the truck. I turned to Mrs. Allen. "How about letting him spend the night down at Entry?"

"Do you think he'll be better down there?" she said, I'm sure suspecting what I felt about Erie. I nodded. "Okay. Leo, take him down."

"Thanks, Mrs. Allen," I said.

As they drove away, I realized again that Sandy was still beside me. "Are you okay?" I asked softly.

"Yes."

"How about you, kid?" said Wes.

"Yeah, Wes, I'm okay."

"Look, man, the House is open. If you're all right, I'd better go back."

"Go ahead, man. Thanks."

Sandy had gotten her sandals, and, without putting them on, walked with me slowly across the oval. The blood and mucus were all over my shirt and my arms, and it stunk. We didn't say a word. My neck ached; all of a sudden I was as tired as I ever could remember.

"I have to wash up," I said. "Come on in, okay?"

She came in with me. I took two Cokes out of the kitchen and handed her one. The smell was becoming unbearable. "I have to get this stuff off, Sandy. Will you wait while I take a shower? It won't take long."

"It's all right. Take as long as you need. I'll wait."

The shower washed the aches out of my body. The fatigue gave way to a strange numbness, and I just let it take hold of me as I stayed under the water. When I got out, I dried off and put on my slacks. I must have been in a long time, I thought.

I opened the door partially and called out. You couldn't see much of the apartment from the bathroom; it was off a small corridor near the entrance, and the room extended back behind it. The room seemed dark; she hadn't put on any lights.

"Sandy?"

"What?" she said softly.

"I'm sorry I took so long. I'll be out in a minute." I kept my shirt off so I could brush my teeth and dry my hair. I was bent over the sink, rinsing out my mouth, when the door swung open. I hadn't closed it tightly. She stood there watching me without speaking.

Finally she said, "Why did you want me to 'get away'?"

"Because I didn't want you to see that, that's why."

"Why not?"

"Because it's monstrous."

"Were you trying to spare my feelings?" We were arguing, I think.

"What's wrong with that?" I snapped, turning toward the mirror.

"He's sick; it's a natural thing, not monstrous."

"The convulsions are monstrous; what they do to a human being is monstrous."

"He was pathetic," she said.

"Then how about his own dignity? Is it right that people should look on a grown man while he urinates or defecates in his pants and doesn't even realize it?"

"If they look on him with empathy and compassion, why not?"

I turned the water off and reached for a towel. "Yeah...you're right," I muttered. "Why not?"

I started to wipe my face when I felt her hand on my forehead brushing my hair back. I never knew how I caught her, but when I did, I drew her by the shoulders into my arms and buried my face in her hair. The clean smell of it, the scent of her, her softness...my mind wasn't working anymore, only my feelings were responding to her warmth. I trembled at the silky feel of the cleft of her back as I ran my hand beneath her blouse. For me there was no turning back. But she stiffened.

"No, Sandee," in the same soft drawl, "please."

"I can't wait for you anymore, Sandy. I'm going crazy this way..."

She put her hand to my mouth and looked into my eyes with those great moist gems of hers, "Not like this...in this hospital. Please."

It was enough to bring me back to the reality of where I was; in the bathroom of a small apartment in a mental hospital. I walked out into the room to the closet and got a jersey. The room was still dark.

"I'd better go," she said.

"Yeah. I'll walk you to your car."

Again we walked in silence. The air helped calm me down and clear my head.

"I'd like you to meet my parents tomorrow night," she said, looking straight ahead. I groaned. "All right, don't come," she said testily.

"I'm no good at that stuff, Sandy."

"They just wanted to see who I've been meeting all these nights, that's all. I told them about you...and that you'd probably be with me somewhere, so they asked me to bring you home."

"You know I don't get off until late. I have to escort tomorrow night."

"They would wait. This has seemed more sudden to them than it does to us. They liked Larry, and they want to see who forced him out of my life. Besides, they're going out later; you won't have to be with them long."

"Did I force him out? Or was he over with before I really met you?"

"I don't know, but why does it matter now anyway?"

Her parents liked him, I thought.

"Please come. It won't be bad."

"I know it won't...I just get all...Yeah, I'll come." I said.

"It's on the other side of the river," she said. "Bear left over the little bridge past the Shell station, and turn up the hill. Take the first street to the right. It's called River Bend. Number twenty-three. Got that?"

"Yeah," I muttered, still not sure about meeting them. She kissed me quickly and got into her car before I could get my arm around her. Then she was playful again.

"You're hairy," she said.

"You didn't see the half of it." She smiled and wrinkled her nose. Then she kissed my hand as I rested it on her door, and drove off.

The next day I went down to Entry to see Rigley. He was asleep. "How is he?" I asked the nurse.

"He's okay, but these things take a lot out of him. I think we're going to keep him here another day."

"That amytal knocks him for a loop, doesn't it?"

"Well, she gave him a good dose. He's so huge; it's surprising how it works on him."

"Yeah."

"We had two student nurses really clean him up. It took them almost an hour."

"He looks good now…thanks," I said. "Did he hurt himself in falling?"

"Not much. Maybe this cut on his lip. But you might have done it when you put the stick in his teeth. That often happens."

"Some blood came out of his nose." "A small vessel must have broken. It's okay now."

He looked clean and peaceful. It was a lot easier leaving him to sleep down at Entry.

The Friday night card games seemed to drag whenever I was going to see Sandy. I tended to miscount my melds and to walk a little faster when I escorted.

I showered, put on some fresh clothes, and then drove out by the river. The road beyond the Shell station, leading up the hill, was a small one, easy to miss. It wound up and back upon itself through dense woods as it girded the hill. At the top was a short curved road lined with huge, sprawling, beautiful houses. On the left side, the backyards sloped down to the river; on the right, where Sandy lived, they angled back into a sloping hilltop among the trees and bushes. There were bigger front yards for houses on Sandy's side.

The house was magnificent, and old: slender white pillars resting on a portico, a curved drive, divided so that it circled back from the portico to the street, or went beside the house to a rear courtyard, fronting an old four-car garage made of stone, once probably a stable for horses. The doors were built for coaching days; they were wide and high. Between the garage and the back of the house was a path lined with tall dense bushes so that you couldn't see the house. I went around front.

Sandy was waiting on the porch. Her feet were bare, and she was wearing a short skirt tied with a hemp rope around her waist. The skirt was green. She also wore a white blouse dotted with small green flowers. The two shirttails tied under her breasts in front, leaving her midriff bare. Her pierced earrings were tiny yellow flowers with white centers, daisies, I thought.

"Hi," she said, taking my hand and kissing me lightly. "Come on in; they're about to leave."

The inside of the house was a symphony of wood; mahogany and oak paneling highlighted by different colors of wallpaper. But wood everywhere: bay windows, ceiling beams, bookcases, tables and chairs—everything glistening and beautiful.

"Sandy, my father, Dr. Covington, and my mother. Daddy, this is Sandy Morelli."

I could see hints of Sandy in them. Her father was dark and auburn haired, a handsome, rugged man, muscular and slightly heavy. Her mother was blonde, with a small, straight nose and those same green saucers with long, dark lashes. She had the athletic symmetry and small waist that gave Sandy so much of her grace. The only mystery in them was the burnished red of Sandy's hair.

I was uncomfortable as hell. "How do you do, sir? Hello, Mrs. Covington."

"Hello, Sandy," they said in unison. Her father thought about the sound. "Those names must cause you both some trouble, huh?"

"What's you real name, Sandy?" her mother said.

"Alessandro, but nobody ever called me that."

"That's Italian, isn't it?" she said, smiling. No malice.

I flashed a corner-of-my-eye glance at Sandy, and she wrinkled her nose at me, knowing my fondness for the phrase. When we shook hands, her father held on to mine for a moment as we talked. He spoke to both Sandy and me. "These things are, uh...tomorrow it'll have been a bore, but still we'll manage to stay the evening late."

We talked a little more; they were both warm and easy to know, so much different from the people of wealth I had known in the past. Her mother spoke to her then.

"Sandy, he's been working. Take him back and fix him something." Then she turned to me. "Relax," she said softly, "and make yourself at home."

"Oh, don't worry," Sandy said. "I'll take care of him. Just have a good time...and be careful, Daddy." She tiptoed up to kiss him. I realized that even if she wore shoes, they would both be taller than she was. Somehow, there with the two of them, she looked younger, more like a little girl.

"Look, we have to go," said her father. "Please come back to see us again; I promise we won't rush out on you." Then he turned to Sandy. "Tell Jill that you two have a long way to go tomorrow, so she shouldn't be late." He clasped my hand again. "I'm glad you could come. Don't forget; we'll visit again."

When they left, Sandy closed the double door behind them.

"They're nice," I said honestly.

"Oh, I told you they'd be. Why couldn't you believe me?"

"Italians aren't used to redheads. Can't trust them."

She made a disapproving face, then took my hand again. "Come on; let's go see the house." We went through the rooms. Everything was carefully chosen, unpretentious, but quietly elegant.

"One more thing..." She called upstairs. "Jill!"

"I'm coming, I'm coming!" She came down the stairs in a floor-length, white terry-cloth robe. Her hair was soaked; so was she. Beads of shower water still rolled down her skin.

"This half-naked hussy is my sister, Jill," Sandy said.

"Quiet, Sandy. Hi." She extended her right hand, and she was smiling—a family trait. Sandy prodded a finger at her ribs, trying to tickle her.

"She's so stuffy," Jill huffed. "I'm sorry we're all leaving. You'll just have to endure her for tonight."

"I'll bear up," I said.

"Why don't you take him for a swim, Sandy? The water's nice and cool."

Sandy glanced at me. I'd never be able to stand seeing her in a bathing suit, and she knew it. I said nothing, but it was mental telepathy. A smile played on her lips as she imagined what would come over me if I could get my hands on her in that pool. She turned back to Jill. "You're excused, child."

Jill's eyes danced just like Sandy's. "I'll see you again before I leave. She's such a prude; I'll upset her if I stand here any longer."

She ran back up the stairs. She was taller than Sandy, more slender, with the same green eyes, but fewer freckles. She lacked only the final perfection of her older sister, the smaller nose and fuller mouth, great waves of red hair and fuller breasts. Still she was lovely, resembling her mother more than Sandy. She didn't have her father's swarthiness.

Sandy sensed what I was thinking. "She's okay if you like blondes," she said. "Would you like me to put a steak on the grill?"

"How about some beer and pretzels?"

"Really? Is that all you want?"

"Yeah, I'm really not hungry."

She kissed me and sprang away, bouncing. I couldn't get over how much younger she seemed. She chattered all about Jill and her parents while she gathered the snack. Then we went out to a screened porch in the back of the house, an extension of the dining room. The leather couch and chairs on the porch breathed, so that you sank into them as you sat down. She sat on the couch with her feet tucked under her. I sat on a chair opposite her and rested my feet on an ottoman.

"Tired?" she said.

"No, not now."

"How's Rigley? He was asleep when I went in this morning."

"He was sleeping this afternoon, too, but he looks a lot better. It took two student nurses to bathe him. I think they're going to keep him there another day."

To the right of the sun porch was a swimming pool and bath-house, and to the left was about an acre of yard. All of it was bordered by a thick row of poplars grown together. It was completely private, a kind of small park with flower gardens spotted among the trees.

Jill came back down. Her hair was lighter than it looked when it was wet. It was long, straight, blonde, and down on her shoulders. She spoke to me. "Well, I'll see you again, okay?"

"Okay," I said.

She made a face at Sandy. "Treat him nice, ugly," she said.

"Daddy said you shouldn't stay out late. We still have some packing to do," Sandy said.

Jill groaned. "It's like having a mother superior around the house," she said to me.

Neither of us spoke until we heard the red VW go down the driveway. The sun porch and house were dark except for the high-lights and shadows cast by a small candle on the dining room buffet.

Clouds outside had snuffed out the faint glow of dusk clinging to the screen on the outside. She was studying me.

"She's beautiful," I said.

"So are you," she said softly, still studying.

I grimaced.

"You seem tight," she said.

"I don't like courtship rituals. I've never done this before." "Oh, God, Sandy, is meeting my family just a courtship ritual for you?" She was hurt and pleading, hugging herself in frustration. "You make it sound so grotesque. I'm sorry I forced you to come," she said, looking out into the yard. "I didn't want you to be miserable."

We were quiet for a while. I smoked uneasily. "You didn't force me to come," I said. "But seeing you here, belonging so naturally...I feel like a working-class kid from Youngstown again."

She seemed bewildered. "You never acted like this before," she said.

"I've never seen you in this house before, either. I used to caddy for people like you."

"Haven't you ever outgrown that?"

"I thought I did...Do Larry's parents have money?"

"Larry who?" she said, smiling. "Oh, Sandy, yes; they own drugstores and apartment buildings. But what of it?"

"It puts him a little more on your social level, doesn't it?"

"Do you really think I care about that, Morelli?" she said sternly.

"No. But maybe your parents do. They like him."

"But maybe they like me more than they like Larry, and believe in me enough to let me make up my own mind about men. Haven't you been listening to me all these nights, Morelli?"

We were both quiet for a while. I took a deep breath. "I'm just being foolish," I said. "It's easy to see why you're like you are. This is a good house."

"Come on," she said, bouncing off the couch, "let's see the yard before it rains again."

She led me through the door, turned on the outside lights, and the garden became softly lit with ground lanterns promenading through trees and around flower gardens. The grass was wet with easy August rain. It had been nurtured through the summer, and was green and spongy underfoot.

"I love to walk barefoot through this grass," she said. "Try it."

"No."

"Come on, silly. It feels good."

I took off my shoes and socks. When she reached for a flower on a small tree, my eyes were drawn to the fullness of her breasts, and I realized that they seemed to be constrained only reluctantly by the blouse.

"Sandy," she said, "I lay awake last night thinking about you... and feeling bad."

I must have looked puzzled. It was hard to figure what she'd come up with. She turned away and walked as she talked.

"I've been selfish...and teasing, and I'm sorry. So I've decided that no matter what happens, even if we don't turn out to be for real, I'll make love to you."

My only reaction was a snort. Christ, she really means it, I thought.

She could read my feelings. "Why not? I've been around you too much, and I know what you're going through. It's unnatural, and I owe you at least that."

"Oh, goddamn. Shut up, Sandy!"

"But you've made love to other girls before."

"Hell, that was different. They weren't offering themselves as consolation prizes." My voice was getting thin.

"You'd enjoy it, wouldn't you?"

"No, as a matter of fact, I sure as hell wouldn't enjoy it."

"But why not?"

"Because it would be artificial. And I can get a deal like that any place."

"It would have to be love, then?"

"Something like that."

"Why did you want me in the bathroom last night? Did that mean you didn't love me?"

"I don't want to talk about this stuff, Sandra."

"Sandee," she whispered softly.

"I wasn't all that metaphysical last night, okay? Did it ever occur to you that I'd respect you enough not to want you as a consolation prize?"

"And you wouldn't make love to me the way you do to Marcia and Barbara, girls you obviously don't respect?"

"I do respect them. This is different."

She stood there smiling, enjoying my torment while she opened up my heart for a look. I was sounding more confused every time I spoke.

"I just think you would be different from Marcia or Barbara after I've left you."

"Oh?"

"You're rich and pampered. You probably couldn't handle the trauma as well," I said.

She was coy again. "Okay. So it'd be therapeutic, right? It wouldn't have anything to do with love?"

"I told you, I don't know much about love. I've never been in love before."

"Before?"

The game was over. Surrender, Morelli. "Until now."

"Sandee," she said, taunting and encouraging.

I stopped walking and held her at arm's length. She was a devil, smiling, eyes shining in the lamplight, delighting in her mastery of me. She curtseyed. Then she laughed and came into my arms, her breasts yielding against me, the silky warmth of her back and belly caressing my hands. She broke the embrace after a moment.

"How about another beer?" she said.

"How about a cold shower?" I said.

Back inside, I put my shoes and socks on while she made me a scotch and soda. We sat back on the porch. The scotch tasted fresh and cool in my mouth. It was raining softly.

"Jill and I had a long talk about you," she said.

"Dissect Morelli time, huh? You were pretty Socratic out there. You and Jill didn't rehearse that, did you?"

I knew she was hurt the minute I said it. Her eyes clouded and filled with tears. "What's wrong with you tonight, Sandy?" she said. "Why are you trying to spoil this?"

I was ashamed at being so bitchy. Man, I was sounding like a caddy again, defensive even with her. I went over and sat on the floor in front of her, resting my arm on the couch to face her. I kissed her hand and she ran the other one through my hair. "I'm sorry," I said.

"You know, Sandy," she said, "all summer long I've been afraid of you...afraid of myself, too."

"Is that why you were so snooty at orientation? Because you were afraid of me?"

"I mean it," she said. "There's something ruthless about you, just beneath the surface...and I'm afraid of it."

"It's called being pissed off. From getting screwed a few too many times," I said, looking up at her.

"You let it out, though—at me. Like now. I get you to say you love me and you resent it."

"I don't resent it."

"What is it, then?"

"I'm afraid, too. I told you I've never been in love before."

"Afraid of me?" She sounded perplexed.

"Afraid of letting myself be vulnerable. That's part of it, isn't it?"

She caressed my cheek with her hand. "You're funny. When I watch you with other people, you seem so tough and cynical. Yet you gave Rigley a bath, and cradled him in your arms like a baby when he had his seizure..." Her voice cracked, and she stopped talking. She looked away and I could see tears.

I drew her face back toward me. "So that's something to cry about, huh?"

She wiped the tears with her hand. "No. But it was sad...and beautiful...and..." She turned away again and wiped more tears with her handkerchief. "I must look awful," she said.

"No. You're really flawless, you know. I stare and stare at you..."

"You know what I'm saying, don't you? I don't want to be the third girl in Ohio you visit once a month. But...I'm afraid I'd settle for it if you wanted me to." Those green eyes were looking right into my soul.

"I told you I wouldn't do that with you," I said, looking away.

She was quiet for a while, studying me again as I rested against her. "You're so different from Larry—more brooding and private."

"The word is sinister. And I don't want to hear about Larry anymore. I hate him."

"Are you jealous?"

"Yes..."

She thought about that for a while as she arranged my hair, listlessly curling it with her fingers. Then she rested her palms against the back of my neck. "You're so hot to touch..."

"Speaking of hot..." I said as I started to untie her blouse where it was bound beneath her breasts.

"What are you doing, you maniac?"

She giggled and tried to get away, but I trapped her between my arms and gently wedged her back into the couch. She really didn't try to stop me from opening the blouse. All she did was croon softly that we couldn't…wrong place, wrong time. Yet she kissed my cheek and the side of my neck as I moved the bra down away from one breast. The nipple was large and honey colored. I kissed it lingeringly, letting my lips draw sustenance from it.

My right hand slid beneath her skirt to the silky, firm buttocks. "Sandee," she whispered, "not here." Her hands held my head up so that our eyes could meet. "Please wait," she pleaded. "Just a little longer. Then I'll never stop you again."

A little longer. The story of my life. I pushed myself away and sat back on the floor, lighting a cigarette and taking long, deep drags.

"Sandy?" she said.

"What?"

"I don't care if you go to Columbus or Youngstown this weekend."

"Okay, I'll go to Columbus," I said quickly, catching her off guard, and trying to keep a straight face in doing it. She looked away, then back, then wrinkled her nose and cradled her forehead in her hand.

"I'm not going anywhere," I said.

She shook her head and smiled at herself. "I die inside when I think of you with those girls, Morelli."

My head was in her lap again. And I was nuzzling and kissing the bare softness of her belly. "See?" she said gently, "you're burning when you touch me."

"Yeah, well, I tend to heat up a little when I'm near you."

She urged me away and walked through the dining room to a bookcase in the hallway, putting her clothes back together as she walked. She came back with a lighted candle and a book.

"Will you read to me?" she said, setting the candle on an end table near the couch. It was a book of poems by Garcia Lorca. She rested her cheek against the back of the couch, curled up facing me, and waited. I read slowly, from time to time looking at her.

"Do you really love me, Sandy?" she said after a while. "Is the feeling so different from what you've felt for other girls?" She gazed at me hopefully, almost like a child. She was like that, trusting, all her defenses down.

"Yes."

"But why? Why me?"

I hesitated for a minute, trying to be very solemn. "Because… well, you have large, honey-colored nipples, and I—"

"Oh, damn you Morelli! I'm such a fool!" she sputtered, blushing and laughing and angry at the same time. I was feeling smug and grinning. She threw a pillow at me in disgust. "Oh, you're such a nut. You're a real crazy, you know that?" Then she spoke to herself in wide-eyed amazement. "I'm talking about something that could affect our whole lives, and he's making jokes about my nipples—Oh, my god!"

I had never known someone like her, someone who made me want to tease her, embarrass her, play with her. With Marcia and Barbara… well, it just wasn't like that.

"Sandy, please. I have to know. Can't we be serious?"

"Hell, Sandy, I don't know," I said. "It's just a feeling inside me."

"You must know. All we did was fight most of the summer. What happened?"

"Your beautiful young body happened."

"Morelli," she said, low and easy, in a warning tone. No more funny stuff.

"Well…this summer, even though we fought all the time, I knew that you were different. You're gentle, you cry easily, you have a heart that feels for people." I paused to listen to my own words. "I just knew you were the one."

She rested the side of her head against the couch, without looking at me. "I'm not like that, really," she whispered. I touched her and she looked up at me with tears in her eyes. "But it's not just the way I look, is it? It's really me?"

"It was always you," I said. "You must know there are other beautiful women around."

She looked out through the screens into a darkness challenged by one lonely light along the walk that led behind the bushes into the courtyard. "I can't believe this is happening, Sandy," she said. She came over to me and buried her face in my chest. "I love you," she said. "I love you."

Jill came home and said goodnight. Sandy put her arm around my waist and we walked through the garden to my car. She kissed my cheek, then my lips. "Goodnight," she said.

When I drove away I felt the night coolness on the wind blowing through the damp trees. I needed the feeling. Inside, I was haunted by the scent of her hair, by reds and greens and golds that would shimmer in my dreams every night I slept without her.

On Monday, mercifully, it rained, for the second time all summer, and the softball game was washed out. Hostetter, earlier in the day, sensing the smugness and exhilaration of the RTs at the downpour, decided to call a departmental meeting. It was one of the few times all of us were together, and Hostetter took the opportunity to wax philosophical and profound, and interminable.

After he left, we still had to sit around and wait till quitting time. Ray was touchy about that all of a sudden. He didn't want "his" RTs not giving a full day for full pay. Jerry thought a softball game would have been more bearable.

The next day, Tuesday, was warm and sunny. We had a movie scheduled for the afternoon, and a dance for that night. I had forgotten to put up the screen and push the piano out on the stage after the movie. The band never liked anything awry when they came to play for the dance, so I had to take care of it.

"Jerry," I said, "when you round up all the dancers, will you stop at Erie and get Rigley? It'll save me a trip."

"Yeah, sure," he said as I handed him the House key to Erie.

As the patients began to fill up the auditorium, I got the stage ready and turned on the lights. When I was done, I went back into the vestibule. Kari was in my office choosing some records for Wes to play during intermission. He was MC for the night.

"Is Jerry still out at the back cottages?" I said.

"Yeah. He should be coming any minute."

I decided to walk over to see if he had gotten to Erie yet. The sun was falling down below the rooflines of the cottages on the far side of the oval. I could see a group of men waiting outside Erie; it must have been Jerry's last stop. All the time it took me to cross the oval, they waited. What the hell's he doing in there? I thought.

When I reached the patients, I said, "Have you guys been here long?"

"'Bout ten minutes."

I figured the attendant was giving him a hard time. As I started for the steps, Jerry came out of the door looking pale and ghastly, and seemed dazed as he walked toward me.

"Jerry, what's wrong?" I said.

"He's all beat up," he mumbled.

"Who's beat up?"

"Rigley…He's a bloody mess upstairs."

I was running before he was finished. I had always been afraid to think of it happening, to think that the son of a bitch would really do

211

something to Rigley. I knew as I ran what I was going to see upstairs, and was frightened of that, and of what I would have to do to repay madness in kind.

Jerry had forgotten to lock the door on his way out. I burst inside to the middle of the room.

"Where's Rigley?" I asked a couple of patients who were milling around the window.

"He's back on his bunk," said one. "But he's all messed up, mister."

When I got to Rigley's bunk, he was lying down, facing away from me. The shades of the dormitory had been pulled down against the evening sun, and it was almost dark in the room.

"Rigley?" I turned him over by the shoulders, holding him so I could see. His eyes were almost swollen shut, blue and shiny, as the skin spread taut over the swelling. Blood had coagulated over his lips and his left nostril; his lower lip was split and swollen, and his left ear was cut and still bleeding near his head.

He began to cry at seeing me. "Oh, Sandy, Sandy..."

"My god, my god! What happened to you, Rigley?"

He looked away and didn't answer.

"Rigley, tell me for God's sake! Don't you want me to stop this?"

He rested his forehead against my shoulder and began to sob. As my hand touched his head, I could feel the blood from his ear and a bump toward the back, where he had been hit but not cut.

"Who did it? Madden?"

"Yeah. I was scared, Sandy; I thought he was gonna kill me...I told him...I told him...I ain't blowing him no more; I just ain't, that's all...and he start hitting me."

Paddy Keating was there watching us again. "When did he do it?" I asked him.

"I didn't see nothing," he said, his eyes wide with fear.

"Don't tell me that, goddammit! You want the same trouble he's gonna get?"

"No...Couple hours ago."

"Where's Madden now?"

"He's back in the john. But when he comes out, he's gonna be madder than hell if you're here."

I left Rigley there. The john was off a corridor between the dorm and a small supply room in the back. Madden had no idea I was there, so I waited for him in the hallway, against the wall, raging silently. As he came out and pulled the door closed behind him he looked up and saw me standing in his way. We stared at each other for a few short seconds. And I think I would have killed him if I had a gun. Suddenly I kicked him. It was more of a stomp, I guess; the heel of my shoe caught the side of his upper calf just beside the knee. Then I hit him in the face with a straight punch, throwing him backward. And before he could move again, I hit him between the shoulder blades with both my hands locked together. He was a large man, thick and paunchy, and he fell hard, face first on the floor, screaming. I grabbed the collar of his uniform and smashed his face against the wall of the corridor; then I wedged my knee into his groin and drew his face back toward me so I could spit the words at him.

"You motherfucker," I said, strangling him with his collar. "You ever hit anybody again I'll cut your fucking throat."

He was gasping, more in fear than in pain. I slammed him back into the wall again and blood started gushing from his nose. "Hear me, Madden? I'm gonna meet you out in your car someday, and take you out into the woods and cut your balls off."

Suddenly he was quiet, and I thought he was unconscious. I threw him over backward, and when he hit the floor he started screaming about his leg again and trying to crawl away from me. I kicked him in the same leg one more time as he tried to get away.

I walked out through the dormitory to call the night nurse. "Mrs. Allen, this is Sandy. I just found Rigley all beaten up, here in Erie, and he's pretty bad. Will you and Leo come up with the truck?" She said she'd be right over.

While I was beating Madden, I had hurt my hand on the wall. I was aching and soaked as I went back to Rigley.

"He ain't gonna get me, is he, Sandy?" he said, still frightened and sweating himself.

"No, man, he's not gonna get you anymore." I could hear Madden moaning back in the corridor.

"I ain't blowing nobody anymore, Sandy. It just ain't right, me all the time. Don't nobody leave me alone."

"It's all right, man; it's all right. Come on; can you walk?"

Only when I was in the outer room could I see all the damage Madden had done. Rigley's whole body was sore; his face was a mangled mask of pain, grotesque and swollen. Slowly we walked down the narrow stairwell. He leaned on me because he hurt every time he raised his right leg. Madden must have gotten him low in the abdomen. Leo came in and stopped abruptly when he saw us. "My God, look at that!"

"Madden," I said, nodding to Rigley's bruises.

"That dirty son of a bitch," he said.

We supported him to the ambulance, and he groaned when he bent over to lie down, so we had to be careful. But in trying to steady him without leverage, we ended up hurting him more with sudden jerks and pulls. Mrs. Allen stood watching in helpless anguish.

"You coming, Sandy?" Rigley asked.

"Yeah, man. I'm coming."

When I went around the side of the ambulance, Wes met me. "He all right?"

"I don't know what damage he did," I said. "He's hurt around the gut, and his ribs seem to ache. His eyes maybe…I don't know."

"That rotten bastard," he muttered.

"Wes, call the ward supervisor and tell him to go up and get that motherfucker out of there. Madden and I had a serious discussion, and he's not doing so well. Let him know that if I get back from Entry late, then I'll just see him in his office tomorrow."

He reached for my hand to see the blood on it; then looked at me and understood. "I'll take care of it. See you later."

Down at Entry I told Mrs. Allen what Madden had been like all summer in the cottage. I was there an hour and a half talking while we filed a report.

The resident stopped by and said Rigley had two broken teeth and bruised ribs. His eyes were blackened but not damaged, but both his lip and his ear needed stitches. All the swelling would take a while to go down. "He wants to see you," he said. "Better hurry, before he gets groggy from the sedative."

I went down the hall to the Emergency Ward. There were observation rooms where they kept newly admitted patients until they could find places for them upstairs. Rigley was in the room beyond the nurses' station. It was small—hardly enough room for a bed and chair. He was on his back, and rolled his head toward me as I went in.

"How do you feel, man?" I said, noting the blood-engorged bruises.

"Hi, Sandy. Oh…not so bad now."

"You look ugly."

He smiled crookedly. "They done made me ugly. Look at all this stuff." He waved his hand over his chest and head.

"They'll take most of it away in a few days. Those bandages'll make you feel better." I touched some of the bruises. "Man, that son of a bitch really got you good," I muttered.

"Sandy?"

"What?"

"You beat him up, huh?"

"Yeah."

"You do that for me? 'Cause he beat me up?"

"He had it coming a long time, Rigley."

He reached for the water jug but drew up short when he tried to stretch. Soreness had set in, and every movement seemed to cause him pain. I poured the water and put in a flexible straw so he could drink. He sipped it with long drafts. Then he lay back and was quiet, looking at the ceiling.

"Rigley?"

"Yeah, Sandy?"

"Why'd you blow Madden?"

"I don't know."

"You didn't want to, did you?"

"Nope."

"Then why?"

"Some of them other guys did. They said maybe he'd like me better...wouldn't be so mean an' all."

"That why you did that with Skinny Tom and his friends? So they'd like you?"

"Yeah...Still they didn't like me none."

"You know, man, liking you is easy. And for nice people you don't have to do that stuff. They'll like you all the same."

"Nah, Sandy. I'm just a dummy. Most people are scared to talk to me..."

"Sandy likes you, and Wes, and Mrs. Allen, and Leo...You have friends all over the hospital. You don't need people like Madden."

"Yeah...I guess so."

He was quiet for a while. I gave him more water. Occasionally he'd wince and I'd steady his head so he could drink.

"When am I gonna get out of here, Sandy?" he said.

"Few days...when they're sure you're better."

"I'm going back to Erie, ain't I?"

"I don't know, man. At least Madden won't be there."

There were tears in his eyes. "I sure hate that place."

Wistful dreams...all he had anymore. Those and a few tears that betrayed the outcome of all his hopes. Sure, he was going back.

"Rigley, I'll see you tomorrow, okay?"

"Yeah."

"Okay. Get some rest now."

When I returned to the City, the ward supervisor was in the RT office talking to Wes. He was an old-timer who had made supervisor the long, hard way. We knew each other but hardly had any contact all summer.

"How is he?" he said to me.

"Bruised ribs, black eyes, sprained abdominal muscle, stitches in the mouth and ears, and broken teeth," I said, feeling weary.

"Where is he now?"

"Down in Emergency still. They're going to keep him there for a while to look him over. What about Madden?" I was in no mood for polite talk.

"He's down there, too. Security's taking care of it after he's out of Emergency," said Wes.

"Did you have to beat him so bad?" said the supervisor. "He can't walk or move his neck. You almost killed him."

"Did you see what he did to Rigley?" I said angrily. "Don't you think he deserves that?"

"But Christ, man, you didn't have to do his knee like that. I think his leg's broken."

I was losing whatever cool I had left. "How many beatings and blow jobs you think they've had up in Erie the three years Madden's been there?" I growled. "And when does the word get ever get around to you?"

He backed off then, sensing that somehow the blame for the whole thing might start coming his way.

"Where the hell did you get a bastard like that anyway?"

"It's damned hard to fill that job," he said. "Most people won't work out here at all, let alone in a security cottage."

"Yeah, well, you sure scraped bottom for this guy," I said as I walked out of the room to go throw some water on my face.

The cigarette was soothing, and I took my time smoking it. When I got back, the supervisor was still there, pacing nervously. "Well," he said weakly, "we'll take care of this. I'm sure it won't happen again." Then he made a hollow attempt to be funny. "You're pretty tough, kid," he said to me, patting my shoulder. "You ever think of being a pro wrestler? Well, I'd better get going; I have a report to make. Did you see Security down at Entry?"

"Yeah," I muttered through a stream of smoke.

"So long, boys."

"Yeah. Take it easy," said Wes.

We both stood silently watching him walk across the oval. "That fucker's scared, Sandy. He has to keep this shit from getting out of Wyandotte."

"Wes, you think he knew about Madden?"

"Yeah, man, he knew. But he was treading water till he retired. He sure didn't want a scene like this."

"God! How could he sleep at night, knowing those patients were up there being handled like that?"

"Most of these fuckers think their job is to keep a lid on this place. This is where they dump the lepers, man. Long as none of them get back outside to bother the solid citizens, no one gives a rat's ass."

"Man, we gotta get Rigley out of lockup, Wes."

"We got no stick, man."

"Isn't there some way? Anything?"

"He shook his head doubtfully. "We gotta do mucho homework first."

"You're in with Mrs. Allen, aren't you?"

"Yeah, but she's just medical staff. They won't listen to her...You ready for this?"

"What?"

"We're gonna need Hostetter going for us down at Entry."

"Oh, man!"

"Oh, man, nothing. Look here: you have to go in to talk to him... and you have to nigger down, understand? If he sees on your face what you really feel, we're dead."

"Man, Wes, I don't know if I can."

"Look, kid, the road to Entry goes through Hostetter. Even then we're gonna get shit on."

"Man, we have to do it. I can't leave here with Rigley still up in Erie." It was the first time I ever mentioned leaving Wyandotte, and Wes looked chagrined the moment I said it.

"I never really thought about you leaving, man," he said.

"Neither did I, Wes. Till lately."

"Well," he sighed wearily, "let's go to work on it tomorrow."

"Come on," I said. "I'll drive you home."

That night I lay awake, scanning stars that glimmered above the warm and husky late summer Ohio breeze. I'd be leaving in two weeks. What was I going to do? How could I get Wyandotte out of my system? Or Wes? Or Jerry and the girls? Too much to work out. I hadn't seen Sandy in three days and I was dying, still dreaming of her on the porch that night.

I went over to the kitchen for a Coke and brought it back. It was two o'clock, and I lit a cigarette. When the phone rang I thought of

Rigley down at Entry and flinched. I was afraid, almost, to pick it up for fear the news would be bad.

"Morelli here."

"Sandy?" Her voice was soft and quiet, almost a whisper.

"Sandy! Are you all right? Where are you?"

"I'm in Columbus, but I can't sleep. You don't mind my calling, do you?"

"God, it's good to hear you," I said.

"Have you been up?" It must have occurred to her that I sounded wide awake.

"Yeah. I was having a Coke and a cigarette.

"Can't you sleep?"

"No. It's kind of warm out."

"Are you thinking about me, Sandy?"

"No. I was thinking about how many games the Browns would win this year."

"Oh, don't tease me. I'm so lonely, I don't know what to do."

"I think about you whenever I'm in bed alone," I said.

She laughed, and it was like tiny bells tinkling.

"Yes, really. I miss you terribly. I don't like this at all. When are you coming home?"

"Probably Thursday morning. I can't wait to get back. This meeting is good, but I'm just not listening well...daydreaming. What have you been doing?"

"Checking out some whorehouses."

She squealed. In my mind I could see that nose wrinkle. "Do you really miss me?" she said seriously.

"Like I've never missed anyone in all my life," I said.

"Have you been busy? That would keep your mind off me."

"No. Nothing does it; Wyandotte's strange when I know you're not here. We had a little excitement, though."

She hesitated for a second. "Is everything all right?"

"Yeah. Rigley was in it, but it's a long story. I'll tell you when you get back."

"Are you okay?"

"Without you, I'm not."

"You're sweet…Sandy, will you do something for me?"

"What?"

"Say 'Cordoba' for me. You voice will linger with me till I sleep."

I liked to hear that kind of talk, man. I spoke slowly and self-consciously; hearing my own voice intoning poetry over the phone bothered me. I didn't do it well. "Someday I'll say it better, Sandy… when you're here with me."

"I love you, Morelli," she said softly.

"I love you, too."

"Goodnight." And she hung up.

The next morning I went to Ray's office full of foreboding. When I walked in he seemed in a friendly mood, asking me to take his place at the evaluation meeting Friday afternoon. Suddenly he settled back in his chair and waited. It was my cue to begin.

"Ray, I have a favor to ask you."

"What is it?"

"I'd like to get Rigley Potter out of Erie," I said.

"Just like that, huh?"

"No, not just like that; I know it's unusual, but I thought you could help." Goddamn, I didn't like doing that.

He got up, went over to a tray on a bookcase and poured himself a cup of coffee, then sat down behind his desk again without speaking. He was going to enjoy turning me down, the bastard. Careful,

Morelli, I thought; it'd be too easy to blow your cool this late in the summer.

"You know that's not RT business," he said finally.

"I know that. But this is a special case," I said. I could feel the muscles in my jaw tightening.

"Special case for you maybe. RT doesn't have special cases. You know, Sandy, I've been lenient with you all summer about this Potter thing. It was only 'cause you were leaving soon that I didn't order you to stop showing him preferential treatment."

"But the only time I devote to him is when I'm free. You know he should never be in Erie."

"If you single him out, it's preferential," he said.

"Look, Ray," my voice was cracking a little, "Rigley's my lifelong friend…"

"How about Doc Covington's daughter? Is she a lifelong friend, too? What excuse do you have for spending time with her? Well, I want you to know I don't like that either."

"Don't like what, Ray?" This was his chance for a showdown, just when I was on my knees kissing his ass.

"I don't like you using RT time to do your spooning, that's what. You didn't get hired for fun and romance."

My blood was boiling. "Goddammit, Ray, do you know of a single instance when I didn't do my job?"

"You didn't give one hundred percent."

"When? I'm here on call twenty-four hours a day and most weekends. Isn't that enough?"

"I don't care about your weekends; I care about RT time, and you used your position to carry out your private little therapy sessions when you could have been helping others."

"That's a damned lie and you know it! How'd you come by all this dead-sure information anyway? Who the hell saw you all summer?"

Goddamn, Wes warned me, and yet there I was calling the man a liar and asking him to help me at the same time.

"I get around enough."

I tried to sound less hostile. "Look, Ray, I know we don't get along too well…"

He laughed. "Get along well? Listen, man, I've got a future in state hospital administration, and I'm sure not gonna let a two-bit summertime supervisor get in my way. I'd run you down first."

That was it, man, all hanging out: his career against me and Rigley. And it was no contest.

"Ray, I don't give a damn if you become governor. All I want is to get Rigley away from a bunch of criminals and psychopaths. You have to know that that's the right thing to do."

He was sneering at me, feeling superior and smug. I sighed, and started toward the door. Then I turned back toward him.

"Can you at least tell me who I have to see down at Entry? Whether you like it or not, I'm going down."

"Ramirez is on that committee. That's all I know," he said.

As I reached the door, he called me.

"Morelli." I turned back. "I'm not going to help you, but I won't stand in your way down there either," he said.

I nodded and left.

"Man, I almost blew it," I told Wes at lunch. "Everything you said was true. He's a bureaucrat all the way…wants to move up in the state system."

Wes nodded. "Man, you can see that in his eyes. He's not gonna lay out cool for anybody."

"Well, at least he won't get in our way; we got that much out of him," I said. "Now I have to find out if Ramirez can see me this afternoon."

"Now look: you cool it down there. Remember what it is you're trying to do."

"Yeah, but he's only one vote, and there are three on that committee. We have to swing another one."

"Yeah. Have you heard anything about Madden?"

"They're gonna get rid of him and not press charges…fix his knee as part of the settlement. If they did, the whole thing would hit the papers, and they sure as hell don't want that. Who're they gonna get for Erie?"

"Some guy by the name of Warren. Came here a couple years ago. Used to guard a stockade in the marines; then he was a night watchman for a while. Leo told me he doesn't think he'll go the cock-sucking route. Might slap them around, though."

"Jesus Christ," I muttered.

"I told you, man, the more things get better, the more they stay the same. When the heat's on, they change the curtains and serve a little better food, then in a month it's back to the same old shit. By then, nobody gives a fuck."

I was staring at my coffee cup, listening.

"You did him up good, though," he said, "tore some ligaments in his leg and really bashed up his face. Bastard will be hurting a while yet."

"Warms my heart to hear it," I said.

"Okay, Warm: check with Ramirez. I'll see you later. By the way, how's the romance department?" he said, chuckling.

"Fuck you, Spook. She'll be back tomorrow."

Ramirez was a man in his early forties, a Cuban who was having trouble getting licensed for psychiatry in the United States. He was rather small and balding, with a thin, carefully trimmed moustache.

"Morelli, eh? Italian?"

224

"Yeah."

"I met an Italian girl in Spain once. Best piece of ass I ever had... better than my wife."

We both laughed, and I relaxed a little. Then he leveled his gaze at me. "What do you want, Morelli?"

"I'd like to get a patient moved out of Erie."

"Rigley Potter?" he said.

"Yes. How'd you know that?"

"Everybody down here knows what happened last night."

"Can you do it?"

"He's an epileptic, is he not?"

"Yes. And that's the only damned reason why he's in there."

"Why are you so interested in this man?" he said.

"We're friends. We grew up together."

"Is that why you almost crippled the attendant?"

"Did you see what he did to Rigley?" I asked.

"Yes. This morning. I would have done the same myself...desgraciado...All right. Are you ready to come to the committee tomorrow and argue?"

"Yes. But maybe since I'm only an RT—"

"Who probably knows more about Rigley Potter than anyone else in this place, right?"

"Right," I said.

He smiled and stood up. "The meeting is in the conference room on the third floor at three o'clock. Be prompt."

"Thanks, Dr. Ramirez," I said, shaking his hand.

"Do not thank me. You must be prepared to justify your faith in Rigley Potter. I am only one vote...the other two will be difficult."

Wes and I rehearsed a little over beer at the Tinkerbell. Ramirez, Stiner, and the assistant administrator of the hospital, a guy named Parker, would be on the committee.

"Goddamn, we might pull this one off, Wes," I said. "That guy from SS should help us out."

"He should. I just don't trust any of those bastards."

"But, man, it's not like we want to send him home. All we want to do is move him."

"That lockup scene is funny business, man."

That night, I slept for a while, then woke up, sweating like hell. Sandy was coming back. I had to think about what we were going to do. So we were in love. So what? Logistics, man. Funny, all we were looking for was the real thing; we never talked about what would happen when we found it.

School started three days after Labor Day, and I had told Marcia I'd be down that weekend. Hell, I'd have to tell her about Sandy. How could I explain falling in love with someone who was a dream to me half the summer? It was going to sound bad. Christ, no one would believe the last few weeks.

I hated the thought of telling her I wouldn't be back anymore. We never expected much from each other, but still, to fall in love with one girl, and then have to forfeit a girl you almost loved because neither of them could tolerate the existence of the other in your life? Hell, we were all crazy.

At three o'clock I was on the third floor of Entry, but no one was in the conference room. Man, it was hot; even in the air-conditioned hall it was muggy.

Finally Ramirez came down the hall. "Hello, Morelli," he said.

"Hi. Where is everybody?"

"They're coming. I just saw Parker down in the lobby."

Parker came, and Ramirez introduced us. "So, you're the RT supervisor," he said disdainfully. "I saw some of your handiwork last night."

I had my standard retort ready, but thought better of it and shut up. I didn't believe he had seen Madden at all. Or Rigley either, for that matter. The wheels just didn't want any state inspectors haunting the place, and I almost blew it for them.

We waited ten minutes and SS still hadn't shown up.

"I saw Ted earlier this morning," said Parker.

"Wasn't the SS staff meeting over?" said Ramirez.

"No, not at two thirty it wasn't."

I sat in a chair around the large table and looked humble.

Parker was an older man who had reached the last rung on the administrative ladder, a preview of Hostetter in twenty-five years. He was stuffy and humorless, probably a good man with a budget. Ramirez smoked, so I lit up, too. Finally a white-haired woman came in—Mrs. Brenner, the second honcho in SS.

Parker chaired the meeting. So I told my story, about our childhood, and Rigley's parents, and the convulsions, and the beatings.

Mrs. Brenner put a question to me. "Do you think it possible he might still harbor aggressive impulses that could suddenly erupt?"

"I doubt it," I said. "I've never seen him deliberately harm someone."

Ramirez helped. He argued that almost all epileptics could function normally when they were on medication. There was no real reason for confinement.

Parker, negative from the moment he saw me, answered Ramirez. "Dr. Ramirez, this case is not simply one concerning epilepsy, there are other relevant behavioral variables."

Mrs. Brenner opened Rigley's file and started paging through it casually. She scanned some of the psychological reports. "According to the latest report by an SS counselor, Mr. Potter displayed passive-aggressive homosexual tendencies and an intense hostility toward authority figures."

My heart faltered. My God, Sandy's report!

"There must be a qualifying statement in the file," I said. "That counselor has seen Rigley informally many times since that interview, and I'm certain she's convinced she had made a mistake."

"There's nothing in this file to contradict the latest report," Brenner said. "It's not even two months old."

"But the report is not accurate; there are several errors of fact in it. I know Miss Covington; I'm sure she would substantiate my story."

She looked at Parker and I knew we were done right then. He spoke for them. "But if the report is accurate, young man, the beating you administered to the attendant might have been unwarranted. Perhaps he was protecting himself from one of Mr. Potter's—"

"Come on, Dr. Parker," I said, trying not to sound too sarcastic. "Rigley was a mass of bruises, and that attendant didn't have a mark on him."

"And you took care of that readily, didn't you, Mr. Morelli?" said Brenner coldly.

"Please. I can see how you could draw the conclusions you do, but—"

"Potter doesn't seem to have changed much at all in the years he's been here, according to SS," said Parker. "I see no reason to permit him free access to the City."

Mrs. Brenner handed him another folder.

"But I tell you he's harmless. That report is wrong and should have been corrected. I have to leave the staff soon and that will be traumatic for Rigley. Don't you see that confinement will only make his outlook worse?"

"I am quite aware that you are leaving, Mr. Morelli," said Parker. "Now we've made our decision. If further data warrants reconsideration, I'm sure that in the future—"

"But I told you I'm not going to be here in the future! Surely you're not going to let my behavior or an inaccurate report—"

"Sandy!" said Ramirez. "We'll take the case up next month again." He looked at the others for their assent. They nodded. "We appreciate your interest in this patient." He was escorting me toward the door by the arm. The other two watched impassively. "Don't blow it now," he muttered quietly to me.

When we were out in the hall he shut the door behind us. "You know you can never reason with them like that."

"But they never gave an inch, never even listened to me."

"I know, I know," he sighed. "But at least there is another hearing next month. Perhaps SS will have a later report. Perhaps Stiner will be there and it will go differently. Brenner is a bitch, a female Parker. We'll see next time," he said resignedly. "Look, you did what you could. It just wasn't our day." He went back inside.

All I could think of was leaving Wyandotte with Rigley still locked up in Erie. Sandy's goddamn report! How in the hell could she do that to me?

It was only four o'clock. When I reached the SS office, I walked right past the secretary; she had seen me enough to have given up talking to me. Sandy was in her office writing something. I walked in and slammed the door behind me. The split-second smile at seeing me faded into a stunned, fearful look.

"Why didn't you change the report?"

"What report? What happened?"

"What report? The bad one. Rigley's interview!"

"But why? Sandy, will you please tell me what's wrong?"

"Dammit, Sandy! Dammit!" I pounded her desk with the heel of my hand. Tears had filled her eyes already. "Your report just sent Rigley back to Cottage Erie. Do you know that?"

"But how? You're being silly. My report—"

"They used your report to deny him a transfer. That goddamn Mrs. Brenner shoved it down my throat."

"Did you see the committee today? Rigley wasn't up for review until—"

"It was a special plea, and I thought I had a chance to get him out before I left. Goddammit, Sandy, he's going back there."

She was getting angry at me in return. It was like before, early in the summer, as though those last weeks had never happened.

"Just a minute. Are you blaming me for all that? How about you? Everyone down here knows about the beating you gave that attendant. Are you proud of that? Do you think that helped you make a case for Rigley?"

"You know, I'm goddamn tired of everybody being horror-stricken at my brutality. Not one of you down here knows what went on in that cottage. You just have your nice, quiet interviews and then turn them loose."

"That doesn't justify what you did. Even an animal shouldn't be beaten that way."

"Well, maybe you ought to be the first to know just what he did do; too damned many people down here are leaving out some of the story. An animal, huh? That's rich. Are your feelings so screwed up that you can't tell the difference between Madden and me?"

She softened, and began pleading. "Please, Sandy, you're yelling. Don't do this to us."

"I'll yell, goddammit! You want to hear a little news, counselor? You want to know just why Rigley was beaten, so maybe you can spread the word around to all those sensitive souls who are so appalled by what I did to Madden? You know what he told me when I found him crying on that bunk? 'I ain't blowing him no more, Sandy!' Got that, Miss Covington? 'No more!' He'd done it before, and he'd been beaten before, and so had some of the other ones up there. Tell that to your goddamn compassionate friends. Tell them that a real animal kept them locked up there just so he could use them to enact his own demented sexual fantasies.

"This is our Rigley, baby. We brought him home to that at night, remember? And when he was sick of it, when even he knew he'd had enough, the guy you're wasting so much pity on tried to beat his brains in."

My words crushed her. But I wanted it. I wanted to shock her, and make her hurt, to pay for all the bitterness I felt.

She struggled to talk, each word seeming to bring pain as she spoke. "It was an honest report, Sandy. And I really was going to write another. But I thought I had time…I left the other because it was my natural—"

"Natural! I'm sick of hearing that word. Let me tell you something: nothing is natural in this place—RT, OT, and least of all this office. We all go on in some kind of dream play, pretending we're really doing something. But look around you. Hell, we're a world unto ourselves, as though we could justify our jobs even if the patients weren't here.

"And what's worse, we send them into those stinking cottages at night, to be molested by sadists and Neanderthal ex-stockade guards. And goddammit, I had one chance to beat the system for Rigley, and you stood in my way."

I was done—sick of Wyandotte, never wanting to see it again. But as I turned to walk out, I was confronted by the poster of the man and woman, embracing naked in the river. Suddenly it represented the whole misguided, arrogant mentality of SS. I ripped it off the wall and wrapped it in my fists and held it before Sandy's face.

"See this?" I said. "It's not 'new love' at all; it's cheap and contrived. You know what I call it? I don't call it love; I call it fucking in the river."

I never saw her move, through the blur of my anger, and felt more the sudden silence than the blow itself. It caught me fully in the face, and the sting didn't register until I saw her recoil and cover her eyes with her hands, trying not to see what she had just done. "Oh, my god," she whispered.

The door flew open on our moment of violence. It was Stiner, Sandy's boss. "What the hell is going on in here? Don't you two know there are patients sitting outside? What are you yelling about, pal?" He glanced at my name tag. "Oh, I know you. You're the tough guy that goes around crippling people."

"Don't get excited, big shot. You just might not know the whole story."

He bristled, the young man of position and influence. "Are you all right, Sandy? Has he done anything to you?"

"If I wanted to assault her, man, I could have done it long before now," I said.

"Then get out of here before I call Ray Hostetter to come down to get you."

Man, I was ready to unload on him and Hostetter both.

"I'm okay, Ted," Sandy said softly. "He's leaving."

"Are you sure you're all right?" he said, looking back doubtfully at me again.

"Yes. I'm sure."

He glared at me, looked back at Sandy, then walked out and shut the door. I reached for it slowly, knowing I had said too much.

"You see why I was afraid of you, Sandy?" she said feebly. For the first time since I had known her, she wasn't beautiful. Her eyes were dull and red, her hair was undone and falling over her forehead, and she was pale and tired-looking. The poster was a mangled heap on her desk.

I turned back at the door. "Maybe three weeks wasn't enough for us, Sandy," I said. "It seemed so easy. Maybe we pretended, too, just like everyone else in this place."

"It could have been enough," she said, sitting down and crying, looking away, with her hands both flat on the desk as if holding on. "Goodbye, Sandy," she said.

I closed the door and headed back to the City.

—————

The next day was sheer hell. I wrote evaluations in my office and spent time in my room. It was hot, and the hours moved slowly. I had a headache all day.

The card party brought me more anguish. They had been such happy times when I knew Sandy was waiting for me. Midway through the evening, when we were about to have refreshments, I asked Kari to take my place at cards so I could serve. Wes saw me and left his table to come to the counter.

"Going to Bernie's tonight?" He knew what had happened with Sandy.

"No, Wes, I'm going to Columbus."

"You all right, man?"

"Yeah. I just have to get out of here for a few days."

"I'll see you next week. I want to talk to you about something."

"Okay."

"Hey."

"What?"

"Take it easy going down there."

I nodded.

I left Wyandotte as soon as I escorted the golden agers back. I had called Barbara, so she was waiting for me in Columbus. The drive made my headache feel a little better; the wind in the car cooled me off. As I drove, my imagination replayed the week. Suddenly my happiness, my future, had all come undone, and my life would never be the same again. Suddenly all the work I did at Wyandotte was wasted, never enough. And suddenly teaching didn't seem worth going back to anymore.

Barbara was feeling good. She and her friends were winding down after a long week, the same week that had left me lost. Their talk was painful to me, their laughter shrill and terrible. I was sullen and restless, and in the end fled to Youngstown, driving all night.

When I got to my parents' house I went to bed. The next day I saw Gini, played with her kids, and talked to her husband for a while. Later, he went to work on the afternoon shift.

After supper, I sat alone at the table, smoking in moody silence. Gini was washing dishes. "Is it Marcia?" she said.

"No."

"Who, then?"

"No one."

"Sure. No one. Only you didn't say three words all through supper. What's wrong?"

"Nothing, Gini…Please."

She wouldn't be put off. "Is it that one you told me about from the hospital?"

"Why are you so sure it's about some girl?"

"Because I know my brother, okay? Nothing else would do this to you."

"It was something I thought would work out. It didn't."

She kept washing. "Are you ready to go back to school?"

"Yeah. There's not much to take. I'll leave next Saturday."

"Will you come to see us more often then?"

"Yeah. I'm sorry about that. I'll come up more often in the fall."

"How's Rigley?"

"About as good as...No, he's still the same, not so good."

One of her kids came to me to show me a picture he had been coloring. I told him I liked it, and he was happy. He went back outside to color another one.

"Is it your job?" Gini said.

"Yeah, it's everything. All of a sudden I don't know where I'm going."

"But it's really her, right?"

I nodded, then got up to get my jacket. She stopped me at the door. "Let me help you if I can, okay? If you need anything, call me. No matter when—just call."

I kissed her and went home and sat with my mom and dad watching television. Once, through the evening, I started to call Marcia, but when she answered, I put the receiver down without speaking.

Dad seemed to know how I felt, so he left me alone. My mother tried to get me to eat cookies. Neither of them asked me why I was staying home. Maybe they had talked to Gini; I don't know.

Later they went to bed. I stayed up to watch a late movie, smoking and drinking Coke. I fell asleep on the couch.

The next day we all went on a picnic—swam, played cards, and stuffed ourselves with food. It was fun talking to aunts and uncles and cousins I hadn't seen in ages; they made me forget my troubles. I missed not seeing them more often.

It was late when I left Youngstown. Wyandotte was dark and misty when I walked onto the oval. I was tired, and fell asleep easily.

———— ∞∞∞ ————

We shoved the last softball game up Hostetter's ass. None of us, Wes, Jerry, or I, gave a damn what happened. We didn't plan it, but somehow we all got the same idea. I deliberately screwed up the roster—had slow guys playing outfield, pitchers fielding, fielders pitching; we walked dozens of men. Jerry deliberately made bad calls. Wes kept calling time outs and conferences, and causing put-outs as he coached third base. It was sweet. Hostetter knew we were gagging him, but he couldn't say much without losing some cool. Score: three hundred to nothing. Game called on account of darkness.

As we were gathering the equipment, Hostetter came up to me. He had never said anything about me to Parker, though I thought that he would. "Potter didn't make it, huh?"

"No," I said coldly.

"They're tough down there."

"Yeah."

I never saw Hostetter again.

———— ∞∞∞ ————

The next day I started saying goodbye to patients I wouldn't see again before I left. Rigley was still down at Entry; he was coming back Wednesday.

Wes asked me to go out, but I told him I didn't feel like it. "Come on, man, you haven't been over my place in a week."

"Maybe later, huh? Not tonight." Instead I watched TV and started getting some of my things together.

Later I stayed awake looking out the bay window. Leo and the ambulance would drive by occasionally. The night shift came on quietly, and there was silent movement on the oval. The nights were getting cooler.

Marcia was going to wonder what I'd been doing; I had only seen her twice all summer. What would I have told her about Sandy? Hell, no need to worry about that. But what would I have told her about anybody? She'd have cried after I left, but never would have asked painful questions while I was there.

She was easy to love. When we were in bed, she wanted to make me feel good; then she'd send me away in peace.

Why did she have to be so good? So vulnerable? Why couldn't I just go down there and get laid, just get laid and leave, like with Barbara? I needed someone who'd forget about me in a few weeks. I needed a good shack-up, with no questions asked. I needed someone who didn't have time to let me wound her. I needed someone new. I needed excitement. Oh God, I needed Sandy.

The next day, Rigley came up in the early afternoon. I went to see him for a while; he wasn't allowed to leave Erie until Friday. I promised him I'd take him down to the grove, and then make him some mead. He never mentioned the beating; he talked to all the patients as though nothing had happened.

Later that afternoon, I went to open house at the rec center down in Entry, played some Ping-Pong, and listened to a man tell me his troubles. It was an old story. A poor black guy whose life had gotten out of control: in debt head over heels, driving a new Buick, wearing fine clothes, creditors on his back, and a wife castrating him.

Poor bastard, I thought. The cure was simply stated but impossible to do: pay his bills, get him a job, organize his finances—set him even. Get the nigger demons off his back. But what the hell is that? Money therapy? No, we weren't going to help him.

When I closed up at four thirty, I had some straightening to do. I put the records away, racked up the pool tables, and closed the windows. It was almost a quarter to five when I left.

As I went out the back end of Entry, heading up to the City, a ring of cars was forming along the blacktop, rides for those who quit at five o'clock. I was smoking and walking slowly, and didn't notice the white MG until I was only a few feet away from it. Larry was waiting for Sandy. I didn't know if he knew me; if he did, he didn't seem to notice. He was young and handsome and rich, perfectly at ease with himself. Life was fabulous, in a world of lovely redheaded girls and MGs, where everybody had money and wore white slacks, Italian shoes, and knit shirts open to the waist.

I thought of him in bed with Sandy and cursed him. I thought of her really wanting that body, bronzed by the sun of freshwater sailing trips, and ached inside. I turned to look back at him after I passed. He was a living American dream, sprawled in his car, everything going his way again.

Wes and I had lunch in the cafeteria. He said I'd been avoiding him; were we going out or not? I told him I was ready that night to drink him under.

Open house. The word had gone out, and people came up to say goodbye all evening. Time passed slowly. Playing anything was a chore, listening to problems, agony. I was too ready to leave. Sometime through the evening Kari told me she thought she saw the new permanent RT supervisor walking around with Hostetter. He was an older man, she said, supposed to be a specialist at setting up new programs. Hell, I thought, at Wyandotte he'd be a specialist at sowing seeds among stones.

That night at Bernie's, Wes was drinking scotch. "Well, man, you've been a hermit for five days now."

"I should have left last week, Wes," I said almost inaudibly.

"Man, you should never leave; you belong out here."

I snorted in disbelief. "I'm about as welcome out here as a plague of locusts after what I did to Madden."

"Madden deserved more than that and you know it. You don't know how many people think you should have got a medal."

"Hostetter and I would kill each other," I said.

"Oh, man, in a year or so he's gonna have a state job in Columbus. Then you can be the boss of RT."

"You should be boss, man. You're the best RT in the whole damn system."

"No, kid, I'm a good RT, but I don't have the brains or temperament to be boss. I've watched you grow up these three months. Before you came, you didn't know what you were pissed off about; now you know. You've seen part of the world out here that most people never see."

"Thanks, Wes. I'm gonna miss you."

"I'm gonna miss you too, White Eyes; we worked good together this summer. Everything clicked—you, the kids, me. Man, RT was moving people. You notice the turnouts for activities? And the noise at open house? It wasn't like that when Ray was supervisor and he knows it. And it was you, man; you let us work into it with our own ideas; no one-man shows. Fuck, man, the patients believed in us."

"Yeah, and we sent a lot of them back into cages every at night," I said.

"Hey. The world ain't a Disneyland. Would it be better to have bad RT and still send them back into cages at night? Where does it start? Fuck, nobody else is doing it. And you believed in what we were doing; don't tell me you didn't."

"But I lost it all last week. Suddenly I think the world never gets any better, Wes. The minute someone cracks, the minute we see what we're doing to each other, someone takes them away and puts them in a place like this. That way we never have to look on our sins again; someone hides them from us. Fuck, Wes, we're the ones who're doing the hiding."

"But goddamn, man, we did more than that. Don't you know it?"

I didn't answer for a while. I just sat there smoking. "I'm tired, Wes," I said finally.

"Isn't there some way you can work it out with Sandy?" he said.

"I don't think so. It was bad, Wes. I acted like I hated her—tore it all apart. There's nothing left."

"Nothing left, huh? That's why you couldn't stand Columbus? That's why you've been living like a monk for five days?"

"I saw that blond kid in the MG down at Entry this afternoon," I said.

"I saw him yesterday, too," he said. "So what?"

"You know, even if I never saw her again, I'm still sorry for the way I did it. I spoiled all the good memories; that's what hurts." I took a long drag on my cigarette. "I made her forget that kid once, Wes, then I pushed her right back to him last Thursday. God! Seeing him in that car kills me."

He took a drag and blew the smoke slowly. "Kid, there were times I said things I never should have said. But I did just what you're doing now, and never made it right. Go after that blond dude, man! Listen to me: Sandy loves you. And you know damned well she's worth it."

"You know what she said to me when it was over? 'Goodbye.' I don't know...maybe when I get to Columbus...Aw, hell!"

When I drove Wes back to his house, he said goodnight and got out of the car. After a few steps, he returned and put his head down so that he could look directly at me from the passenger side. "I'm gonna get Rigley out for you, man," he said. Then he turned and walked away.

———— ✖✖✖ ————

My last day at Wyandotte was a beautiful one; the air was clear and the breeze was fresh and cool on my skin. Buckeyes were falling from their trees already.

Nothing much happened. I signed out at Personnel, so there was nothing left to do but leave. Rigley was allowed out. I ate lunch with him in the patients' cafeteria, then took him back to Erie. I told him I'd see him later. He still had no idea I was leaving.

Wes saw me walking back from Erie and came out of the office to talk to me. "Hey, White Boy, you want to take me shopping at suppertime?"

"Anything for a scotch drinker," I said.

"Man, I have something heavy lined up tonight. I need top-shelf stuff, no pouring cheap shit into Cutty bottles."

"She must be something. Studs like you don't get honest easy."

"I even like her, how about that?" Then he paused. "She's too nice, though. She brings out too much respectability in me. I want to be bad all the time."

"Yeah. A regular badass."

"Screw, Wop."

———— ✖✖✖ ————

I told Wes I wasn't going to the card party because I had to say goodbye to Rigley. I went up to get him after the party started, about seven thirty. Down at the grove I just sat morosely.

"Where's Sandy?" he said.

"She couldn't make it tonight."

"But I wanted to play some games."

"You can't play any games. You just got out of the hospital, remember?"

We talked for a long time. He told me that when he got out of Erie, he'd go on leave to see his sister in Youngstown. Then when he got out of Wyandotte, he'd get a job, maybe buy a car.

The time was growing short and I was nervous. Man, I hated saying goodbye. We started walking back up the oval. "Rigley?"

"What?"

"I have to leave here."

"What?"

"I'm going to leave tomorrow."

"Leave? You can't leave! Who's gonna be my friend then?" He was getting excited and mad, the one reaction I hoped he wouldn't have. "Where you going?"

"Back to Columbus where I live. I told you before, remember? I'm a teacher, and kids start school soon."

As we neared Erie he was getting louder. "Hell, you're just moving away from me again, ain't you? Hell, you don't like me..."

I saw Leo parked further up the oval with the truck. God, maybe I'd need him.

"I'll come back to see you. Honest, Rigley. I'll come once a month to see you, okay?"

His voice was loud again and he was crying. "It'll be just like before. You moved away and never came back. You forgot all about Rigley. Don't go, Sandy. I'll be good. I won't never make no trouble."

The truck started moving toward us. When it stopped, Leo and an orderly got out; they had been watching us and waiting. "Shake hands, Rigley. I'll see you in a few weeks."

He didn't want to hear any more. His eyes looked wild as he grabbed my hand. "Where's Sandy? You're going with her, ain't you? You're runnin' away from me, and you're taking my girl, too. Now I have to make new friends..." He fell on his knees, crying again. "But they won't treat me nice, Sandy. They won't be like you. They'll be just like Skinny Tom."

Leo and the orderly knew I was in trouble, so they moved in to help. When they touched him, he went wild. "No! Get the hell out of here! Sandy! Sandy! Stop them!"

"Go back up, okay? Please, Rigley. Please go up." The patients were beginning to gather. The card party had just let out, and some came over when they heard the noise.

"Get them away! Sandy! Don't leave me, Sandy." He was struggling against them. I looked at Leo and he nodded for me to leave.

"So long, Rigley," I said. I was walking through a maze of blurred faces as I heard him crying behind me, his voice echoing across the oval. "Sandy, don't go. Sandy, I hate you. Sandy! Please, Sandy."

I didn't know if I was running or not. My ears were full of the screams of loneliness that no one could understand if they had not lived it the way Rigley did. His cries summed up our lives together. I was always leaving him. I'd never been able to really help.

And through the hell of Rigley's voice resounding in my brain, I carried my own special torment. I saw faces, curious, vacant, pitying. I saw Wes, standing mute and helpless, and at last, as I fled to the doors that would shut the oval behind me, I saw Sandy. I looked at her, but walked by, unable to speak, suddenly a stranger in Wyandotte again.

The House was cool and quiet when I entered. My room was full of shadows, as the twilight sun bathed the bay window but no longer reached in. Now the pain within me was more than I could contain. As I stood with my forehead against the sill, one great sob rose within me and shattered into tears. Then the merciful silence was broken by the closing of my door latch, and I turned around to see Sandy, all in white.

"Sandy, I can't talk to you now..." The tears seemed to drown my voice as I tried to make it work.

"Please let me stay. I won't bother you," she said softly. She sat in a chair by my table, as though afraid that I might force her to leave.

My sorrow ebbed quietly, seeming for hours more than minutes. The shadows from the sun had been replaced by even fainter shadows from the lamplight. Finally I said, "He's going to die out here, Sandy."

I heard her crying then, feeling all the pain and remorse my words had conjured up in her once more.

I stared for a long time out the window watching some workers come on the oval for the new shift. She had been watching me since she stopped crying.

"I tried to forget you with Larry," she said softly to my back, "but it didn't work. I love you too much. Oh, Sandy, I'm so tired of fighting. Please. Take me with you—even tomorrow. I don't care about anything else; I never want to be away from you again."

I turned to look at her, for a moment almost doubting that she could be there, that she could have come back to me.

Then she was in my arms, crying, and whispering, and kissing me, surrendering all the sweetness of her body. And then I knew that all my life I'd been lonely, all my life I'd been waiting for this small girl to come to my room that night and tell me that she loved me and wanted me forever. And then I was complete.

PART IV: JENNY

SOME MORNINGS I WATCH her as she sleeps beside me, her shining hair falling over her forehead and emblazoning the pillow. I wonder sometimes how she could be more beautiful now than she was then, how those great hazel eyes reflecting light in tiny, instant stars and the clean scent of her body, its summertime gold, the smoothness of her belly, and the tensile loveliness of her legs could enkindle me more than they once did, and yet I know they do.

Sometimes, as I touch her, I notice a tiny blue vein under the skin behind her knee, or the shadows of small stretch marks low on her belly, reminding me of when she gasped beside me as Jenny was being born. But they don't mar her beauty; somehow they become her. She has enchanted them the way she always enchants me, with the quiet assurance of someone never worried about being beautiful, someone never afraid of age or nature, someone totally loved.

Sometimes, after we make love, I watch her expression as she lies in my arms, as though not believing she's like she is, sensual and yielding, enticing and confident, her breasts delivering the sweet nourishment of her body when I feel the stir that only she can assuage.

At night when I awaken, I reach out for her, and she moves toward me, unaware, reflexively, until somehow in her sleep she feels me there, and is content to let the life flow between us at our touch.

I still feel the thrill of seeing her in a short skirt and blouse, barefoot, her midriff and her legs playing colors off the sun, just the way she was at Wyandotte. And after six years, there's still never enough time to look at her, or think about her, or touch her. It's always too short.

That inner font of magic sustains her, and in turn, me, even in our sorrow. The second child we were so happy about, that we felt stirring within her all those nights we lay awake, wondering what it would be like, boy or girl, redhead or brunette, was born dead. We knew he was dead within her body the last week. And each night she cried... for me, for herself, and for the dead child, a dream of love denied us.

Last year we went to Youngstown for the Christmas holidays. We stayed at my parents' house, and enjoyed the company of our family and some old friends, many of whom had never seen Sandy or Jenny, who were both delighted with all the attention. In the week between Christmas and New Years' we relaxed a little more, one hectic season over, the other about to begin.

One morning I slept late, awaking to find Sandy not in bed. When I dressed and went downstairs, she was sitting at the table while Jenny slowly finished her breakfast.

"Good morning, Daddy," she said as I kissed her. Sandy purred as I nuzzled her neck for an instant. Then I poured myself some coffee.

"Want breakfast or lunch?" she said.

"It's pretty late now. How about lunch in a little while?"

"Okay."

"Where are Mom and Dad?"

"They went shopping...said they'd be back this afternoon."

I watched her as she quietly coaxed Jenny through breakfast. She was wearing white, slacks and slippers, and a long-sleeved blouse.

"It seems funny being alone with you in this house," I said.

"Why?"

"I don't know…Maybe because you remind me that I don't belong here anymore."

She looked puzzled, but she also knew me well enough not to search for logic beneath my moods.

"Do you ever wish we had as much money as your dad?" I asked, not really knowing why I did. Maybe to reassure myself that it still didn't matter to her.

"No. We do all right, don't we? Why do you ask that?"

"I don't know," I said, still in the same mood.

She fixed her gaze on me, her eyes alert and sparkling, and she sensed the doubt that suddenly had intruded upon my contentment. "Sandee. There's more to us than money, isn't there?" she said softly.

"Yes. But don't you ever wish you could just buy more things… more clothes maybe?"

"Don't I look all right?"

"You look fabulous, but—"

"But if you're inviting me to feel sorry for myself, I'm not doing it. I buy nice clothes, all I can use. Besides, I don't wear clothes quite as much as I once did." She winked at me and came into my arms. "None of it would matter without you anyway."

I decided to go down to the Royal Oaks to get some cigarettes before lunch. It was cold outside, but the sun was out. It was one of those Youngstown days where in ten minutes sunshine would turn to snow blowing from a whirlwind. The air made me feel good.

I went in and said hello to the bartenders. It had been nearly two years since I'd been there. One of my father's friends greeted me and forced me to drink a beer. To refuse would have meant disrespect, so I drank it, though it tasted bad early in the day.

I saw Big Sam, O'Brien, and a few other guys from the old days. Hell, they were still always together, pissed off as usual, and funny now that we were older. I had to fight off more seasonal drinks.

Then Burt walked in, dressed in work clothes and preoccupied with getting his check cashed. I was at the bar, and he walked right past me. "Hello, Burton," I said casually. He knew the voice instantly, and turned in amazement.

"Sandy? Jesus Christ, how the hell are you?"

"Fine. How about you? Those checks must be big enough to hypnotize you, Burt."

He laughed. "I got five kids, man. Peanut butter's expensive nowadays."

"Five? You're a hell of a man, Burt."

"Hey, did you ever get married? I used to ask your dad, but he'd just shake his head, like maybe you were gonna be a priest or something. So I quit asking embarrassing questions."

"Yeah, I'm married. Six years now."

"Yeah? She from Youngstown?"

"No. Not even a dago," I said. He laughed again.

"How the hell are you, really? I haven't seen you in seven, eight years. You still teaching?"

"Nah, I gave it up. My wife and I write some articles for a little newspaper outside Chillicothe. And we got a good deal on a couple hundred acres down there so I'm trying to whip them into shape."

"Goddamn. A farmer? Remember how we used to bitch about farmers out the golf course?"

"Didn't know what I was missing then."

"You making any money?"

"Yeah, a little. But most of it goes back into the farm."

"How many kids?" he said.

"A four-year-old girl. How about you? Where are those big checks coming from?"

"I'm a trucker. After we got out of the army, I worked at Steel Valley for a while. Then a couple years ago I got my own rig. Been trying to pay it off so I can get another one."

"We both have big deals cooking, huh? That's not bad for a couple of slow linemen, Burt."

"You're the one that surprised me, man. I never thought you'd go to school after we got back from 'Nam. But hell, I never thought you'd get married and be a farmer either."

"Well, Sandy and I both like it; it gives us a chance to be together a lot."

"Sandy?"

I knew he was confused; the names do it all the time. "I married a Sandy, Burt, a redheaded Sandy."

"Goddamn. You're weird, man."

The way he said it struck me funny. It felt good laughing with him as though I had seen him yesterday.

"How's Patti, man?" I said.

"Well, every kid I got is so blond you'd never know I was their father. Pisses me off a little bit. Yeah, she's fine."

Then he got serious, and studied me for an instant, thoughtfully. "You look happy, kid. That redhead must be taking care of you."

"I've been lucky. How about you? You happy?"

"I changed a lot, man. I go home now, help the kids with their homework, take out the garbage...stuff like that. Hell, they got me liking it."

I drank another beer, this time for Burt, and the glow started. We caught up on old times, who married who, who's divorced, who's in jail, who's dead.

"That was something about Rigley, huh?" he said.

"What about him?" I said apprehensively.

"He died here last summer. Didn't you know? I thought you were still pretty close to him."

I set my glass down. The words stunned me. "No...I didn't know," I said.

"Yeah. It was a shame. Poor bastard. He was in a state hospital for a while, Wyandotte, I think. That's the bad one ain't it? Anyway, last summer he was home here with his sister...took a fit. Died right there. Just like that."

I didn't feel like talking after that. Burt, of course, never knew about Wyandotte. In parting, we promised each other we'd meet next time I was in Youngstown, though we still both knew we'd only meet again by chance, just as we did then. Our lives made us too busy in different directions.

⸺◦⊱⊰◦⸺

It was clouding up and I knew the snow would soon be blowing. It seemed cold driving home. Sandy was upstairs with Jenny when I walked in.

I gazed out the picture window at the highway below us as the yard sloped far away from the house and down to the street. I lit a cigarette, thinking back to the days when Rigley and I played together down the creek, and he would share with me wonderful childhood secrets like where to find clay, and cattails, and crayfish. I remembered the trouble we'd had caddying at Meander Valley. And I remembered Wyandotte, and how I had to leave him.

"Sandy? I didn't know you were home," said Sandy.

"Yeah. I've been here a few minutes."

"Aren't you hungry? Come on, I'll fix you something."

"Not now; I'm not hungry."

"You haven't eaten, have you?"

"No."

Then she walked over to me to meet my gaze. "What's wrong?" she said as I tried to avoid looking at her by staring out at the cars sliding on the snow.

"Rigley died last summer, Sandy."

She was quiet. Suddenly her arms encircled me from behind, and I could feel her cheek resting against my shoulder. "I knew this day was going to come sometime," she said, her voice cracking a little, "and I've always been afraid I'd never be able to make it better."

"It was so easy to break my promises to him..."

"It happens as we grow up; don't you know that?" she said.

"You know, all my life, the more I understood him, the further apart we grew...and the less I could feel his pain. It all seems so damned fateful."

"It's not just a story of dying, Sandy. Didn't his life mean more than that?"

"I don't know. That's what I'm afraid of."

"I knew I loved you the first time I saw you with him. That was something."

"Something for me. But for all he went through in his life...not much for him."

She tightened her grip on me. "I don't know why he was like he was, Sandy...why horrible things happen...why our own baby had to die even though we could have loved him so much. But without Rigley you wouldn't have become you...and I'll always be grateful for that."

Jenny had been playing with some large soft blocks she got for Christmas. She came over and stood looking at both of us. I touched the auburn hair, the flawless face, looked into the same green eyes. "Is Daddy crying, Mommy?" she said.

I stooped down and drew her near me. "Will you say something for Daddy?"

"Yes. What is it?"

"It's a big word. Say *Dracaena marginata.*" I said it three or four times slowly, and she repeated it each time. Finally she said it perfectly.

I glanced at Sandy. She knew what I was thinking. I held them together in an embrace for a moment without talking. Then Jenny broke away and went back to her blocks. Sandy stayed close.

"Time passes, Jenny," I said.

28907628R00156